S. L. ROTTMAN

PEACHTREE
ATLANTA

Published by
PEACHTREE PUBLISHERS
1700 Chattahoochee Avenue
Atlanta, Georgia 30318-2112

www.peachtree-online.com

Text © 2009 by S. L. Rottman

First trade paperback edition published in 2014

Cover design by Maureen Withee
Book design by Melanie McMahon Ives

Printed in February 2014 in Melrose Park, Illinois, by Lake Book
Manufacturing in the United States of America

10 9 8 7 6 5 4 3 2 1 (hardcover)
10 9 8 7 6 5 4 3 2 1 (trade paperback)

Library of Congress Cataloging-in-Publication Data
Rottman, S. L.
  Out of the blue / written by S.L. Rottman.
    p. cm.
  Summary: After moving to Minot, North Dakota, with his mother, the new
female base commander, Air Force dependent Stu Ballentyne gradually
becomes aware that something terrible is going on in his neighbor's house.
  ISBN 978-1-56145-499-0 (hardcover)
  ISBN 978-1-56145-786-1 (trade paperback)
  [1. Children of military personnel--Fiction. 2. Military bases--Fiction. 3.
Moving, Household--Fiction. 4. Child abuse--Fiction.] I. Title.
  PZ7.R7534Ou 2009
  [Fic]--dc22
                                    2008052839

Dedicated to all armed force members
and their families.
Thank you for serving.

Thank you to Russ and Pam Maclean for their insights into the B-52 world. Any remaining mistakes are all mine.

Thank you to all the Air Force "Brats" who tried to help me get the story right: Larissa Barnes, Nathan Cantu, Derek Lair, Josh Nelson, Tori Osment, Pat Rottman, Sam Rottman, AJ Slye, Denali Sperl, Katy Wickberg, and Paul Wickberg.

And a special thanks to my Major Pain.
I couldn't be prouder.

COMMON MILITARY ACRONYMS AND TERMS

AFB—Air Force Base
ALS—Airman Leadership School
Base Regs—Base Regulations: rules/laws on base
BX—Base Exchange: department store
Class Six—liquor store
Commissary—grocery store
DV—Distinguished Visitor
LOR—Letter of Reprimand: report of misconduct that is placed in your file
OPR—Officer Performance Report: annual evaluation
PCS—Permanent Change of Station: a move to a new location
PT—Physical Training: mandatory exercise
SF—Security Forces: base police
Shoppette—convenience store
SOP—Standard Operating Procedure: the way things are always done
TDY—Temporary Duty: business trip
TLF—Temporary Lodging Facility: hotel
USAFA—United States Air Force Academy
VOQ—Visiting Officers' Quarters: hotel
XO—Executive Officer: assistant

Enlisted Ranks and Insignia
Airman Basic—no insignia
Airman—one stripe
Airman First Class—two stripes
Senior Airman—three stripes

Noncommissioned Officer Ranks and Insignia
Staff Sergeant—four stripes
Tech Sergeant—five stripes
Master Sergeant—five stripes down and one on top
Senior Master Sergeant—five stripes down and two
    on top
Chief Master Sergeant—five stripes down and three
    on top

Commissioned Ranks and Insignia
Second Lieutenant—gold ("butter") bar
First Lieutenant—silver bar
Captain—two silver bars
Major—gold oak leaf
Lieutenant Colonel—silver oak leaf
Colonel—silver eagle
Brigadier General—one star
Major General—two stars
Lieutenant General—three stars
General—four stars

Author's Note

Some liberties have been taken with the physical lay-
out of both Minot Air Force Base and Minot, North
Dakota. Air Force bases have the amazing capacity to
change a lot in a short amount of time—and yet stay the
same for decades.

Through the years, the Air Force, along with the other
branches of military services, has had several recruiting slo-
gans, including "Above All," "Aim High," and "Cross
into the Blue."

Uh-oh. Looks like they made a mistake."

Mom glanced at me out of the corner of her eye. "What do you mean?" she asked.

I pointed to the sign above the gate. "'Only the Best Come North,'" I read aloud. "But for some reason, they invited you."

"Ha ha, Stuart. Very funny," she said as she got her ID out for the gate guard. "Do you have yours ready?"

I handed her my ID. The guard gave a rather sloppy salute to the driver in front of us and turned to say something to his buddy in the guard shack. I hoped for his sake that he'd shape up when it was our turn. In an effort to distract Mom, I asked, "Do they always do one hundred percent ID checks here?"

"There's an exercise going on. I saw a sign a few yards back." She pulled up next to the guard. "Good afternoon," she said to him, handing over the IDs.

"Good afternoon," he repeated in an offhand tone as he scanned her ID. I could tell when he reached her rank, because he suddenly stood a little straighter.

"Welcome to Minot, ma'am!" He handed back our ID cards without looking at mine and snapped a sharp salute. "Lodging is located on the right at the first stoplight. I'm sure they're expecting you."

"Airman Weekes," Mom read his tag in a very cordial tone. "According to the sign we just passed, there's currently a one hundred percent ID check in progress for all personnel. Is the sign wrong, or are you merely too busy to check all IDs for this vehicle?"

"N-n-o, ma'am," Airman Weekes stuttered.

"No to which question?" Mom's tone was still friendly.

"Both, ma'am. We're doing hundred percent checks, and I saw both IDs."

"You saw my daughter's ID?"

"Yes, ma'am."

I groaned and leaned my head back against the headrest. This poor airman was digging his own grave with a power shovel and he didn't know it. He was too flustered to lean down and look into the car to see that I wasn't her daughter.

"Airman Weekes, who is your supervisor?"

I handed Mom her notepad and a pen. She was always taking notes and had notepads everywhere.

Airman Weekes recited his supervisor's name and then said, "I hope you ladies have a good day." He finally bent down far enough to see into my side of the car.

I gave him a big grin and batted my eyes.

The look of shock that crossed his face was almost worth the last long two hours of our trip.

I knew better than to say anything to Mom as we

made the short drive to lodging. Not only was she considering Airman Weekes's poor performance, she was also inspecting her new base.

Mom was assuming command of the 5th Bomb Wing. Minot was one of the few bases in the Air Force that housed two wings, the 5th Bomb Wing and the 91st Space Wing. The Bomb Wing was essentially the B-52s and support groups. The Space Wing was the Minuteman Missiles and their support. But the Bomb Wing owned the base, and as commander of the Bomb Wing, Mom was now commander of the whole base.

Leaving the gate, we drove toward a few office buildings. When we turned at the light I could see rows of houses—new ones. I had spent most of my life moving in and out of old homes, but here they were renovating base housing. I wondered if our house would be new or if we'd be in an old one again.

As Mom turned into the hotel parking lot, I tried to read the sign.

"Sac…Sack-a…"

"Sa-ka-ka-we-a," Mom pronounced the word for me, turning into the parking lot.

"Sakakawea Inn," I tried again, looking at the image of the Native American woman on the sign. "She looks a lot like Sacagawea to me."

Mom laughed. "One and the same. There's a difference of opinion about her name. Up here, the favored pronunciation is Sakakawea."

"Okay." I rolled the name around in my mouth a few more times, trying to get it right. After living so many places, I've found that it's easier to fit in if you can at least pronounce local names the same way the residents do.

Fortunately, check-in at Sakakawea Inn went smoothly. The moment Mom gave her name and rank—Colonel Tina Ballentyne—everyone was eager to help. I'm used to seeing Air Force personnel, from one-stripe airmen to lieutenant colonels, immediately show deference to her. By the time I was old enough to realize that people treated her differently, she was already a lieutenant colonel. Captains and majors jumped whenever she snapped her fingers.

"If you'll wait just a moment, ma'am, we'll escort you to the VOQ."

"That's okay," Mom said. "I'm sure we can find it if you tell us how to get there."

"Yes, ma'am." The sergeant pulled out a map and gave Mom the directions to the building where the Visiting Officers' Quarters were located. Our household goods were scheduled to arrive the day after tomorrow, so I'd have one day to look around before settling into the new house.

Most U.S. Air Force bases are laid out in similar style. The BX, or Base Exchange, is usually pretty close to the Commissary, the grocery store. Base housing is normally confined to one side of the base, and when the base has been well planned, as in Minot, housing is on the opposite side from the flight line. There's usually a restaurant in the Officers' Club—sometimes one at the Enlisted Club as well—and a couple of fast-food places. They usually have a library, barbershop, post office, chapel, theater, gas station, child development center, and gym. Some bases have a swimming pool and a school or two. Essentially, an Air Force base is a little city, and everybody ultimately answers to our version of a mayor, the base commander.

As we rolled our suitcases across the parking lot, I thought I could hear birds singing in the distance. The pleasant noise was drowned out when retreat blared over the PA system. We put down our luggage and turned in the direction of the loudspeaker. There was a two-second pause, and then the national anthem began to play.

Mom stood at attention, shoulders back, hands loosely cupped at her sides. The sharp breeze blew a strand of her curly red hair across her face, but she made no move to brush it back.

I stood next to her, hand on my heart. A couple of cars drove by, and she glared at them. When the anthem is played at a military base, cars are supposed to pull over and stop. I knew that Minot Air Force Base was not off to a good start in Mom's opinion.

The anthem finished, and we once again pulled our suitcases toward the VOQ.

A small brown animal skittered across the sidewalk in front of us.

"Prairie dog?" I asked as it disappeared down a hole.

"Ground squirrel," she said.

Now that I knew what to look for, I saw holes all over the place. Three or four of the critters stood at attention next to one of the bigger openings. I realized that it hadn't been birds that I'd heard earlier; it had been these little rodents chirping.

Mom was shaking her head. "This is going to be a lot of work," she said.

"Yeah," I said. "This is going to be hard."

Mom turned quickly to look at me. "Why would *you* say that?"

I shrugged, embarrassed that I had said it out loud. "It just is."

"It's going to be fine," Mom said, pulling out the room key. "Remember, we can do anything, as long as we work together."

"Yeah," I said, looking down at her, something I'd enjoyed being able to do for the past year.

Mom was a big believer in teamwork. But this time we didn't have much of a team. This time, we were down to a duo.

***

As an Air Force brat, moves were second nature to me. This was my seventh in fifteen years, and I knew the moving drill. Usually it wasn't a big deal. But this one was different.

My brother Ray had packed all his stuff last week, and now he was off to the University of Oklahoma for his freshman year. I'd given him grief about choosing a cow-town school, and he'd rubbed it in hard that our new assignment was taking me to a much smaller cow town. "Like a one-cow cow town," he'd said. After my first glimpse of Minot, I was beginning to agree.

My parents met at the Air Force Academy and married right after graduation, even though their first assignments had been at separate bases. After three years of a long-distance marriage, just before my brother was born, they were both assigned to Minot

Air Force Base here in North Dakota. Mom was a B-52 pilot and Dad was a missile maintainer, and from what I hear, everything was good. When they weren't able to get a follow-on assignment together, Dad decided to hang up his uniform and stay home with the growing family. As a pilot, Mom got extra flight pay, and it made more sense for her to stay in.

But I guessed all those years of watching her career soar while he stayed home finally caught up with Dad.

A few weeks ago, Ray and I were having a pizza dinner alone with Dad when he announced that he wasn't going to Minot. "It's time for me to get away for a while," he told us. "Besides, I didn't like it in Minot the first time. I can't imagine that it's gotten any better."

"So what are you going to do?" Ray asked, recovering from the shock much faster than I thought he should have. He hardly seemed surprised.

"To start with," Dad said, "I'm going home."

I blinked. We didn't have a "home." Some Air Force families had places they called home—the state where both parents were from, or the city where they'd spent the most time—but we didn't. Mom was from New York, Dad from Vegas. But both sets of grandparents had always come to see us, not the other way around. I'd been to my grandparents' houses maybe three times in my life.

"Where's that?" Ray asked, making me feel better. At least I wasn't the only one who didn't know where "home" was.

"Nevada," Dad said. "Your grandmother's not doing well, and I think it's time for her to move out of that big house. After I talk her into it, I'm going to help her find a nice retirement home and then fix up her place."

"And help her sell it?" Ray asked, picking up another piece of pizza.

"We'll see."

Ray and I exchanged a glance. "What do you mean, 'we'll see'?" he asked.

"You're both bright boys," Dad said with a sigh. "I'm not going to pretend that you two don't know that things haven't been great between your mother and me lately."

I froze.

"You're splitting up?" Ray asked.

It was a good thing my brother kept asking all the questions. I could barely breathe, let alone speak.

"Not exactly," Dad said. "For right now, I'm going to help my mother sort things out. I don't know how long I'll stay in Vegas. It's been years since I've lived there." Dad looked at me. "What's wrong, Stu? I've never seen you let a piece of pizza sit on a plate that long."

Dutifully I picked up the pizza and took a bite. I could have just as easily been eating the box it came in. Had he really just asked me *what's wrong?* After saying he was leaving us, he asked me *what's wrong?*

"You know," he said to me, "Minot's a good place."

"You've always said you and Mom took the only two good things out of Minot—me and Ray."

"I should have known that statement would come back to haunt me. Minot is…well…"

"Cold. Desolate. Hicksville."

"True. But it's also a close-knit community, especially on base. People pull together and help each other out. You'll get a warm welcome and do just fine."

"Bet I'd do just fine in Vegas," I muttered.

He surprised me by agreeing. "Yes, you would," he said. "You're a good kid, Stu. You'll do fine anywhere. But between the two choices, you'll do better in Minot."

"What choices? I wasn't given a choice!"

"Another good point. You weren't."

We stared at each other, me angry and Dad patient as always.

"Is it over between you and Mom?" I finally asked.

"I don't know yet. But things can't go on between us the way they have been. Maybe some time apart will help; maybe it will be the final straw. We'll have to wait and see."

I didn't trust myself to speak, so I just nodded.

He clapped his hand down on my shoulder. "We'll always be a family, Stuart. No one can ever take that away from us. But families change. They have to. Ray goes to college this year, and you go in a few more. But through it all we're still going to be a family."

Really? I thought, glaring at him.

We'd moved every two or three years, so often that leaving friends and familiar places behind seemed normal. But we'd always left together, the four of us. It had always been Captain or Major or Lt. Colonel Ballentyne and her boys. Now it was Colonel Ballentyne and her boy.

It just didn't feel right.

Where does this one go?" the head packer asked. She'd introduced herself as Linda, and the other packers were Steve and Marty. Dad always made sure that he took the time to learn the packers' names, so I did too.

I consulted the packing list, checking off box number 121. "First bedroom on the right," I said.

Linda nodded and headed off with the box. Watching packers was one of my least favorite parts of a move. Don't get me wrong—it beat packing up and unloading everything by ourselves—but standing around for hours, checking to make sure everything got unloaded and recording any damage we found was a giant pain.

Mom had said she was going to help me this morning, but right after the packers showed up, she'd run into the office to "do a quick check" on something. It was almost noon and she still hadn't made it back. Technically it wasn't her office yet; she wouldn't be the base commander until the change-of-command ceremony Tuesday afternoon. But Mom wasn't one to sit around and wait to take charge.

"Hey, Marty!" I heard a voice call outside.

"Hi, Billy!" the packer called back from the truck. "Everything good at your new home?"

"It's totally awesome!"

Marty was still grinning as he came inside. "Box 87," he read.

I flipped to the previous page and made a check mark. "In the kitchen." I looked out the window and saw a kid bouncing around the moving truck. Steve, the third packer, was laughing.

"I see Billy's here," Linda said, coming down the stairs.

"Who's Billy?" I asked.

"We unloaded their household goods about two months ago," Linda said as she went out on the front porch. "They live over there." She pointed to the duplex catty-corner to our right. "We packed up their neighbors last week too, so we've seen Billy a lot."

"Box 111," Steve said. "Marked for the master bedroom."

I checked the box off the list and Steve headed upstairs.

"Hey!"

I turned and saw the kid from outside—a skinny boy who looked about seven—standing on our front porch. His great big grin took up half of his dirt-streaked face, and there was a large tear in his faded T-shirt. He had a few scratches on his legs, and one nasty bruise on his arm.

"You got any kids?" he asked me.

I laughed. "I *am* the kid! You must be Billy."

"Yeah! How'd ya know?"

"I'm all-knowing. I'd say you're from somewhere

11

down South and you've lived here about...let's see...two months?"

Billy gave me a skeptical frown, but he recovered quickly. "What's your name?"

"Stu."

"You the only kid?"

"My brother's at college," I said. "He won't be visiting till Thanksgiving."

It was weird to think that Ray would be visiting instead of living at home from now on.

"How old are you?" Billy asked.

"Fifteen."

"Cool! My brother's sixteen! His name's Curtis."

"Excuse me," Marty said, coming back in with another box. "Number 14?"

"In the basement, please," I said, checking it off.

"I'm almost nine," Billy said, unfazed by the interruption. "I'm pretty mature for my age, though, so you can still hang out with me."

I tried not to laugh. *He may think he's mature on the inside,* I thought, *but he's tiny on the outside.* "Thanks, Billy."

"Where're y'all from?"

"Everywhere."

Billy made a face. "No, really."

"Really. We've lived all over the place. But we're moving from Barksdale right now."

"Where's that?"

"Louisiana," I said, keeping it short. I didn't want this kid hanging around all day.

"Oh. We're from Texas."

"I wouldn't have guessed."

Billy laughed. "Most people do. They all think I talk funny. Me, I think people here talk funny."

"You're probably right."

"Box 219," Linda said.

"Hang on," I told her. "That's got a big dent in the side. Let's open it up."

She sighed and set the box down gently. Even as she did so, I could hear broken glass. Sure enough, when we opened the box and pushed aside the paper, we could see the shattered pieces of Mom's holiday punch bowl. There'd be hell to pay for that. I circled the box number and wrote "damaged" on the comment line.

"Just put it over there," I said, pointing to a corner in the entryway.

"Where're your folks?" Billy asked me.

"Working," I said.

"Hey, Stu," Marty called to me from the truck. "We're gonna break for lunch."

I waved so he knew I heard him.

"How'd y'all get the big house?"

Raising my eyebrows, I said, "My mother's the new base commander."

"Commander? She's the boss of everyone?" He paused a moment to take in this news. "That makes you better'n us, right?"

"No," I said, trying to hide my irritation. "Just a higher rank."

I thought that had shut him up. But a few moments later Billy spoke again. "I'm hungry."

I stared back at him. "Then you'd better go home and get lunch." I felt kind of rude, but obviously I

13

didn't have anything here to eat. If Mom didn't come home soon, I'd be going without lunch myself.

"Wanna go to Burger King?"

"I can't," I snapped.

"Oh. Okay." Billy started down our front porch steps. "Guess I'll see ya later!"

I sighed and turned back to our new home. I wasn't ready to deal with the boxes in the living room yet, so I went up to my bedroom.

The packers would probably take at least forty-five minutes for lunch. I decided to see how much of my stuff I could unpack by the time they got back.

After only ten minutes, I almost had my entire closet set up. When I was eight, Ray had helped me devise a system of plastic boxes that doubled as shelves for all my stuff, and they made my room extremely portable.

"Hello?" an unfamiliar voice called from downstairs.

"Be right there!" I yelled. Taking the stairs two at a time, I tripped halfway down but managed to catch myself before I plunged to the bottom.

"Careful!" a woman gasped. She was standing on the other side of the screen door.

"I'm just clumsy," I said, hating the flush I felt lighting up my face. I had inherited my mother's red hair, but while she only turned pink when angry or embarrassed, I went maroon. "And I usually bounce if I fall." I pushed open the door.

She laughed and extended her right hand, balancing a casserole dish on the other. "I'm Bridget Murphy," she said. "We're your neighbors. You must be Stuart."

"Nice to meet you," I said, reaching out to shake her hand.

"I wanted to bring you and your mom a little something to help you get through the first few days while the dust settles."

"Thank you," I said, relieving her of the casserole. "I know we'll enjoy it."

She was eyeing me. "Sixteen, right?"

"Next month."

She grinned. "Then you're in luck. I'm pretty sure one of the kids who moved in across the street is sixteen too. Have you met him yet?"

"Not yet," I said. We said good-bye, and she waved when she got to the street. For some weird reason, adults believe that all children within two years of each other will be instant friends. Every once in a while, though, they're right.

When I was ten, I had two best friends. I cried like a baby when we had to move away. After we were settled in our next house, I decided I didn't want any friends at all. By the time I realized how lonely I was and how important friends were, almost three months had passed, and all the kids thought I was stuck up because I hadn't made any effort to be friendly. Ever since then, I've tried to give everyone a chance. I don't go for close friendships—they're too hard to deal with when one of us moves away—but I like to have a lot of buddies to hang out with. This is one reason playing sports is so important to me. It makes it easy to meet a lot of people who have something in common with me.

I sorted the rest of the plastic boxes that held my

clothes, DVDs, books, games, and sports gear, and then turned to the finishing touches.

My room's easy to decorate. I only put four things on the walls. One is a framed poster of the Thunderbirds, signed by all of the pilots from 2004, including the first female Thunderbird pilot. A large clock goes across the room from my bed, and the coat rack/mirror combination that my grandfather made for me when I was little goes directly underneath it.

The last thing I hang is an old oil painting of a house out in the country. I don't know who the artist is, or even where we got it. All I know is that the house looks like the kind that would be in a family for generations, a place where kids, grandkids, and even great-grandkids would build memories. While we're here in Minot, I'll probably pick up some new things for the walls. But when we move away, I'll leave them behind and start over at our next house with my standard four.

By the time I finished my room, I was starving. I rummaged through one of the boxes in the kitchen, searching for a fork or a spoon so I could try some of Bridget Murphy's casserole.

"Hello?"

I groaned. No lunch for me today. "Coming," I called, closing the box. I almost ran Billy over in the hallway.

"Whoa!" he said, backing up quickly.

"What are you doing?" I demanded.

"Thought ya might be hungry," he said, holding up a Burger King bag.

I blinked. "Wow. Thanks!"

He grinned. "No problem."

"Let me pay you for this."

"Nah," he said, waving his hand. "Curtis works there. He gets me stuff."

"Thanks," I said, making a mental note to pay this Curtis guy back. I had flipped burgers in Barksdale before we moved and we'd had to buy our own food.

We walked out to the front porch and sat on the steps. I made short work of the burger and fries. All it needed was a Coke to be the perfect meal, but I wasn't going to mention that. Just as I wadded up the paper bag, the movers pulled up.

"Here we go again," I sighed.

A car turned into Billy's driveway. Before it came to a full stop, a woman stuck her head out of the driver's side window. "Billy!" she yelled.

"I'd better get goin'." Billy jumped up and was almost to the street before he finished the sentence. "See ya, Stu!"

"See ya!"

It was time for me to get back to work anyway.

"Box 93," Steve said.

"Living room," I replied, checking off the box and putting Billy completely out of my mind.

hated being in the front row. Everyone in the hangar could study me, but I couldn't see anyone without turning around and obviously staring.

In the center of the temporary stage in front of me were the U.S. flag and the guidon, the wing flag. Next to the flags sat my mother and Colonel Stoddard, the current—at least for the next ten minutes—wing commander. On the other side a visiting general stood at the podium, making a speech highlighting the outgoing commander's career and accomplishments. Colonel Stoddard's eyes were overly bright. It looked like he'd have a hard time making it through the speech without shedding tears. Mom had on her perfectly polite attention face.

When the general finished, he asked my mother and the outgoing commander to stand in front of the flags. Colonel Stoddard gave the general the unit guidon and said, "I relinquish command." The general then took the wing flag and handed it to Mom, symbolically turning over the command of the base to her. She gave the customary response: "I assume command." While they both had hold of the flagpole, they paused for a second and looked toward the Air Force photographer, waiting for the flash. Then my mom was holding the flag all by herself. Everyone started clapping.

A major inconspicuously escorted the outgoing commander and his family from the hangar, and another colonel took the podium to officially introduce the new wing and base commander.

As he ticked his way through the list of bases where she'd served, I tried to maintain a polite attention face like Mom. She was a USAFA grad (that's where she met my father), and she was first stationed in Enid, Oklahoma, then right here at Minot (where Ray was born and I was conceived). Not long after that we moved to Barksdale (where Dad separated from the Air Force and I was born), then spent time at a base in Florida (where I started kindergarten). Mom pinned on major in D.C. (where I finished kindergarten), and then did a short tour at Sheppard (where my friends and I got in trouble for breaking the colonel's windshield while playing basketball). When I was about nine years old, she pinned on lieutenant colonel, moved on to War College (where Dad was always home for us), and taught courses at the Air Force Academy (where Ray and I learned to love Colorado). She had just finished a second tour in Barksdale, where she pinned on colonel. And now here she was back in Minot. The colonel paused for a moment while the audience applauded.

"Colonel Ballentyne's oldest son, Ray, is off enjoying his first semester as a Sooner at the University of Oklahoma," the speaker went on. "Her youngest son, Stuart, will be a sophomore here at Central Campus this year and hopes to make it to State in the 100 breaststroke. Mr. Dave Ballentyne, who separated from the Air Force as a captain, is currently in Nevada, caring for his ailing mother."

At least Dad had been mentioned. He was still considered part of the Ballentyne family. If Mom thought they were getting a divorce soon, I figured that she probably would have left him out of the introduction altogether.

When the change-of-command ceremony was over, I had to join Mom in the receiving line—actually we made up the entire receiving line. I stood next to her, trying to ignore the fact that I was sweating under my tie and Ray's old jacket, shaking everyone's hand and smiling when they said how glad they were to meet me. I couldn't understand why I had to be part of this. Unless these people had kids who were in my class or on a team with me, they'd probably never see me again. Not until someone took command from Mom, that is, and we were the ones discreetly escorted out the back door.

"Howdy, neighbor!"

My hand was swallowed in the grip of a monster of a man. He was huge, easily six and a half feet tall and almost half as wide, but he was all muscle. He stood straight, practically at attention, and his dark, piercing eyes didn't blink. In short, he looked like a poster boy for drill sergeants. But he was smiling, and the smile took up half his face.

"Captain Vinson," I blurted out, recognizing the grin. This had to be Billy's dad.

"Call me Tim," he said. "Hope my boy Billy hasn't

been pestering you too much." Vinson's Southern accent was thicker than Billy's.

"You have an older son too?" Mom said, joining the conversation.

"Stepson, ma'am." Captain Vinson shook her hand. "Stuart here is Curtis's age."

"Wonderful. And your wife? Is she at work or—"

A strange expression crossed his face, but I couldn't interpret it.

"She's not working at the moment, ma'am."

"Well, I hope you invited her to come join us for cake."

"Yes ma'am, I did, but she had some errands to run in town. She—"

"We're looking forward to getting to know your family," Mom said smoothly, indicating that it was time for him to move on. The line was still pretty long.

He bobbed his head. "Nice to meet you," he said. "We'll see you around."

A few more faces blurred past.

"Ah, Captain Cardinal," Mom said warmly. "Stu, you need to remember Jonathan Cardinal; he's my XO."

As my mother's executive officer, he was basically an office administrator and her main errand boy. He had to be on top of her schedule and help prioritize items for her attention. He would have to be at the office before she got there, and probably wouldn't be leaving until well after she did. Working weekends would be expected too, and the Air Force doesn't pay overtime.

"You have my sympathy," I told him, shaking my head.

Mom frowned.

"Thanks, but I'll be fine," Cardinal said with a chuckle. "I volunteered for the position."

I raised my eyebrows. "You volunteered? When's your next psych evaluation? I'm afraid you might not pass."

He laughed again. "I knew what I was getting into. I enjoyed working with Colonel Ballentyne in Barksdale." He nodded to his new boss and moved on.

Finally the receiving-line ordeal was over and Mom and I were free. She began working the room, of course, saying hello to everyone all over again. I headed straight for the cake.

"Surely you could have found a bigger piece," I heard a voice say. "That one doesn't quite cover the whole plate!"

"Receiving lines are hard work," I retorted.

Cardinal smiled. "Not hard, just duller than a plastic spoon."

"You got that right."

"They've got some pretty good lemonade over there," he said.

I made a face. "Chocolate cake and lemonade isn't exactly a winning combination."

"Good point." He drained his glass and tossed it in a nearby trash can. "Do you wear your hair long to bug your mom?"

I shook my head. "No. I just cut it for the big meets and let it grow in between." If it did bug my mother, she'd never said anything about it.

"So you're a pretty serious swimmer."

I nodded, scarfing down my last bite of cake.

"I was a diver in high school."

I managed to swallow the dry cake. "College?" I asked.

"Nah. Didn't even finish my senior season."

"Why not?"

"Hit the board doing an inward. Fifteen stitches, concussion, broken cheekbone. I didn't have time to recover before the league meet."

"Not that you wanted to get back on the board or anything."

He laughed. "Well, I wasn't in any hurry to do another inward, that's for sure."

"How long were you at Barksdale?"

"Almost three years. It was my first assignment. Your mom took command of the squadron I was in two months before I PCSed up here."

"Oh." I scraped the remaining cake crumbs together with my fork.

"You don't have to lick the plate," Cardinal said. "You can get another piece."

"That takes all the fun out of it." I tossed the paper plate and napkin in the trash. Mom was across the hangar from us, laughing with someone I'd just met but whose name I couldn't remember. "Think I'll head on home," I said.

"Want a ride?" he asked quickly.

"No thanks," I said, holding back a grimace. Apparently Cardinal was going to be one of those extra-helpful XOs. Now I just had to figure out if he was doing it for his career or because he was a nice guy. Either way he'd want to get on my good side, and I'd want to be on his. We were going to be talking frequently, passing messages back and forth for her. If we didn't get along, things could get nasty. "But you could let my mom know that I went home."

"Sure thing," he said.

I headed out of the hangar, leaving behind the loud sounds of Air Force camaraderie.

As I walked down the main drag, I saw a couple of guys about my age walking in the opposite direction on the other side of the road. I raised my hand to wave. They never acknowledged my presence. They were both smoking, and I wondered if that meant that the SFs here didn't enforce the law, or if those guys didn't care if they got caught. Of course I'd known underage kids who smoked on base, but always behind closed doors. We all knew the unwritten rule: Don't do anything bad in public. It reflects poorly on you and your family.

It was a long, lonely walk through my new base. If I had my license, I'd be driving home right now.

Just a couple of months, I told myself. *I can handle it.*

StuForceOne: i hate it here.
H2Oxcelr8r: it can't b that bad.
StuForceOne: no, it's not that bad—it's worse!
H2Oxcelr8r: how worse?

It had taken Mom two weeks to get the cable guy out here to hook up our DSL. Now I was finally able to be part of the world again.

Three years and two bases ago, Dad had encouraged me to sign up for the virtual pen-pal program at the Sheppard Youth Center. It was one of the best things he ever suggested. Now Taylor and I were good friends even though we'd never met. He was a friend I could take with me whenever we moved, and it didn't matter what rank our parents were.

I typed "I miss Ray," then deleted it. It sounded too whiny. My brother's e-mails were only a few lines long, and the two times I'd been able to get him on the phone, our conversations felt awkward and Ray had cut them short.

StuForceOne: so bad i can't wait 4 school 2 start!
H2Oxcelr8r: that IS bad! what's so wrong?

I had to stop and think about that for a moment. The easy answer was *everything*.

StuForceOne: there's no 1 here to hang out w/
H2Oxcelr8r: what about ur neighbor?
StuForceOne: curtis? haven't seen him yet.

We'd been in Minot exactly two weeks, and the house was completely unpacked. I had nothing to do. High school registration was still five days away. It was too late to get a summer job. I was too old to just hang out at the teen center during the day, and it seemed like half the base was on summer vacation. Doing laps at the pool made me feel better, but I hadn't met anyone there between the ages of eleven and eighteen.

I'd seen too much of Billy, though. He came over at least once a day to ask if I wanted to play.

H2Oxcelr8r: how's ur swimming?
StuForceOne: good.

Taylor was always good for a change of topic. One of the things I liked about him was that he shared most of my interests: swimming, Stephen King novels, tennis, camping in the mountains, and football (even though he liked the Bears and I was a Packers fan). Best of all, Taylor had an older brother and was an Air Force dependent just like me.

Although we were both swimmers, we had opposite specialties. Taylor was a distance swimmer, doing insane events like the 500 freestyle for his high school and the 1650 for the USS team. I'm a sprinter, pretty much useless after a 200 free, and I usually focus on the 100 breast and 200 individual medley. It was a good thing that we wouldn't ever race each other. Even putting his best time in my worst event, I'd blow him out of the water. I'd never told him my times, simply because I didn't want to start a rivalry. Letting him know I'd qualifed for State and Junior Olympics was enough.

H2Oxcelr8r: got a workout schedule yet?
StuForceOne: no, but there's an indoor and outdoor pool.
H2Oxcelr8r: bonus.
StuForceOne: got a locker at mcadoo gym and

Before I could finish, Taylor broke in.

H2Oxcelr8r: oops. gotta bolt.

And he was gone, signed off without saying good-bye. But the good thing was, I knew I could e-mail him a long letter if I wanted and he'd read all of it, then take the time to answer. I knew that when we had another IM session, we'd pick up right where we'd left off. In short, Taylor was always there for me—even when he had to sign off abruptly like that. Friends from previous bases, friends I'd known from school or swim team, had been good for two, three letters max.

Right as I was getting ready to sign off, my mail icon flashed. I almost didn't click on it. Probably spam. But I had nothing better to do.

To: StuForceOne
From: RGBallentyne
Subject: Grandma

Bro—
Dad wanted me to let you know that Gram isn't
doing so great. But she's also flat refusing to
move. He's started repairs around the house, but
isn't pushing the nursing home issue yet. He
hasn't gotten Internet hooked up, so you gotta
call his cell phone. I know all this sucks, but look
at it this way—at least you don't have to wait
for Mom and Dad to agree on things anymore.

How was change of command? Any hot girls on
the block? Make sure Mom keeps the spare room
for me—she can't make it her office yet.

Ray

It irked me that Ray was passing me messages from
Dad. Why didn't Dad just call me?

I e-mailed Ray back, asking him to define "not so
great." The last time we'd seen Grandma was almost
four years ago. Even then she'd had to hold books up
to her nose to read them in spite of the thick glasses
she wore, and she was using a walker.

I went down to the kitchen and checked the assort-
ment of casseroles in the fridge. After the change of
command, the food had really come flowing in. A base
commander whose spouse was out of state while her
youngest was home alone—well, that almost called for
full base mobilization.

There was a lot of pasta and rice in the casseroles, which didn't make Mom happy. She'd been bitten by the low-carb diet bug, as if doing regular PT wasn't enough for her to stay in shape. (Mom was a big believer in leading by example, and she was out there running with her troops at least three days a week, staying "Fit for Force.") Fine with me. I happened to like carbs.

I had just finished eating when the doorbell rang. Since only our glass storm door was closed, I could see someone around my age standing on the porch, leaning against the post. It was one of the guys I'd seen smoking on the street after Mom's change of command.

"Hi," I said, pushing the door open.

"Hi. You're Stu, I'm Curtis Sweeny, and we're supposed to be friends." His long dirty blond hair hung just past his shoulders. He was smiling at me, but it seemed forced.

"Says who?"

"Curtis!" A loud wail came from across the street. "You were s'posed to wait for me!" Billy flew out his front door and sped across the street. He tripped over the curb and sprawled, hard, on the sidewalk.

I immediately jumped off the porch and jogged toward him, convinced he must have broken something.

Curtis started to laugh. "God, Billy, you're such a loser!"

I reached down to help Billy up, but he ignored my hand, pushing himself to his feet.

"I'm fine," he gasped, eyes bright with unshed tears. "I can take it."

Curtis whistled low. "You ripped your jeans, man. My mom just bought those for you."

Billy's face had been red after his hard fall, but now he went pale. "Don't tell her, Curtis," he begged.

Curtis appraised Billy for a moment, making him squirm. "Maybe."

"Please!"

"We'll see," he said. Curtis was smiling, but the tone of his voice made me feel like he wasn't likely to be helpful.

Billy turned to me. "So are ya coming?"

"Where?"

Curtis punched Billy casually on the shoulder. "I haven't invited him yet."

Billy smiled brightly at me as he reached up to rub his shoulder. "We're goin' four-wheelin'!"

"Yeah?"

"Yeah," Curtis said. "We're leaving tomorrow morning at nine if you want to go."

"Where are you going?"

"Dad's going to take us out to Roosevelt Park," Billy said. "There's cool trails out there!"

"Tim promised to take me hunting this year," Curtis said, "and we're going to scout a little bit. He wanted me to invite you."

Curtis was obviously lacking in social skills. "You don't have to invite me just because—"

"Yes I do," Curtis cut in, still talking in that laid-back manner, showing no emotion. "He said if I wanted to go four-wheeling tomorrow, I'd have to invite you. So are you coming or what?"

When we first moved to Barksdale, a lot of kids had

invited me to go places, which I thought was cool—until I realized that some of them were doing it only because their parents wanted them to. It took me a while to sort out who was sincere and who was following orders. At least Curtis was being up-front about his motive.

Four-wheeling interested me; going because Captain Vinson wanted to look good for the base commander didn't. But I got the feeling that if I didn't go, Vinson would call off the trip and Billy would be disappointed. I was trapped.

As if to prove it, Billy said, "Please!"

Almost reflexively, Curtis punched his shoulder again. "Quit whining, ya baby."

"Sure," I said, noticing that Billy seemed to be in real pain this time. "Sounds good."

That night Mom went over to talk to the Vinsons to make sure there really was going to be an adult with us. She came back satisfied, not in the least concerned about the embarrassment she'd caused me. I didn't know which was worse: her growing irritability since taking over as base commander or her total cluelessness about being the acting parent. Dad had essentially been in charge of me and Ray and our social lives up till now, and she seemed determined to take on that role.

"Tim seems like a pretty good guy," she said. "Just make sure you have your helmet on at all times and that you listen to him."

"Jeez, Mom! I'm not six!"

"And don't forget sunscreen, either."

"Mom!"

16 August

Mom was gone when I woke up, but she'd left a note on the kitchen counter with a tube of sunscreen and a signed blank check.

> *Stu—*
> *Don't let Captain Vinson pay for your rental. I packed you a lunch. It's in the fridge. Maybe tomorrow we can run into town to see a movie.*
> *Hope you have fun!*
> *Love,*
> *Mom*

The Vinsons had two ATVs of their own, and on the way out of town we stopped at Outdoor Recreation to rent two more. The plan had been to only rent one more for me, but Billy was devastated when he heard he'd have to ride pillion with his dad all day. He didn't whine or anything, just ran his hand longingly over the handlebar of the ATV. When Captain Vinson saw the look on his face, he gave in.

In spite of my misgivings, four-wheeling was a blast. While we were out riding, Captain Vinson asked me three times to call him Tim. He seemed pretty cool. He let Curtis and Billy decide where to go on the trails. When he did make suggestions about which fork in the road to take, Billy always followed his father's advice, but Curtis never paid any attention to anything his stepfather said. I noticed that somehow when I was in the lead, Captain Vinson never had a suggestion to make.

The captain slowed down several times, pointing out the different types of plants and identifying various animal tracks. Once he stopped to show Billy a hunting stand.

Curtis and I pulled over to wait for them. "It blows that Mom dragged me up here to Minot. If I was eighteen, I could live on my own," he said. "I can't wait to get back to L.A."

"I thought you were from Texas."

Curtis snorted. "The Vinsons are from Texas. We're from L.A. Mom met Tim online last year."

"Oh," I said, trying not to sound shocked. Less than a year ago these people had never heard of each other, and now here they were. No wonder things seemed a little off in the family.

"But as long as I'm stuck in this hick dump, I might as well find something to enjoy." He raised his voice as Billy and his stepfather caught up to us. "I can't wait to go hunting!" Curtis shouted, sighting an imaginary rifle on a crow.

"Keep your grades up," Captain Vinson said mildly. "That's the deal."

"I wanna come huntin' too," Billy said.

"Too bad," Curtis sneered.

"Sorry, buddy," Vinson said, tapping on Billy's helmet. "The law says you've got to be twelve to hunt."

Billy sighed. It was clear that he'd already been told that but was hoping something had changed.

"You hunt, Stuart?" Vinson asked me.

I shook my head.

"Wanna try?" Curtis asked.

I shrugged. "Never really thought about it."

"You should come with us," Curtis said. "We get to ditch school."

"Only if you keep your grades up," Vinson repeated. "And stay out of trouble."

"Let's go!" Billy said, bouncing impatiently on his ATV.

"Lead on," Vinson said.

Billy took off, lurching a little bit on the ATV, and Vinson followed him.

Curtis sighted his imaginary rifle on his stepfather's back. "Pow!" he said, pretending to shoot. "What an ass!" He peeled out, spraying rocks and dirt, before I could say anything.

For the rest of the day I focused on the riding. I answered Curtis when he asked me questions but didn't encourage him to talk. I stayed on the trail with Billy and Captain Vinson as much as I could.

It would be better, I decided, to be lonely in Minot than to have Curtis as a friend.

I was counting down the hours left in my vacation. It was Friday, and school started on the twenty-third, approximately 150 hours away. I was excited, but nervous like I always was before starting in a new school. I spent hours in the pool trying to work out my nerves. The cool water washed away the nervous sweat, and I could control the water in a way I couldn't control my life.

Warming up easy, I'd always start with freestyle and backstroke, using long, slow strokes to get down the length of the pool with the least amount of effort possible. Then I'd switch to breaststroke, almost diving each stroke forward. And then, when I felt good and loose, I'd throw in a few laps of butterfly. My coaches had never wanted me to do fly during warm-up, but I liked it because it stretched my back and shoulders.

As I settled into the workout, I pushed myself, making each length faster, each stroke stronger. I increased distance and decreased rest time between each set. As I sprinted through 100s and 50s, I'd focus on grabbing the water in front of me, shoving it so hard I could actually feel the ripples as they rolled down my torso to my thighs and all the way down to my toes. Lap after lap coursed by, rhythmic and comfortable.

I used to play tennis and basketball, but I found that swimming was more satisfying—and easier to take with me. It didn't matter where we moved, I could always find a pool. I wasn't reliant on a partner or someone else to practice with. I could challenge myself. I could work out as often and as hard as I needed to.

Each day that week I'd been the first one in for lap swim and the last one out, finally leaving when the lifeguard stuck a kickboard in the water in front of me and said lap swim was over.

When I made the turn down our street, I saw two cars parked in our driveway. Mom had finally gotten her staff car.

The staff car was supposed to have been ready for her right before the change of command, but someone had screwed up. Mom had called about it immediately. First she was told it was in the shop getting tuned up. Then they said it needed some parts that were on order. She usually stayed cool in situations like that, but I could tell she was getting frustrated. Yesterday, when they told her it was being detailed, she ripped someone in two right over the phone. I hadn't heard her yell like that in years. So I shouldn't have been surprised that the staff car had turned up today.

Then it hit me. Two cars! We had two cars again! And I was getting my license in forty-three days!

I ran the rest of the way home. I didn't want to let Mom get away without hearing my pitch.

"Mom!" I called as soon as I ran into the house. "Hey, Mom!"

"Stuart?" Mom called from upstairs. At the same time, Cardinal charged out of the living room. "Everything okay?" he asked, eyes wide.

Mom pounded down the stairs. "Stuart? What's wrong?"

I blinked. "Nothing."

"Then what are you yelling about?"

"You got the staff car."

She arched an eyebrow at me. "Yes. And I'm about to use it to take Captain Cardinal back to the office."

"So I'll be able to use our car!"

"No, Stuart. We've discussed this."

"I don't mean right now," I backtracked quickly. "But when I get my license. I can—"

"Stuart," Mom began, but I kept talking.

"You said I couldn't have my *own* car. You never said—"

"I said I didn't want you driving on Highway 83," Mom cut in.

"How else am I supposed to get to school?"

"On the school bus."

"But swim practice—"

"No, Stuart," Mom said firmly.

"But—"

"Stuart!" She checked herself and glanced over at Cardinal.

Mom hated to have family disagreements in front of others. Even when I did something wrong as a little kid, she would send my friends home before yelling at me. Family business stayed behind family doors. I knew that. We had to keep family issues separated from base gossip. I knew that. As eager as people are to offer help, they're just as eager to spread word of problems. Security gates and guards can't keep gossip off base. I knew that. She hadn't told anyone here about the separation. I knew that too.

"I bet Dad would—"

"Enough!" Mom swung her hand up so fast I flinched. But she wasn't trying to slap me. She was pointing up the stairs. "Go to your room! And stay there until I come home!" Her face was white, her freckles standing out like spots made with a Magic Marker.

Poor Cardinal was just staring at us.

I started up the stairs. "Sorry about that," I heard her say to him, and then the front door swung open so I couldn't hear his reply. As soon as the door shut, I turned around and went back downstairs. I wasn't going to stay in my room while she was gone. I wasn't some little kid.

I grabbed the remote and slumped down on the sofa. After flipping through the channels for a few seconds, I turned off the TV and went upstairs. After all, the computer—my window to the world—was much more entertaining than HBO could ever be. As a result, by the time Mom came home again I was sitting in my room looking like a good little boy.

When I heard her pull up in the driveway, I considered running down to the living room just to make a point. But I decided chances were she'd catch me as I was going down the stairs, and she would think I was coming to meet her. I stared at the e-mail I'd started to Ray and waited for her to come up and face her current problem: me.

Mom has never been one to put things off for long.

Whether it's discipline for Ray and me or for her troops, she never drags it out.

Sure enough, she came straight up to my room. "So," she said, setting her briefcase down just outside my door. "What was that all about?"

I kept typing. Ray had finally taken the time to tell me about college life—some of the good stuff—and I'd enjoyed reading about it. But I wanted advice on handling Mom. My brother always knew how to get her to see his side. I also wanted to find out how often Dad was calling him. I'd called Dad twice this week and left messages, but he hadn't called back. I was starting to get pissed.

"Stuart, I'm talking to you."

"Be with you in a minute," I said. Mom hates to wait. My fingers danced across the keyboard. An unexpected bonus to having a regular e-mail pal was the improvement in my typing skills. Last year Ray had paid me to type his papers. I was going to miss that money.

"Stuart!"

"Almost done," I muttered. I could've easily typed another five minutes catching up with Ray, but I could've just as easily said good-bye as soon as I heard Mom in the driveway. I was determined to make my point. But there was a very fine line between making that point and pushing Mom over the edge.

I hit Send, waited for my computer to say the mail had actually been sent, logged off, and then shut down the computer before I turned around to look at her.

Mom's arms were crossed in front of her chest, and she was holding her flight cap in one hand. But she wasn't tapping her foot yet, and her face hadn't begun to flush. I had achieved my goal.

I was at my desk and she had come to my room. For a moment there was a feeling that I was in control. That feeling didn't last long.

"You are grounded for a week."

"Excuse me?"

"You heard me."

"What for?"

"For blatant disrespect."

"I wasn't disrespectful, I was—"

"Stuart, you were belligerent and argumentative in front of one of my troops."

"I wasn't being belligerent!" I yelled. "I was trying to make a point and—"

"And I had already said no—"

"You hadn't even listened to what I had to say!"

"I heard what you said, and the answer was no."

"You always tell me it's important to consider all angles. You call it making an informed decision."

"When parenting, there's only one angle to consider, and that's the safety angle."

"I'm turning sixteen, Mom, not six. I don't have to hold someone's hand when I cross the street anymore. I'm old enough for you to trust me."

"Only if you learn to behave."

"I do behave—"

"Ray would have never talked back to me in front of—"

"I'm not Ray!" I exploded. "I never have been!"

Mom took a deep breath, held it for a few seconds, and then slowly released it. "No, you're not Ray. I'm sorry. I know better than to compare you two."

I stared at her, not acknowledging her apology.

"The point remains, however, that I had already made my decision about the car and shared that decision with you. You know better than to argue with me in front of somebody else."

"The point remains," I said, doing my best to match her even tone, "that I wasn't arguing with you, I was merely trying to give you another perspective. The point also remains that you haven't listened to *anything* I've said about the car."

"In this situation, Stu, there's nothing to listen to. The decision was made. Your father and I agreed—"

"Dad?" I interrupted. "You talked to Dad about this? When?"

"As soon as I found out we were coming up here. I knew I'd have a staff car, and I knew that I didn't want you driving on Highway 83. It's a very dangerous stretch of highway—"

"It's not any more dangerous than I-25 in Colorado Springs, and you let Ray drive there when he was learning!"

"We're not comparing you with Ray, right?"

"No, we're not," I said. "But I'm comparing the situations. Highway 83 is totally safe compared to I-25."

"In the winter, the black ice here is horrible. They frequently have to shut down the highway."

"So I won't drive when the highway's shut down," I said, trying to keep the impatience out of my voice. "And it's a long time until winter!"

"It comes earlier here."

"What if I promise not to drive when it's snowing?"

"The decision is final, Stuart. It's not open for negotiation."

"I just want to be able to drive to school—"

"Stuart!" Mom shouted so suddenly and so loudly that I jumped. "I said no! That's it! And you are grounded for another week for your defiant attitude!"

She did a formation-perfect about-face, picked up her briefcase, and closed my bedroom door firmly behind her.

"This sucks!" I shouted.

All I heard was her bedroom door shutting—more than a little firmly.

Fuming, I threw myself down on my bed, but almost immediately jumped up again. Mom had changed since we came to Minot. She was yelling more than she ever had before. Nothing I did or said seemed to make her happy. I'd thought Mom and Dad's separation would cut down on tension in the house, but I was wrong. And now she only had one target.

I paced back and forth between my closet and my bed, then sat down at my desk, both feet tapping. The walls were closing in; I had to get out.

I didn't exactly sneak out of my room, but I didn't stomp down the stairs, either. I opened the front door slowly, waiting for it to squeak, or worse, for my mother's voice to call from the top of the stairs. The door swung open soundlessly, and as I stepped out on the porch, I didn't feel my mother's disapproving stare drilling into my back.

Even so, I didn't really take a full breath until I was halfway across the street.

The late August night was warm, humid, and buggy. I swatted at the mosquitoes, then broke into a run, trying to outpace them and release my tension at the same time. I didn't have a plan, but I headed toward the middle of base, toward the Shoppette, BX, gas station, and theater. I could decide what to do when I got there.

The mosquitoes kept pace with me, so I ducked in the first door I came to, which happened to be the Shoppette.

I browsed aimlessly in the DVD rentals because I didn't have any cash with me. I'd seen almost all of them already anyway. There hadn't been much else to do the last couple of weeks.

"Hey," a lazy voice said.

I turned and saw that it was Curtis. The fluorescent lights made the acne on his forehead stand out. "Hey. What's up?"

He shrugged and ran a finger along the top of a shelf. "Nothing. As always in this crappy place."

I looked around. A couple of young airmen were picking up snacks, and a tired-looking woman stood in the medicine aisle. "Pretty slow."

"I'm goin' to meet some friends. Want to come?"

I shrugged and followed him into the snack row. Anything would beat going home right now. "Might as well."

"Ya got any cash?"

I shook my head.

"Nothin'?"

"Nothin'."

He grunted and picked up a few candy bars. "Me

43

either." He tossed the bars back in the box. "Thought your mom was loaded."

I tried to laugh. "No. She's just another working uniform."

"Got the biggest house on the block. Hell, on the whole base. It's not a duplex and it's the only one with a two-car garage."

"Comes with her job," I said.

Curtis nodded but didn't seem that interested. "Well, at least no one lives in the other side of our stupid duplex. Of course, that could change."

"Yeah, but maybe you'll get cool neighbors."

Curtis just looked at me skeptically. Then he sighed. "Ready to go?"

As soon as we were out of the Shoppette he started off at a pretty good pace, and I fell in beside him. Within seconds, mosquitoes swarmed me again.

He reached in his front pocket and pulled out a pack of cigarettes. "Here," he said, holding the pack out.

"No thanks," I said.

Curtis shook his head and pulled one out for himself. "They're great for keeping the bugs off," he mumbled, returning the pack to his pocket and coming out with a lighter. "Better'n the spray crap my mom uses."

"I'll let your smoke work for both of us."

"Suit yourself."

The mosquitoes still bit me after he lit up, but there seemed to be fewer of them swarming around. "Where're we headed?"

"Out past that big building," he said, pointing toward the other side of base.

"Past the hangar?"

"If that's what it is." He took another drag from his cigarette. "You got your class schedule yet?"

"Picked it up yesterday."

"What lunch you got?"

I thought for a minute. "I'm pretty sure I've got B lunch."

Curtis nodded, blowing a plume of smoke. "Yeah, I think all sophomores have B. You got science right after?"

"I've got geometry after lunch. I have chemistry in the morning."

"Oh, you're in those smart classes," Curtis said. "I've got shop and pre-algebra and earth science. Maybe you can wave to me in the hallway."

I laughed, feeling awkward. Every step I took felt wrong, but I didn't want to go back to the house. "Who are we meeting?"

"Chance and Mike," Curtis said. "You wouldn't know them."

"What's behind the hangar?"

"Just a place."

The lights of the Shoppette, the BX, and the gas station were well behind us now. It was much darker out here. There weren't any streetlights like the ones on the other side of the base, and the buildings were mostly closed. The moonlight was barely strong enough for me to see his profile.

"Tell me again what we're doing out here?" I asked.

"Hangin' out."

I heard a rustling and then his lighter flared as he lit another cigarette.

"This way," he said, giving me a push. He turned off the sidewalk and began to walk through a field.

We passed several buildings with chain-link fences around them, each with their own security floodlight that turned on when we came within range. I stepped on a rock and twisted my ankle a little, but I made myself keep up with Curtis. The crunching of his steps was steady and even. He slowed down a bit when we came to a small wooden building without a fence around it.

"Dude!"

"Hey!" Curtis said, slapping hands with two shadows that appeared from behind the shed. "What's up?"

"Chillin'," one of the shadows said. It was too dark to see his eyes, but I could tell he had light hair and was a few inches shorter than I was. The other shadow seemed to have dark hair and was tall, probably six feet four, and really skinny.

"Simon ain't been here yet," the skinny one said. "Ya got any food?"

"Want a Snickers or a Reese's?"

"Reese's."

Curtis tossed him the package, then handed one to the other guy. "Sorry, Stu. I only grabbed the three," he said, ripping open his candy.

I shrugged, then realized he couldn't see me in the dark any better than I could see him. "No problem," I said, trying to convince myself that everything was okay. I hadn't seen him take the candy from the Shoppette, but I hadn't counted how many packages he picked up and tossed back, either. *He could have brought the candy from his house*, I reasoned to myself.

"How much cash you got, Chance?" Curtis asked.

"Enough for me," he said. "I spotted you last time, remember?"

"Mike?" Curtis almost whined.

"Nuh-uh," the skinny kid said, taking a step back. "Not till you pay me back."

"Crap." Curtis ran his hand through his hair. "Why'd I quit Burger King? Stu, you sure—"

"Told you. I'm broke." And I was getting nervous. It was late, we were on a part of the base where we shouldn't be hanging out, and Curtis was sounding desperate for cash.

I bounced lightly on the balls of my feet. My ankle had quit throbbing. The warm August night was getting a slight chill to it, but on the plus side, the mosquitoes seemed to have disappeared.

A lone car came down the street toward us. I tried to breathe normally. When the car turned into the field and the headlights splashed over us, I flinched.

It rolled to a stop, but I was too blinded to see what kind of car it was. Then a floodlight came on, and I figured it out. SF. Security Forces, also known as base police.

I thought about Curtis's candy bars, and I wanted to run as fast as I could to get out of there. The Security Forces had brought Ray home four years ago, and he'd been without a life for nearly two months. And that was when Mom was just a lieutenant colonel, not the base commander.

But I didn't run—partly because no one else seemed fazed by the car, and partly because I figured running would make me look guilty. But the main reason I stayed put was because I was still mad at Mom and I didn't want to go home yet.

The floodlight allowed me to get a better look at Chance and Mike. Chance was the guy I'd seen Curtis with a couple of weeks ago. I'd never seen Mike before.

"'Bout time, Simon," Mike growled.

"If I'm too late, I'll just leave," a disembodied voice behind the lights replied.

"Naw, man, it's good," Curtis said. He wasn't whining now. He sounded totally relaxed.

"You boys really shouldn't be out here," a different voice called from the driver's side. "If something were to happen to you out here, no one would know about it. We hardly patrol out here most nights."

I didn't like his tone—it sounded vaguely threatening.

"Who's the new guy?" Simon asked. He stepped out of the SF car, but I couldn't make out his face. I felt exposed under their light, like an insect under a microscope.

"Stu," Curtis said easily. "He's my new neighbor."

"New neighbor? And you brought him here?"

"No prob, man. He's cool—"

"Wait!" the menacing voice from inside the car snapped. "A new neighbor? On Chevy Chase? Like just a couple weeks ago?"

"Yeah, but—"

"Jesus, Simon! He's brought Ballentyne's kid out here!"

Any hope I might have had that this meeting was okay evaporated. When people treated me differently because of my mother, it was either because they wanted something or had something to hide.

Simon edged back toward the car door.

"Wait!" Curtis and Mike said at the same time.

"No way, José," the guy in the car said. "And you'd better not be saying our names."

"But, Lu—"

"Shut up!" the voice roared.

Simon got back in the car and said something to the driver that I couldn't understand. But I didn't have any trouble hearing the guy's response.

"I told you all, no names!" The guy sounded really pissed off now. "Ballentyne better never hear our names. We'll send another patrol car in ten minutes to check a vandalism tip we're about to get. Get the hell out of here."

The floodlight snapped off, and in the relative dimness of the headlights I could see the dust and gravel fly as they gunned the car in reverse.

In silence we watched them pull back onto the road and drive away.

As the darkness enveloped us, I once again felt the urge to run. I couldn't see anyone's face, but it was clear that I'd wrecked whatever they had planned for the night. And all because of my last name.

I tensed up, listening for sounds of movement in case Mike or Chance or even Curtis suddenly decided to remind me to keep my mouth shut. I could take care of myself as long as I wasn't ambushed. If all three of them came at me, though, I was going to be in big trouble.

"Crap, Curtis," Mike said. "I knew you were stupid, but this just beats all."

"I didn't know—"

"Bull," Chance said. "You knew he was Ballentyne's kid. You told me—"

"So you knew too," Mike said to Chance, obviously disgusted. "God, what a pair you make."

I could hear gravel crunch as he walked away.

"Where're you goin', Mike?" Curtis asked, the whine back in his voice.

"To find a party."

Chance took a couple of steps after Mike.

"And none of you losers is invited," Mike growled. He continued to crunch away until he got to the street.

We just stood there. Finally he was too far away to hear his footsteps anymore.

"Sorry, guys," I said, because it felt like I should say something.

Curtis sighed. "Now what?"

"We'd better bolt," I said.

"Yeah," Chance agreed.

"I know that," Curtis said irritably. "But where?"

There was an awkward pause.

"I think I'm going to head home," I said.

"You sure?" Curtis asked, with the slightest bit of hope in his voice.

"Yeah," I said. "I've got...ah...an appointment tomorrow morning."

"Okay."

"Let's go hang at my house," Chance said to Curtis, ignoring me. I tried not to be bitter.

We crunched across the field to the street, not speaking. Chance and Curtis smoked until we got to the first streetlight, then crushed the cigarettes on the pavement. To my relief they didn't light up again. We didn't need to be drawing attention to ourselves.

Two cars passed us as we got closer to the Shoppette. We were in the lights of the parking lot when we heard another car approaching us from behind. This one slowed down and trailed behind us for a few seconds before the blue and red lights flashed.

My heart stopped for a second, and I hung my head. Curtis and Chance both swore, just loudly enough for me to hear.

"Hands in the air," a voice barked. It wasn't Simon or the other guy, and I didn't know whether to be relieved or worried.

"Turn around."

We did as we were told, blinking in the flashing lights. Two SF guys got out of the car and walked slowly toward us.

"We need to see IDs," the guy from the passenger side said.

"Can't help you," Curtis said.

"You don't have your ID with you?" the driver asked incredulously.

"I have it," Curtis said, "but I can't help you with my hands in the air."

"Drop your hands, smart-ass, and produce your ID."

We all pulled out our IDs, which passed inspection. I got my first military ID when I was ten, and I thought it was the coolest thing. Now I saw it as just another way for the Air Force to track me.

"Where've you boys been?" the driver asked as his partner handed our IDs back.

"Out," Chance said.

"Out where?"

"We went to Burger King," I said. "And then we went for a walk."

"For a walk?"

"We're all new," I said, "and we were just looking around." Since they'd seen my ID and name, they knew that I was new to the base. Hopefully they wouldn't ask Curtis or Chance how long they had lived here.

"Did you see anyone else while you were walking, Mr. Ballentyne?"

"No sir," I said, trying not to grimace.

"You probably don't want to be walking around late at night like this. It looks suspicious. We've had some vandalism around the base lately."

"Yes sir," I said. "We're heading home right now."

"Want a ride?"

"No!" Curtis and Chance said immediately. Then they seemed to pull themselves together.

"No, thank you," Curtis said. "We're going to the Shoppette."

"Yeah," Chance added. "We're going to get some chips and rent a movie."

"Mr. Ballentyne?" the driver asked.

"Sure," I said, feeling very tired. "I'll take a ride."

The SF guys tried to make conversation with me on the short ride home. First the driver apologized for stopping us. "But we really have had a lot of vandalism," he said over his shoulder. Then he asked where we were coming from and how I liked it so far.

"I just got here from California myself," his partner offered.

"It's not as bad as you might think," the driver said. "It kind of grows on you…like a fungus."

The staff car in our driveway reflected the streetlights, proving it had been well waxed. We pulled in behind it. The cop on the passenger side had to get out to open my door for me.

"Thanks," I said.

"No problem." He hesitated, looked over his shoulder at my house, where the porch light had just turned on, and then looked back at me. "I know it's hard to make friends at a new base," he said, lowering his voice, "but you might want to be careful. We had to take that Sweeny kid home a few weeks ago, and it wasn't just because we wanted to give him a ride."

He looked over his shoulder again and then pivoted, snapping to a salute. "Ma'am," he said.

Mom was standing in the front doorway, arms crossed over her robe. She returned the salute and gave him a curt nod.

"Thanks for the ride," I muttered as I walked past him.

"No problem, Stuart," the cop said in a loud, friendly voice. "We're always ready to help."

He got in the car and they backed out smoothly. Mom stepped aside wordlessly to let me into the house. As I walked past her, I turned and looked across the street. The Vinsons' house was dark except for one upstairs window, where a small silhouette stood.

18 August

Mom wasn't home when I woke up, which was fine with me. Last night I'd gone straight up the stairs to my room and shut the door. I don't know what she did.

I was midway through my second bowl of cereal when I heard the front door open. Mom marched into the kitchen and stood behind the chair across the table from me.

"Want to tell me what happened last night?" she asked. She hadn't even taken her hat off.

I shrugged. "Went for a walk."

"And asked the SFs to bring you home?"

"They offered me a ride."

"What were you doing, Stuart?"

"I told you. Walking."

"Stuart!" Her face went from slightly pink in the cheeks to a salmon color all over.

I dropped my spoon and it clattered into the bowl. "I was walking, Mom. If I had done something wrong, you know they would have told you, just like they did when they caught Ray drinking with those guys at the skate park."

"We're not talking about Ray," Mom snapped.

"No," I agreed. "We're talking about how the SFs handle delinquent kids, and that's the only example I know of."

Mom glared at me.

"The point is, I wasn't doing anything wrong."

"The point is, you were supposed to be in your room."

I rolled my eyes and slumped back in my chair.

"Did you forget to tell me you were leaving?" Her voice cracked ever so slightly on the last word.

I looked up at her. "I didn't *leave*, Mom," I said, alarmed at the way her eyes were glistening. "I just needed to get out for a while."

"You couldn't have told me?"

"You would've said no. And anyway, we were too angry to talk about anything."

Mom took a deep breath and stepped over to the kitchen counter. She took off her hat and tossed it on the counter, then ran a hand through her hair, loosening the curls that had been tucked under it. She turned back to me. "Have we cooled down?"

"I have."

She pulled out a chair and sat down. "Look, Stu. You have five weeks until your birthday," she said. "You'll be riding the bus to school during that time anyway. Find out about swim team schedules and any other activities you might be doing this year, and I'll talk to your father. Then you and I can make an informed decision."

"We can talk about me driving the car to school?" I tried not to smile, I really did, but I was grinning like an idiot.

"We can talk about it," she agreed. "But right now we're going to talk about your punishment for leaving the house without permission last night."

My smile faded. Mostly.

"You're already grounded for two weeks," she said. "I think adding one more week would be appropriate."

"What?" Now my smile was completely gone.

"Or," she said with a smug look that made me uneasy, "you can agree to be my escort for the Dining Out a week from Friday."

I stared at her. "One dinner with you or three weeks in my room?" I asked, making sure I understood my choices.

"Three weeks without your Xbox or going out," she clarified.

She and Dad had been to a bunch of Dining Outs, and they'd always seemed to have fun. "Okay," I said. "I'll be your escort."

How bad could it be?

I hate early mornings. Even though I'd been looking forward to the first day of school, I barely dragged myself out of bed in time to catch the bus. Two boys and a girl were already waiting at my stop at the corner. The girl stood off to one side, but the guys said hi as soon as I walked up. They introduced themselves as Jorge Reyes and Wyatt Porter. They both lived on my side of the street, but I hadn't seen them around because their families had been on vacation for the last two weeks. Mom had said her vice commander's name was Porter, so I was pretty sure Wyatt was his son.

When the bus pulled up, there were still only the four of us. I looked over at the Vinsons' house a couple of times, but Curtis didn't come rushing out the door. Apparently he'd found another way to get to school.

On the ten-mile ride into town, Jorge, Wyatt, and I compared schedules. They were in three of my classes, and we all had the same lunch. I found out they were both swimmers and that Wyatt was a photographer for the school paper. *Maybe*, I thought, *this year won't be a complete loss after all.*

The boys' swim season didn't start until November, but Jorge urged me to sign up for the year-round team.

I was happy to hear that practices were from five to seven every night, because that meant there wouldn't be a bus. Journalism club, which I'd have to join in order to be on the school paper next year, met Tuesday mornings before school, and there wasn't a bus for that, either. My chances of getting to drive to school were looking pretty good.

Jorge asked us if we wanted to go to a movie Friday night. Wyatt said to count him in, and I said yes too.

It wasn't until later that evening that I remembered my promise to be Mom's escort for the Dining Out on Friday.

"No problem, dude," Jorge said when I apologized the next day at lunch. "Turns out my parents are going too. Last night they asked me to babysit my sister and brothers. I figured I might as well make the extra cash. That way if we get to go to the movies the next weekend I can get a large popcorn and soda."

I laughed. "Maybe you'll make enough money to take a date instead of hanging out with us."

"My girlfriend wouldn't be able to go anyway," he said.

"She doesn't like movies?"

"Yeah, but Tricia lives in town and her parents are pretty strict. They don't really let her date much yet. We see each other at church and youth group, but most of the time I have to go to her house to see her. Mom's willing to drive me, but her parents don't like to come up here very often."

"Too bad."

"Maybe we could get a group together in a couple

weeks," Jorge suggested. "Tricia's got friends. She could set you guys up."

"I tried that last year," Wyatt reminded him. He looked at me. "Jorge's girlfriend likes to think she's a matchmaker. Be warned."

I grinned. "It can't be any worse than me trying to find a date."

Wyatt shrugged and looked over his shoulder at the cheerleaders sitting at the next table. "I think I'll try to find my own this year."

So anyway, the journalism club looks cool, but it meets before school."

"Um-hmm." Mom was making marks on some report.

"And I want to join the Minot Swim Team so I'll be ready for the high school season."

"When do they practice?"

"Evenings, from five to seven."

She drew a line through something on the report. "What are you going to do from three to five?"

"I was hoping I'd come home and study."

Mom took off her glasses and looked at me. "Then how will you get back to town for practice?"

"What do you mean?"

She sighed and rubbed the bridge of her nose. "I very rarely get home before six, Stu. You know that."

"But we've got two cars!"

She shot me a warning look. "One, you're not sixteen yet. Two, I still don't like the idea of you driving Highway 83."

"But—"

"I know I said I'd consider it, Stuart, and I still am. But I don't know why we have to keep having this discussion when your birthday's still a month away."

"Because—"

"Don't argue with me, Stuart."

"I'm not arguing, Mom! I'm explaining why I brought it up again," I said quickly. "If we don't talk about it now, then we'll have to talk about it after I'm sixteen and you'll drag your feet and—"

"I am not dragging my feet! And you need to watch your tone."

"Come on, Mom. You know I'm right," I said. "You *know* you're dragging your feet right now. When I turn sixteen, you'll say you haven't looked at all the factors yet, and you'll spend weeks doing that, until it snows six feet and you say I can't drive until after spring thaw and by then you'll come up with some other reason why I can't use the car that's just sitting unused in the garage!"

Mom arched her eyebrows at me. "Did you breathe at all during that?"

"Swimmers have good lungs," I said. "And I need to join the team so they'll get even better."

"We can't settle this now." Mom put her glasses back on and picked up her paper. "I want to talk to your father a little more first."

"When?"

"What?"

"When will you talk to Dad?" As far as I knew, she hadn't talked to him at all since we moved.

"Stuart, I'm trying to get work done—"

"Feet dragger."

She scowled at me.

"Just tell me when you'll call him, and I'll leave you alone until then."

"In that case, I'll call him in four years."

"Mom!"

"Sunday," she said, going back to her report. "I promise I'll call him no later than Sunday."

I had to be content with that.

That first week of school, Billy had been out in his front yard every afternoon when I got home. He always asked if I could play with him, but I always came up with an excuse. When I got off the bus on Wednesday, he was there again, sitting by himself on the front porch.

I felt bad about blowing him off so many times, so I ran inside and grabbed a football. His face lit up when he saw me crossing the street toward him.

"Where's Curtis?" I asked. I'd only seen Billy's brother twice in the hallway at school. As he'd predicted, he wasn't in any of my classes.

Billy's shoulders sagged. "Why? You and Curtis gonna play catch?" he asked. When he lifted his head I saw a large bruise on his left cheek.

"Nope," I said, tossing the ball to him. He caught it reflexively and grinned. It was strange that even though they were so different—his dad was big and tough looking and Billy was small and so skinny he looked breakable—they had identical grins.

"Go long!"

I jogged across the driveway. He threw me a pass, a perfect spiral.

"What happened?" I asked him, pointing to my cheek.

"Oh," he said, reaching up to touch his own face. "Nothin'. I just fell off my bike."

"Ouch."

"Yeah."

We'd been throwing the ball back and forth for almost twenty minutes when the front door of their house opened. I couldn't see who it was, but I had no trouble recognizing the voice.

"Billy!" Curtis shouted.

It was the only time Billy dropped the ball.

"You gotta clean up your room, butthead. Send your dorky friend home."

Billy scooped up the ball and tossed it back to me, a lousy throw that landed five feet short. "Thanks, Stu! See ya later!"

Curtis stepped out onto the porch and gave me a quick glance. "Don't forget your clothes, butthead," he said, swatting at Billy as he ran through the door. Billy ducked, but Curtis's hand still caught the top of his head.

"How's school?" I asked Curtis as I walked up to retrieve the football.

He shrugged. "Sucks, as usual. Only forty-five days till October break, though. See ya." Without waiting for me to respond, he disappeared inside and shut the door.

Before I turned to cross the street, I glanced up. Billy was in an upstairs window, waving and grinning like a madman. I grinned back and waved. I meant to wave to him again, but I heard the phone ringing inside our house. I ran to answer it.

"Hello?"

"Stuart!"

"Dad! I was going to call you again today. How are things?"

"Okay, I guess. But more importantly, how are *you?*"

I flopped onto the couch, tucked the phone between my ear and shoulder, and tossed the football lightly in my hands. "I don't know."

"What's wrong?" he asked. "Is there a problem with your classes?"

"Classes are fine," I said. "At least so far."

"Swim team look good?"

"Yeah, they've got a pretty good school team here," I said, "and there's a year-round team too. Practices are from five to seven. We catch the bus home and then this guy's mom drives us back in for practice." It sucked and meant a lot of dead time driving back and forth, but until Wyatt, Jorge, or I got a license and a car, we really didn't have a choice.

"Ah, so that's where you were last night."

"Yeah. Hey, has Mom called you yet?"

A pause. "No. Was she supposed to?"

I sighed. "Yeah. She won't make a decision about letting me drive till she talks to you."

"I didn't know that was up for debate," he said in a tone that made me wish I hadn't brought it up. "I thought she and I had already made that decision."

"Well, it's really hard not having a car here," I said. "There are a lot of things I want to do at school, and it's not like I can just walk. And it's only a twenty-minute drive, Dad. I'm on the bus for forty-five minutes each way!"

"Well, she hasn't called yet. That's all I can tell you right now." There was another pause, and then he changed the subject. "Have you met many people?"

"I've got a couple guys I can hang out with," I said, and I told him about Wyatt and Jorge. I almost told him about Billy too, but I changed my mind. Dad had always been the one to get the neighborhood groups going, organizing BBQs and carpools and everything else. He wouldn't hesitate to step in to help people. I wasn't sure what, if any, help might be needed, and he couldn't give it from Nevada anyway.

"Sounds super!" Dad said.

"It'll be a lot easier when I can drive, though."

"Stuart," he warned. "Give it a rest."

"But Dad—"

"You know your mom's got a lot to deal with right now. It always takes a while for her to settle into a new job, and it's a huge deal to be base commander. Don't give her a hard time."

"I won't," I said sullenly. "I'm obviously not going anywhere, anyway. I'm here to be her escort to dinners and represent our family."

"Represent it well."

"I have to, since I'm the only one who can't bail on her right now."

"Hey," Dad said sharply. "Watch it."

"Sorry," I muttered, trying not to snap back at him. "How's Gram?"

"Not so great," he said.

"Yeah, that's what Ray told me," I said. "What does that mean?"

"It means she's nearly eighty and things aren't as

66

easy as they were. I've taken her to the dentist, the doctor, the lawyer—it seems like she's had an appointment every day. She had to quit driving a couple of years ago, and she doesn't have any friends nearby. I'm not sure how she's survived. Just getting her to eat right has been a struggle."

"Oh," I said. There wasn't really anything else for me to say. It sounded like he was pretty busy, but how hard would it have been to find five minutes between appointments to give me a quick call before now?

"What's wrong?" he asked.

"Nothing."

He let it go, didn't press me even though I was sure he could tell from my tone that I was upset with him. "How's Ray?" he asked, changing the subject again.

"You've been talking to him. You tell me."

"I'm his dad. He doesn't tell me everything."

"You think he tells me everything?"

"I'm sure he tells you more than he tells me. All I get to hear about is the price of textbooks and the professors who only give two tests all semester and that's your entire grade. I want to hear about the girls and the parties."

"Did you ask him about me?" I asked.

"Of course."

"Then I think I'd better keep quiet," I said. "I don't want to give him a reason to rat me out."

Dad chuckled, and I could almost see him tucking his chin down and running his hand through his hair. I swallowed hard against the sudden tears.

"So what else is new?" he asked. "Are you still e-mailing Taylor?"

"Sort of."

"What do you mean, sort of?"

I shrugged. "I don't know. We're not IMing or e-mailing as much as we used to."

"Well, as we get older, we tend to get busier."

"I know," I sighed. "It's not all Taylor's fault. I haven't been e-mailing much either." These days it seemed like every time I tried to type a message all I did was whine.

"Well, if you're not going to give me dirt on Ray, and you're not going to tell me your secrets, I suppose it's time for me to say good-bye."

"What's a good time to call you?" I asked.

"If you call the house, make it after nine in the morning and before eight at night," he said. "Gram goes to bed early. And don't forget about the different time zones. Remember that we're two hours behind you. But you've got my cell number, right? You can call that whenever you feel like it."

"Okay," I said.

"And Stuart, don't hesitate to call me, okay? For any reason, at any time. Just because I'm in Nevada doesn't mean I don't care."

"I know," I said.

"I love you, son."

"Love you too, Dad."

"Bye."

"Bye." I hung up the phone and could almost feel the emptiness of the house pressing down on me.

I got up and wandered to the kitchen, looking for something to eat. I grabbed a bag of chips and an apple. Mom had stuck a note on the refrigerator.

Stu—

I forgot to tell you that I'll be at ALS graduation dinner tonight, so you're on your own again. I'm really sorry. Can I take you to dinner tomorrow night to make up for it?

Love,
Mom

P.S. There's some leftover ham and potatoes in the fridge, so you don't have to cook!

The empty house threatened to suffocate me. To shake off the loneliness, I switched on my computer. Maybe I could manage just one IM to Taylor without whining. When I logged on, I had mail.

To: StuForceOne
From: H2Oxcelr8r
Subject: Out of touch

Stu—

Just wanted to let you know my computer's been in the shop. Things are so hectic right now, I haven't even had a chance to borrow one to check e-mail. I'm on my dad's laptop right now. I won't be able to use it much, though, because he's going out of town tomorrow morning— HOUSE HUNTING!

Yes, you read that right. He got short notice orders. His report date is 15 Oct. And you'll never guess where we're going. After all you've told me about Minot, I can't say that I'm looking forward to it!

Hope you get Minot warmed up before we get there!

e-ya soon, and c ya l8r!
Taylor

PS—Can you even believe that the Titans are undefeated in preseason? And what happened to your Packers?

I read through the e-mail twice. Finally I figured out that Taylor meant they were moving up here, to Minot! It was too much for me to even think about, so I composed a new message to Ray first, promising not to spill his dirt to Dad if he would promise me the same. Then I went back and read Taylor's e-mail a third time.

Taylor and I had been great pen pals for the last three years. But I wasn't sure how I felt about having him move here. What if we met and didn't get along in person? How was he going to feel if I beat him all the time in the pool? His times were never as good as mine, even when comparing his best events with my worst. Taylor's dad was enlisted. Would it be weird for Taylor that my mom was base commander? And even if we were able to be real friends, what would happen when one of us moved again? Would we be able to go back to being pen pals?

I tugged uncomfortably at my tie and looked around the mostly empty room. There were about twenty-five round tables, all set with white linen tablecloths and alternating red and blue napkins folded into triangle shapes. "I thought you said dinner started at six."

Mom shook her head. "Social hour starts at six. Dinner starts at seven."

My stomach rumbled. "You mean I have to stand around here with you for another hour?"

Mom gave me a disgusted sigh. She reached into her small purse and pulled out a twenty. "Go into the bar. Get me something to drink and something for yourself too. In the far left corner there's a popcorn popper. Just don't ruin your appetite."

I slipped the bill into the pocket of my handed-down-from-Ray jacket and headed for the bar while she glided off to greet some other early comers.

The dining room was empty, but there was already a short line at the bar. As I stood in line, I looked around the room. Everyone else was in uniform or formal wear, and I was easily the youngest person in the room.

When I got to the front of the line, I ordered a lemonade for Mom and a Coke for myself. It was painfully clear that I would need caffeine to get through the night. I glanced over at the empty popcorn machine as the bartender rang up the drinks. "No popcorn?" I asked.

He shook his head. "Not with the Dining Out."

"Is there any food at all?" I asked.

He shook his head again. "Nothing but what they're serving for the—"

"—Dining Out," I finished with him as he handed me the change. I dropped the quarters in the tip jar, stuffed the bills in my pocket, and picked up the drinks.

When I got back to the dining room, I was amazed at the sea of midnight blue. Half of each couple was in uniform, and in several cases both members of the couple were in uniform. Fortunately, with her curly red hair, Mom was relatively easy to find.

"Here he is!" she said brightly. "Russell, Pam, I'd like you to meet my son, Stuart. And Stu, this is Lt. Colonel Porter, my vice commander, and his wife."

I shook his hand. "I've got a couple of classes with your son, sir."

He smiled. "Wyatt told me you're going to be a good addition to the relay team this year."

"I'm going to try to be." I turned to shake his wife's hand and tried hard not to stare. Porter looked to be the same age as my dad, maybe a little older, but his wife looked like she was only a few years older than me. She was resting her hand on her visibly pregnant belly. "Glad to meet you, ma'am." I didn't know what else to say.

Her smile was tired, but her eyes sparkled. "I'm

sure Wyatt's told you he's going to be a big brother in just a couple of months."

Wyatt hadn't said anything, so I nodded because I didn't want to lie out loud.

"Well, you look gorgeous in that gown," Mom told her. "The coral suits you so well."

Mrs. Porter smiled. "Thanks. I've always thought active-duty women have it easy because you don't have to get a new gown for every occasion."

"No, we don't," Mom said with a small smile. "No need to worry about color or style. Just another day in uniform."

It was hard for me to tell if there was a hint of bitterness in Mom's voice or not.

"Oh, Russ, that lemonade looks awfully good," Pam said.

"Yes, dear," Colonel Porter said. He grinned at Mom. "That's what I love about her: the subtle clues she gives on how to keep her happy. We'll see you in a little bit."

Mom and I smiled as they walked away.

"Where are we sitting?" I asked, noticing that others were setting purses and drinks at various tables. "Can we sit over there?" I pointed to a table in the back, close to the kitchen doors.

Mom put her hand on my shoulder. "I'm afraid it's assigned seating at these events, Stuart."

"Where are we assigned?"

She nodded toward the long table in the front of the room. All of the chairs were facing us. There wasn't even a chance that I could sit with my back to the rest of the room. I had a bad feeling about this.

I moaned. "We're in the front?"

She nodded again.

"Can I go sit down over there?" I said, indicating a row of chairs against the back wall.

"You can for a few minutes, but then you'll have to come to the door with me."

The bad feeling got worse.

"We're distinguished guests sitting at the head table, Stuart, and we're going to be introduced."

"It's too late to take being grounded for three weeks now, isn't it?"

Mom laughed.

"I'm going to kill Ray. He said these events were fun."

"How would he know? He's never been to one."

I blinked. "He said he went to one with you last year."

Mom thought for a moment, then shook her head. "No, he went to the Air Force Ball with me, when Dad took you to one of your swim meets."

I bit down on what I wanted to say. She'd never made it to one of my high school meets.

"Your brother was dressed up just like this," she said, smoothing his old jacket on my shoulders, "and we were at the head table. Relax, Stu. You'll have fun tonight if you pay attention and give it a chance. There are a lot of traditions bundled into this evening. Come on," she said, taking me by the elbow. "It's almost time for it to start. We'll go wait in the hall." She had to talk to everyone we passed, so it took us nearly fifteen minutes to get halfway to the door.

Somebody walked by, striking the chimes of what

looked like a small xylophone. The same five notes repeated twice.

The Porters were waiting in the hall, and Mrs. Porter still had her hand on her belly, rubbing it with small circles, ignoring the lemonade her husband kept offering. Mom introduced me to the other members of the head table: the mayor of Minot and his wife; the 91st Space Wing commander, his vice commander, and both of their wives; and the president of Minot State University and her husband. I was sure the evening couldn't possibly get any worse.

Someone arranged us in a line, and of course Mom and I were in the center, which meant we'd be in the middle of the head table. The emcee asked everyone to stand for our entrance, and as I listened to the familiar voice introduce each couple, I tried to figure out who was talking.

"Colonel Tina Ballentyne and her son, Stuart Ballentyne," he announced.

As we walked past the tables of people clapping and staring at us, I looked for the speaker's podium. The emcee was Mom's XO, Captain Cardinal. That's why I recognized the voice. The past few days, Mom had relayed a dozen messages to me through him. I'd talked to him on the phone more than I'd talked to Dad and Ray combined.

When we got to our table, Captain Cardinal's voice boomed out again. "Remain standing for the posting of the colors."

I glanced down at the table. A booklet entitled "The 6th Annual Minot Air Show Dining Out" was on each plate, but more importantly, right in front of me sat a bowl of salad, just waiting. My stomach growled and I was tempted to sneak one of the little croutons. I flipped through the booklet to distract myself until Mom nudged me with her elbow.

The honor guard came in, two of them bearing the U.S. and Air Force flags. It was absolutely still in the room as the four of them marched in slow precision to the head table, heels clicking at the same time so it sounded like one set of feet. The two flag bearers went to either side of the table and placed the flag-poles carefully in the holders. They fussed with the flags, straightening them until the folds hung exactly right, then marched slowly back to the rest of the guard.

"Airman Johanson will now sing the national anthem."

Airman Johanson's clear tenor filled the room. Everyone in uniform stood at attention, shoulders back and hands loosely cupped at their sides. Most of the civilians had their hands over their hearts, like me.

As the last notes faded away, the honor guard snapped their heels smartly and executed a sharp turn. For some reason, my eyes were drawn to their spotless white gloves as the guard marched in perfect synchro-nization out of the room.

"Ladies and gentlemen, please be seated." Our emcee waited for the shuffling to settle down. "My name is Captain Cardinal, and I will be the Vice for the Mess tonight. Colonel Ballentyne is the President of the Mess."

"President?" I whispered to Mom.

"Just listen."

"Each of you has been given the rules of the Mess, so that all may be in order," Cardinal continued. "Those of you who are called out of order at any point during this evening's festivities will be required to take a trip to the grog bowl. You will notice that we have two bowls. The large silver bowl has alcohol in it, so if you are not twenty-one years of age, you will take the grog from the smaller glass bowl next to it."

"Grog?" I whispered to Mom.

"Shhh."

"I ask you all to charge your glasses for our toasts," Cardinal said.

During the general commotion while the glasses were being filled with water, wine, or iced tea, Mom tapped the booklet on my plate. "This will explain most of what's going on," she whispered, "but right now you need to open to the page with the toasts, so you'll know the proper responses."

The salad bowl beckoned and I reached for a crouton. Mom hissed and gave me a paralyzing glare and I drew my hand back.

"Mr. Vice, I would like to offer a toast," a voice said from the far end of our table.

"Yes, Mayor Hoeven," Cardinal said.

"To the Commander in Chief."

Everyone else responded, "To the President!" and then took a drink.

I raised my glass and took a swallow.

"You might want to just take a sip each time," Mom said out of the side of her mouth as I picked up the booklet and found the order of toasts. "There are several toasts."

"Mr. Vice, I would like to offer a toast."

"Yes, Chief Seagren."

"To our troops deployed around the world"—I located the chief, standing at a table to our left—"that their missions may be successful and they will soon be able to come home safely."

"Hear, hear!" everyone replied, lifting their glasses for another drink.

There were six or seven more toasts, and then finally, "Mr. Vice, I would like to offer a toast."

"Yes, Lieutenant Kiernan."

"To the success of our air show this weekend."

"Hear, hear!"

There was a shuffling as we all took our seats. Mom was on my left, Mrs. Porter on my right. They were the only ones I'd be able to talk to, since there wasn't anyone sitting across from us. And there was no way to pretend that people weren't staring at us. We were on an elevated stage, and all of the other tables were arranged to face ours.

"Ladies and gentlemen, please direct your attention to the far side of the room." The lights in the dining room all went out, except for a single light directly over a small square table. It was set, but the chair was empty.

Two members of the honor guard seemed to materialize out of the darkness next to the table and stood just out of the ring of light.

"You'll notice the table is set for one, for our POWs are lonely.... Remember....

"The glass is overturned, for our POWs cannot drink.... Remember....

"The plate has a single slice of lemon, for the price of freedom is bitter.... Remember....

"There is salt on the plate as well, representing the tears that the POWs and MIAs have shed.... Remember....

"While we enjoy our evening together, we must remember our POWs and MIAs, who cannot be with us tonight.... Remember."

The room was so quiet I couldn't even hear anyone breathing. Ever so slowly, the honor guard saluted the empty table and then seemed to completely fade back into the darkness of the room. I felt goose bumps rise along my arms.

"*Remember.*" The word hung in the dark room. The hair on the back of my neck was standing up.

Then the lights came back on. I blinked in the brightness and saw that a couple of ladies were surreptitiously wiping tears from their cheeks. Mom tapped my program, and I read the line she'd pointed out. We had one last toast, and it was silent.

"Ladies and gentlemen, please charge your glasses with water," Captain Cardinal instructed. Almost everyone had to switch glasses. "To the men and women who have given their lives, so that we may live free."

I raised my glass and took a sip. A handful of people around the room finished saying "Hear, hear." They obviously hadn't read their booklets. Sometimes it was nice when Mom looked out for me.

"Ladies and gentlemen, please be seated." Cardinal waited until everyone sat down. "Ladies and gentlemen, I invite you to enjoy your meal."

"Just a moment, Mr. Vice." My mother's voice, unaided by a microphone, rang across the room.

Cardinal, already two steps away from the podium, comically wrenched himself back, as if he'd been hooked midstep. "Yes, Madam President?"

"I do believe that there are several guests this evening who have never attended a Dining Out before."

The hunger in my stomach was suddenly replaced with swarming nerves. My mother wouldn't drag me into this…would she?

Cardinal took a moment to glance around the crowded room. "I do believe that you are correct, Madam President."

"You explained about the two grog bowls, but you neglected to give instructions on the correct way to drink from the grog. That's hardly hospitable."

Cardinal gazed down at the floor for a moment before looking rather sheepishly back at my mother. "You are correct, Madam President. I will explain the proper etiquette—"

"Oh, I think a demonstration would be much more educational," Mom said smoothly.

I relaxed. This wasn't about me after all.

"Ma'am?" Cardinal looked worried, but I was getting the idea that all of this had been planned beforehand.

"Mr. Vice, to the grog!"

Cardinal straightened his dress uniform, threw his shoulders back, and marched briskly to the center of the room. Meanwhile, my mother provided the narration for the rest of the room.

"When called, you must take the shortest route directly to the grog."

Cardinal stopped in front of the silver bowl.

"You then salute the President of the Mess and wait…" Mom paused as Cardinal moved according to her instructions. She smiled and hesitated briefly before returning his salute. "Select a glass. Then fill your glass and toast the Mess." The pink-green-gray sludge that Cardinal ladled into his glass did not look appetizing. He sniffed the glass and made a show of wrinkling his nose.

He raised his glass. "To the Mess!" he proclaimed.

"Empty the contents of your glass in one drink without removing the glass from your lips. To demonstrate that you have, in fact, emptied the glass, you then hold the glass upside down"—Mom paused for a split second—"over your head."

A few people in the audience laughed.

Cardinal knocked back his drink and then lifted the glass over his head. When he turned it upside down, we all saw a few drops fall on his head. From the way he flinched, I was pretty sure a couple went down the back of his neck.

Regaining his composure, he set his glass on the table, saluted Mom again, and then strode back to his place at the podium.

Back at the mike, he tried again. "Ladies and gentlemen, I invite you—"

"Mr. Vice," Mom said.

Cardinal looked down and sighed like a man much put-upon. "Yes, Madam President?"

"I think, since you broke protocol and dripped contents from your glass, perhaps you need another trip to the grog bowl."

Cardinal nodded, but as he stepped away from the

podium, a voice to my right suddenly spoke up. "Point of order, Mr. Vice."

I turned to see Lt. Colonel Porter standing behind his chair.

Making a show of stepping back to the podium, Cardinal lowered his head so his lips were almost touching the mike. "Madam President," he said in an apologetic tone, "Lt. Colonel Porter has a point of order."

I could tell Mom was trying not to smile. "The Mess recognizes Colonel Porter."

"Madam President, while educating the new members of the Mess about the protocol of the grog bowl, you neglected to mention that you must call a point of order and wait to be recognized before speaking."

A brief smile got away from Mom before she was able to resume her stern expression. It was almost like watching a play. "So I did, Colonel Porter. That is a valid point of order."

"And the point of order should be followed with a trip to the grog bowl," Porter continued.

I choked back a laugh as I realized that it was now Mom's turn.

Mom turned to look at Porter, then looked back at Cardinal. She stood up. "Point of order, Mr. Vice."

"The Mess recognizes Madam President."

"I do believe, Mr. Vice, that Lt. Colonel Porter is out of uniform."

Porter looked down at his uniform and held his hands out to either side, the very picture of innocence.

"Please remove your jacket, Colonel Porter."

With a big grin, Porter unbuttoned his jacket. As

he shrugged out of it, he revealed a blue shirt covered with B-52s instead of the regulation white shirt. The members of the Bomb Wing all cheered and pounded spoons on the table. This time I had to laugh.

Cardinal looked at Mom. "It seems that three points of order have been made. To the grog!"

Before departing the table, Mom turned to the Space Wing commander and said sweetly, "Colonel Lair, will you act as President of the Mess during my absence?"

"Yes, ma'am!" Lair said with a grin and a salute.

Porter followed Mom to the center of the room, where they met Captain Cardinal coming from the other side. They all turned to face the head table. They saluted, filled their glasses, and then raised them. "To the Mess!" they all declared. Colonel Lair returned their salute. Mom, Cardinal, and Colonel Porter drank the grog, upended their glasses above their heads, and returned the glasses to the table. They gave another salute before marching back to their places.

At the podium, Cardinal tried one more time. "Ladies and gentlemen, if there are no more points of order..." He looked around the room. No one said anything. "Very well, then, the grog is closed for dinner. I invite you to begin eating."

***

The waitstaff had my dinner on the table before I finished wolfing down my salad.

"See?" Mom said with a smile as I dug into the prime rib. "It's not so bad."

"The food's great, but everything else seems a bit stiff-necked." I raised my eyebrows and nodded toward the booklet beside my plate. "There are a lot of mess rules in there."

"It's the Air Force, Stuart."

"It says you're not allowed to clap," I said. "It says you may only show appreciation by tapping your spoon on the table."

"That's true."

"But what if I've already used my spoon?" I asked.

"You haven't."

"But what if I had?"

"Stuart, don't be difficult."

I flipped the pages of my booklet and found the program. "You're giving a speech?"

"Yes," Mom said, taking a dainty bite of green beans.

"Maybe you should have some more grog," I suggested, "so you can be entertaining."

She gave me a stern look and then changed the subject. "What did you think of the POW/MIA table? It's always one of my favorite parts."

"You've seen it before?"

"Lots of times," Mom said. "It's part of the tradition of a Dining Out."

"Oh," I said.

"The traditions are one of the things I love most about the Air Force. The sense of history, stability, and continuity that the traditions represent."

"Sense of stability and continuity?" I repeated. "In the Air Force?"

"Of course!" Mom said. "What else is the Air Force if not tradition?"

"Change and chaos," I replied promptly. "That's what the Air Force is."

Mom looked surprised. "Is that all you see?"

I thought of all the times our family had moved from one base to another. Things were always similar, but never exactly the same, so you had to learn everything all over again. "The Air Force is pretty much chaos to me."

"I'm sorry, Stuart," she said, putting her hand over mine. "I thought you loved the traditions of the Air Force too, or at least appreciated them. The national anthem every evening, reveille in the morning, taps at night. Knowing someone's name as soon as you see them in uniform, running in formation, watching the Thunderbirds perform—" She shook her head again. "I'm sorry. I guess I got carried away."

I didn't answer. I did appreciate those things. I just didn't love them like Mom did. And she lived the Air Force lifestyle out of choice. I didn't.

As people finished their main courses, Cardinal moved back toward the podium. He paused beside it, apparently waiting for a signal.

He must've seen what he was looking for, because he stepped quickly to the microphone. "Ladies and gentlemen, please stand while the members of our head table depart."

Intermission. What a relief.

We reversed our order and filed out of the dining room. As the doors of the dining room swung closed, I heard Cardinal say to the crowd, "We will have a ten-minute intermission. Please do not be late, because the grog will open again after break."

85

"You look tired. Are you feeling all right?" Mom asked Mrs. Porter.

The colonel's wife smiled wanly, rubbing her lower back. "I've been told I'm feeling as well as can be expected for the middle of the seventh month."

Mom clucked sympathetically.

The doors to the dining room swung open, flooding the hallway with noise and a crush of people heading to the bathrooms. It seemed like an equal number were heading to the bar.

I was watching the crowd when I heard a voice that sounded familiar.

"No, man, really, we can't bail now!"

"Sure we can!" somebody else said.

"I'm telling you," that familiar voice said, "Sarge will notice."

I glanced over my shoulder to the small group of airmen, most with only one or two stripes, none of them looking much older than eighteen. The one with the familiar voice was a tall skinny guy with acne across his forehead and chin and an unfortunate birthmark on the right side of his face. "Simon, you're such a chicken!" someone razzed him.

I froze. The floodlight. The SF car.

"C'mon, Luke, I can't get another LOR," Simon whined.

"So if you don't get caught you won't get a letter of reprimand!" Luke said with a smirk. "Besides, it's not like we were ordered to come here. We paid for the tickets, and we got our dinner. Let's go."

"Sarge said I should be here," Simon said. "It was strongly recommended."

"And you were here. But you don't have to stay."

"Hey."

I turned suddenly to see Captain Cardinal standing next to me.

"I'm heading to the bar," he said. "Can I get you another Coke?"

Simon and his buddies had moved away, so I couldn't eavesdrop any more. "Good idea," I said. "I'll come with you."

As we made our way through the crowd to the bar, Cardinal said, "What do you think?"

"About the Dining Out?"

"Well, yeah."

I shrugged. "It's been okay so far."

"Only okay, huh? You haven't gotten a kick out of any of it?"

"The grog bowl stuff's kind of funny," I admitted as we took our place at the back of the line. "I wonder what's in it."

"Just ask the person who made it."

I grinned. "And who would that be?"

He grinned back. "Well, it's usually the person in charge."

"So what makes it all sludgy?"

"Sherbet," he said. "The rainbow colors look nasty when they melt together, but it really doesn't taste that bad."

I scanned the line of people waiting for drinks. Not everyone in uniform had a date, but most of them seemed to be with someone. "Where's your date?"

"Didn't bring one," he said easily. "Being Vice of the Mess doesn't leave much time for socializing at a Dining Out."

"You're socializing now," I pointed out, before I

87

realized that watching out for the commander's kid was probably part of his job as Vice tonight.

"Yeah," he said. "But I'm not so sure that socializing for the ten-minute intermission of a three- or four-hour dinner would go over well with a date."

"Three or four hours?" I asked in dismay.

He grinned and clapped a hand on my shoulder. "Unless your mom makes you stay for the dancing. That could add another couple hours, easy." He laughed at my expression.

"You're not supposed to enjoy other people's misery!" I complained.

That only made him laugh more.

"So, you got a regular girlfriend?" I asked him.

"Naw, I like mine irregular," he said, still laughing.

I shook my head.

"I can see you've spotted someone you'd like for a regular girl," he said abruptly.

"What?"

He lifted his chin, pointing down the line. "That blonde in the red dress," he said. "You've been staring at her while I've been talking."

"Who wouldn't stare?" I countered, trying to hide my embarrassment. "She's hot."

"No argument," Cardinal said. "But she's a little too young for me, and probably a little too old for you."

"What about that brunette over there?" I asked, tilting my head and pointing with my eyes. It was like I was hanging out with Ray again, checking out the girls. Who cared if they had dates? There was no harm in looking.

"I don't know," he said, after careful consideration.

"She's a little too skinny for me. I like 'em with more—"

"More what?"

Captain Cardinal turned to find my mother at his elbow. "Ma'am," he said, flushing brilliant red.

"More what?" Mom asked again.

Flustered, Cardinal could only repeat, "Ma'am?"

"Mom, it's not polite to butt into a conversation," I said, trying to help Cardinal.

"Oh, by all means, finish your conversation."

"I think we just did," Cardinal said quickly. "Can I get you a drink, ma'am?"

She smiled. "I came over to ask my escort to get me one."

I patted my pocket. "I still have the change from earlier," I said. "I'll bring you another lemonade."

"Wonderful." She squeezed my arm lightly and turned to go. "But make sure you're back before the chimes ring," she added.

"I'll see that he's not late, ma'am," Cardinal assured her. His color was beginning to return to normal.

I looked at Cardinal after she left. "Will you get me a shot of vodka?"

"Excuse me?"

"Not for me," I said in a hurry. "I mean for Mom's lemonade."

He gave me a funny look.

"Trust me, her speech will be much better if we spike her drink."

"Stuart, I think—" He broke off, staring at a woman who had gotten her drinks and was coming back along the line.

She definitely wasn't too skinny. The top of her

scarlet dress plunged in a V almost to her navel, and she was dangerously close to popping out of it. The tight dress might have been attractive on someone a bit thinner, but on her it just accentuated the rolls around her middle that jiggled as she walked.

Her face was kind of ordinary, except for the fact that she looked totally pissed off and her makeup was dark and dramatic. She was carrying two drinks, wobbling a little bit on her high heels.

I couldn't figure out why Cardinal found her so noteworthy. He had stopped mid-sentence and stared at her with his mouth hanging open.

Then I saw her date, and it was my turn to stare.

"Stuart!" Captain Vinson said, sounding genuinely pleased to see me. "I hope you're enjoying sitting at the head table tonight. Not many people get that chance."

I nodded because I wasn't sure I could speak normally. I noticed that although his wife carried two drinks, Vinson had his own drink in his hand.

"Darla, this is Stuart Ballentyne," Captain Vinson said. "I took him four-wheeling with Curtis and Billy, remember? I'm sure you've seen each other around the neighborhood."

I nodded again, even though I was sure I'd never seen her. I would have remembered this woman.

Darla Vinson sniffed. "You promised to take Curtis out again," she said to Vinson.

"I said that—"

"You've taken that kid of yours out twice since the last time you took Curtis," she went on.

I exchanged a look with Cardinal.

Captain Vinson sighed, and I could tell this was a conversation they'd already had. "Darla, sweetheart, you know—"

Darla broke in, turning her sharp gaze back to Cardinal. "Do you think a marriage can work if one spouse clearly favors his own child above the other's?" One of her drinks sloshed over the edge of the glass.

I shifted uncomfortably, and Cardinal looked at his shoes.

"Come on, honey," Vinson said, tugging on her arm and spilling the other drink. "Let's go back to the table. Good to see you again, Stuart. Captain Cardinal." He nodded and led her off.

"Let's get your mom's lemonade," Cardinal said. "I'll get a separate shot of vodka, in case she wants it."

"And if she doesn't?"

"I think I may need it."

* * *

"Mr. Vice, point of order!" The words rang out across the dining room.

"The Mess recognizes Lieutenant Kiernan."

"I have observed that the diners at table ten have beer bottles in front of them, in direct violation of the Mess rules."

"I observed that as well," Captain Cardinal agreed. "Madam President?"

"I believe all members of table ten should go to the grog," Mom said.

"Madam President?" Lieutenant Kiernan added, "I believe that Mr. Vice is a member of table ten."

"Is this true, Mr. Vice?" Mom asked.

"Yes, Madam President, it is true, and I had planned to go to the grog with my table."

"Very well. Lieutenant Kiernan, since you doubted the honesty of Mr. Vice, you may join table ten at the grog."

There was a lot of laughter, and then a pounding of spoons on tablecloths as the military members of table ten and Lieutenant Kiernan stood and marched to the grog bowl.

And so it went, as four or five more people made points of order and sent their friend or nemesis to the grog bowl.

"Mr. Vice, point of order!"

Cardinal's grin seemed to slip a little as he turned to face the speaker. "The Mess recognizes Mrs. Vinson," he said.

I heard a strange sound next to me, and I turned to look. Mrs. Porter looked bad. She was extremely pale, and her face was pinched.

"Mom," I said, "I think there's a problem."

Mom looked past me to Mrs. Porter and suddenly stood up.

Mrs. Vinson spoke in a slurred voice. "I believe that you—"

Mom cut her off. "Mr. Vice, I have decided that the first intermission wasn't enough. The grog is now closed while we break for an additional fifteen-minute intermission."

Cardinal didn't miss a beat. "Everyone please rise as our head table departs."

There was a buzz of confusion as all of us at the head table stood up and left the room. I was watching

Mrs. Porter, who was leaning on Colonel Porter's arm.

Once in the hallway, Mom slipped an arm around Mrs. Porter and helped Colonel Porter get her to a chair.

Mom leaned in close, apparently asking Mrs. Porter a question. She shook her head. Colonel Porter bent forward and said something else. Mrs. Porter began to shake her head again, but then she cried out in pain.

"That's it," Mom said. She and Colonel Porter helped Mrs. Porter to her feet. "Stuart, will you go get Mrs. Porter's coat?"

Colonel Porter reached in his jacket and tossed me a tag.

I trotted over to the coat check and gave the attendant the tag. When I had the coat, I went to the front door, where Colonel Porter was just pulling up. Mrs. Porter was leaning heavily on Mom, apologizing.

"Don't worry about it, Pam!" Mom said. "Just go home and take care of yourself and the baby, that's all I ask."

"We're going to the hospital first," Colonel Porter said as he came around the front of the car to help his wife.

Mrs. Porter began to argue but then looked at his set face. "Yes, dear," she murmured.

I stood next to Mom and watched as the Porters drove away. Mom chose not to stay for the dancing. We left as soon as her speech was over, which was fine with me.

1 September

Once again, Mom was gone before I got up. I had gone straight to bed when we came home from the Dining Out, but she hadn't. She was on the phone when I drifted off.

I ate a quick breakfast and headed out to the air show. I thought about riding my bike, but decided I'd rather walk. It turned out to be a good idea, because the traffic got crazy as I reached the main part of the base. Minot AFB was open to the public for the air show, and a lot of people were taking advantage of the opportunity to visit. Several roads had been closed or turned into one-way streets in an effort to keep everything flowing smoothly.

The best parts of the show wouldn't be starting until later. The F-16s that had arrived earlier in the week would do aerobatic stunts at one o'clock. At two, an old biplane was scheduled to demonstrate flight patterns with someone doing acrobatics on the wing. But there was always plenty to see in the morning at air shows. A lot of planes were set up on the tarmac as static displays, and a couple of bands were going to be playing before noon.

And I knew from experience that all the free stuff would be gone by the time things really got rolling.

I stopped at the missile payload transporter first, because I'd never seen one before. It was a big semi-trailer with several decks inside. A tech sergeant was explaining it to a family in front of me, so I edged closer to hear what she was saying. The decks kept the payload—the nuclear warhead—stable during transport. When the warhead was to be unloaded, the truck would be pulled directly over the missile silo and the side flaps on the trailer would be lowered in accordance with environmental regulations.

After that, I headed to the recruiting booth, because that's where the free stuff was. I scored a T-shirt, a poster, and a key chain, but passed on a spongy ball and lapel pin. I glanced through a pile of Air Force coins. Since they only said "Aim High Air Force" and were made of a flimsy light-as-plastic metal, I passed on them too. It's an Air Force tradition to create coins for each squadron, group, and base and have commanders give them out. I had a pretty good collection at home.

"Hey, Stu!"

I turned and saw Jorge. He was carrying a little boy and holding onto the hand of a little girl. She was trying to twist away from him, but he pulled her over to me like he didn't notice her tugging at all.

"Hey, Jorge. What's up?"

"Looking for my mom, man. She took Tino to the bathroom and I took Dominick and Rosa to check out the helicopter."

"It was boring," Rosa said, still pulling against Jorge's grip.

"So we went to the C-5," Jorge said, ignoring her,

"but when we went back to the helicopter—"

"They weren't there," I finished with him.

"Exactly." He shifted Dominick on his hip just as Rosa gave another pull, and she almost got free. "Quit it!" he snapped.

"Here," I said, shifting my bag of free stuff to one side and holding out my arms. Jorge handed Dominick over and the little boy leaned back and studied me for a moment. Then he popped his thumb in his mouth and rested his head against my shoulder.

Jorge fiercely whispered something in his sister's ear, then straightened up and grinned at me. "Wow. Dom really took to you."

"Yeah."

"We should probably go back and wait by the helicopter," Jorge said. "Want to come with us?"

"Sure."

"This way!" Rosa tugged Jorge to the left.

"Yeah," I said, feeling awkward. I hadn't meant to take Dominick for more than just a few moments, long enough for Jorge to get Rosa in line. But now Jorge didn't seem to be in a big hurry to take him back.

We walked past the missile truck and the C-5. The helicopter, a Huey, had drawn a pretty big crowd, but not nearly as many as the B-52 spectators. A lot of people from town apparently were interested in finding out about the base's main mission. The B-1 bomber, however, had more people around it than all the other displays combined. The tarmac looked like a carnival fairway without the rides.

Jorge and I found a place in the shade and waited for his mom. Fortunately she didn't take long. And as

96

soon as she came up, Dominick immediately reached for her and she took him from me. I flapped my shirt a little, where his body heat had sweated it to me.

Mrs. Reyes settled Dominick in the back of the two-seated stroller. "I think it's time to get some lemonade and maybe a bag of popcorn," she told the kids. "Would you like to come with us?" she asked me.

"Um—" I didn't want to ditch Jorge, but I really didn't want to spend the rest of the day watching his little brothers and sister. "Actually, I should probably go find my mom. I think she's supposed to be over by the bandstand."

"Okay," Mrs. Reyes said, already pushing the stroller toward the food booths.

"See you later, Jorge."

"See ya," he said glumly.

I headed in the other direction. I thought it'd be nice to find Mom, because I could probably talk her into holding my poster for me, but I quickly gave up on that idea. She'd be running around making sure everything was going smoothly, and then when the show was over she'd be running around making sure everything got back to normal as fast as possible.

I passed a long line of kids waiting to climb up into the cab of a fire truck. I glanced over my shoulder to see if the Reyes were still in view, but they'd disappeared into the crowd.

"Stu!" a voice called.

"Hey, Wyatt!" I said. "How's your mom?"

"My stepmom? Oh, she's fine, but the doctor put her on bed rest until the baby comes. Dad's staying home with her today."

"I'm glad everything's okay."

"Yeah. Seen anything good?"

"I was heading to the B-1."

"Me too. Let's go!"

Wyatt and I looked at all the planes. When I told him about the missile truck, he wanted to check it out. I took him over there and told him everything that I remembered the tech sergeant had said about it. I'd been going to air shows ever since I could remember, but not every base has them and there's always something different to see, so I tried to remember as much as I could about everything I saw at each one.

I showed Wyatt my "Cross into the Blue" T-shirt, and he wanted one, too, so we headed back to the recruiting tent. The shirts were gone, but he got a poster and picked up a coin. After that we hit a couple of food booths and got in line for the mobile flight simulator.

A familiar voice boomed over the loudspeaker. "Ladies and gentlemen, in just a few moments the 91st Security Forces will be demonstrating a field exercise on the strip of land between the runways." If I wanted to find Mom now, it wouldn't be hard. She was at the microphone.

Wyatt looked at me with raised eyebrows.

"Yeah," I said. "Let's go watch."

We maneuvered to find a place fairly close to the fence and ended up just a couple of feet behind two women, one of them with a stroller and small camcorder. Another family of four was just in front of them, and a few feet to our left were two airmen sergeants wearing the berets of the Security Forces. We were about as close as we could get to the demonstration.

A few minutes later, a helicopter swooped in, sending dust swirling as it touched down briefly. The popping of gunfire filled the air as camouflaged airmen spilled out of the chopper and moved toward their objective, a shack guarded by other men in camouflage. I was wishing that someone would get on the loudspeaker and explain what the objective of the exercise was—I couldn't tell if the airmen at the shack or the ones from the helicopter were supposed to be the good guys—when one of the women in front of me turned to her friend.

"Wow, they're pretty lousy shots. All this gunfire and no one's been killed yet."

Her friend laughed. "I know. It's not giving me a lot of confidence that the Air Force can keep us safe."

Wyatt and I glanced toward the two Security Forces airmen. The one closest to us was staring at the two women. The other airman stepped forward slightly, and I saw the birthmark on his face.

Simon.

The women in front of us were oblivious to the attention they were attracting.

"I can't believe they're doing this for the public," the woman with the camcorder said. "If you're showcasing something, wouldn't you want it to be a skill that's well performed?"

Next to me, Wyatt snorted, trying to keep from laughing.

"I know. And what's with belly crawling when you're in plain sight, anyway? Wouldn't it be better to charge since the other guys can see them?"

Out of the corner of my eye I saw Simon take another step forward. His partner put a hand on his shoulder, stopping him.

I took a step forward so that I was directly behind the women. "Excuse me," I said almost in their ears, making them jump. "The bullets are blanks and their moves are all predetermined. It's too risky to do a live-action exercise this close to so many people."

"Then what's the point?"

"It's just for entertainment," I said patiently. "But if you'd like to ask more about the Security Forces and their duties, I'm sure the two airmen behind us would be happy to explain it."

The women both looked over their shoulders and saw Simon and his partner glaring at them. The women looked at each other and the dismay on their faces was clear.

"Thank you for your help," one of them said.

"I think I need a lemonade," the other one suggested. "What about you, Sonia?"

"Sounds good." And they both turned to weave their way through the crowd.

Wyatt gave in to his laughter. I looked over at Simon and his partner. His partner nodded. Simon just stared at me. I smiled. He turned to whisper something to his buddy, and then they both left.

"Hey, man, do you think the burger booth is still open?" Wyatt asked.

"Yeah," I replied. "Let's go."

So what's with those Vinson people?" Ray asked over the phone.

"I don't know," I said, looking out the window. I could see Billy playing by himself in the front yard. I flopped down on my bed and switched the phone to my other ear. "It's a very odd dynamic across the street, that's for sure."

I tossed my SuperBall against the wall, aiming for the second *o* in "Cross into the Blue" on the poster I'd picked up at the air show. It showed the silhouette of an airman saluting under the waving flag, while a formation of four F-16s flew overhead.

"Guess I'll have to see for myself."

"Are you coming here to visit?" I asked, sitting up.

"Well, yeah," Ray said, sounding surprised. "Of course. For Thanksgiving."

"Thanksgiving?" I repeated. "But that's months away!"

"That's the only time I've got a break, Stu," Ray said. "Don't be an idiot."

"I'm not an idiot," I grumped, lying back down.

"How are classes, non-idiot?"

"Fine. Nothing too exciting."

"No repeats?" he asked.

One of the worst things about moving a lot was finishing a unit at one school, then having to do the same unit again at the next school. I studied the transcontinental railroad in both third and fourth grade and had to read *The Giver* three years in a row. Dad tried to stay on top of things, and if he found out either one of us was repeating a unit, he'd call and ask the teacher to give us an independent study. Ray and I decided it was better to do the unit twice. It made for easy A's.

"No repeats so far," I said. "But the teachers didn't give us full-year syllabuses, either."

"Maybe Mom will ask when she goes to back-to-school night."

"It was last week," I replied. "She didn't get home in time."

"Oh."

"Have you picked a fraternity?" I asked him. He was going through "rush," something I didn't completely understand. According to his explanation, it was like picking a group of guys to hang out with.

"I got bids from three frats, but I've narrowed it down to two," he said. "I'll have to declare one by next week. And then I'll be out of touch for a few days, doing initiation."

"What's that?"

"A twisted kind of boot camp."

"Oh. That sounds...not fun."

"It'll be okay, I guess. You only go through it once."

"Yeah."

Silence filled the line for a moment.

"So how's—" we both began at the same time.

"Go ahead," Ray said.

"No, you go," I said.

"How's Minot?" he asked. "I mean, really, is it that bad?"

"I don't know," I said. "The base isn't too bad. You know, the houses are away from the flight line and everything. The indoor pool's decent, but the gym's in bad shape, and the BX has a lousy selection."

"Really?"

"It's one of the smallest BXs I've ever seen."

He laughed. "Which is saying something."

"Yeah."

"Hey, check your spring break schedule. Maybe you could come hang out here for a few days."

"Really?"

"Yeah, man. It'd be cool."

We were quiet again for a few seconds, then he asked, "How's Mom?"

"Fine."

"I mean it, Stu, how is she? How's she taking everything?"

"In stride," I said, "like she takes everything."

"Keep an eye on her, okay?"

"What, escorting her to the Dining Out wasn't enough?"

"This is really hard on her—"

"Well, that's not my fault!"

"I didn't say it was. It's not anyone's fault. It's—"

"You don't think it's her fault?" I countered. "You don't think that maybe if she'd try putting her family first for a change then maybe she'd still have one?"

"Stuart, that's not fair! She's—"

"Life isn't fair, remember? That's what she always told us. So why should I suddenly worry about being fair? If she's unhappy, it's her own fault and—"

I heard footsteps running down the stairs. Crap. Mom must have heard me. I hadn't even known she was home. Then I heard the front door open and slam shut. I ran to the window and watched as Mom got in her staff car and took off.

"Stu? Stu? You there?" Ray asked.

"Unfortunately," I sighed.

* * *

Around eight that night, I picked up the phone and dialed Mom's work number. As much as I wanted to avoid it, I knew I had to talk to Mom about what I'd said. But before it rang, I changed my mind and hung up. We needed to talk in person. I'd wait until she got home from work.

I watched a DVD and was halfway through a second movie when there was a sudden loud pounding on our door. I vaulted over the back of the couch and ran to the front hallway. Someone pounding on your door after eleven at night couldn't be good, wherever you were.

When I flung the door open, I expected to see the flashing lights of emergency vehicles, if not in front of our house, then at least somewhere along the block.

Instead I found Billy, panting hard. Tears had left streaks down his cheeks.

"Billy! What's wrong?"

"I'm scared!" he cried, and he flung his arms around my waist, almost knocking me over.

I wasn't used to comforting little kids. Feeling strange, I put my hand on top of his head. "Scared? Scared of what?"

He pointed behind him. All I could see was the empty street. Most of the houses were dark, though a few had lights in the upstairs windows. Billy's house was completely dark, but with the help of the street-light, I could see that the front door was open.

"You're scared of your house?"

With his face still pressed against my midsection, he nodded.

"Where are your parents?"

"Daddy and Mother Darla went out."

"They left you alone?"

"Curtis was s'posed to stay home with me."

"Where is he?"

"I don't know," Billy wailed. "We was watchin' a movie, an' then...an' then..."

"Then what?"

"Then I looked over and he wasn't there!"

"He left?"

"Uh-huh. Then the TV went out, an' I couldn't turn the lights back on or nothin' else!"

I had a flashback to a night when Ray was supposed to be watching me. I had a sneaking suspicion that Curtis was messing with poor Billy, trying to scare him the same way Ray had scared me by turning off the lights in the middle of a horror flick. Sometimes it sucked to be the youngest kid. "What kind of movie was it?" I asked Billy.

"A scary one! Real scary!"

"Were the lights on before Curtis left?"

"Naw," Billy said, leaning back and looking at me like I was stupid. "Ya don't watch a scary movie with the lights on!"

I bet I know who told him that, I thought as Billy took a couple steps away from me and swiped his face with his sleeve.

"So Curtis disappeared while it was dark and you were watching a scary movie?"

Billy nodded his head vigorously.

"Did you go looking for him?"

"Nuh-uh. It was too dark."

"Why didn't you turn the lights back on?" I asked.

Again, Billy looked at me doubtfully. "I *told* you," he said. "The TV turned off and the lights *wouldn't* turn on!"

"Oh. Right." I rubbed the back of my neck and stared over at the Vinsons'. The house was still completely dark. I was pretty sure that Curtis was playing a trick on Billy, but I couldn't figure out why he hadn't put a stop to it when Billy ran out of the house. Ray had turned the lights back on for me as soon as I'd started crying.

"Will you help me?" Billy asked, sounding much younger than his eight years.

"Sure," I said. "Just let me get my shoes."

While I tugged on my sneakers, I asked, "When are your mom and dad supposed to be home?"

"Daddy said he and Mother Darla would be out late. He said I'd be asleep when they got home."

I stood up and started for the door.

"You got a flashlight?" Billy asked.

"Um, sure," I said. "Hang on." When I returned

from the kitchen with the flashlight, I could see the relief on his face. "Do you always call her Mother Darla?" I asked as I pulled the door shut behind us.

"That's what she told me to call her. That way, I'm showin' her respect but still rememberin' she ain't my real mama," he said, clearly reciting a lesson.

"I never heard Curtis call your dad Father Timothy."

"Nope," Billy said. "He just calls him Tim."

When we got to his house, I flipped the first light switch on and off several times. Nothing.

"Told ya," Billy said in a tone of disgust. He pulled the flashlight from my hand. "The lights are out. *All* of 'em."

Still, as I followed Billy and the small spotlight through the rooms, I flipped every switch, just in case the power was on in part of the house. We were halfway up the stairs when we heard a loud thump. We both froze.

"What was that?" Billy whispered.

"I don't know," I whispered back.

"I'm scared again," he moaned.

"Don't be," I whispered. Then I cleared my throat and made myself speak in a normal tone. "I'm sure it's nothing."

The words were hardly out of my mouth when there was another loud bump. It felt like it was right on the other side of the wall I was leaning against.

"Come on," I said, heading back down the stairs.

"We gotta find Curtis!" Billy cried. "We can't leave him in here alone!"

"We're going to find him," I said, forced to stop because Billy had the flashlight. "Come on. I'm pretty sure I know where he is."

"Why didn't you say so?" Billy said, practically bounding down the stairs after me. "Let's go!"

It killed me that even though Curtis held Billy at such a distance, Billy seemed to adore him.

At the bottom of the stairs, Billy started toward the living room.

"Uh-uh," I said. "Other way."

"The garage?"

"Yep."

Billy pushed open the door to the garage. "Curtis? Whatcha doin' out here?"

"Oh, crap," Curtis said.

I followed Billy in. There were five or six scented candles burning. They provided an eerie light, but they couldn't completely mask the sweet smoky smell. At first I thought it was strange that Curtis would be getting high by himself, but then I spotted Chance lounging on a weathered patio chair and Mike astride one of the ATVs.

"Crap," Curtis said again when he saw me.

"Billy was worried," I said.

"Aw, was the wittle baby fwightened?" Curtis asked in a terrible singsong voice.

"No way!" Billy said instantly. "Not me!" He shot a nervous look at me but he didn't need to. I knew how much a big brother's opinion meant.

"He was worried," I repeated, "because the power went off, not because of the movie."

"Oh. Sorry 'bout that," Curtis said, grinning in a way that wasn't sorry at all. "I bumped the circuit breaker by mistake. Didn't realize it bothered you." He stood up, reached across the workbench, opened the breaker box, and began flipping switches. "It was an accident, Billy-boy. Sorry." He flipped at least eight switches on. "Go on back and watch the rest of the movie now."

"Ain't you comin'?" Billy asked uncertainly.

"I'll be there after a while."

"But—"

"Damn it, Billy, I can't be rude to my friends! Now go watch your stupid movie!" As Billy turned to the garage door, Curtis added, "And since you're such a wuss, go ahead and watch your scary movie with the lights on!"

"I'm not a wuss!" Billy only hesitated briefly at the door before walking back into the house.

"Dude, close the door," Curtis said. "I gotta keep the smoke out of the house."

I pulled the door shut.

Mike snorted. "I think you're supposed to be on the other side of the door."

"You know that if you get caught, your whole family will get kicked off base," I said.

"Good, then we could leave this dump," Curtis said.

"God, this guy's a real good boy, isn't he?" Mike sneered.

Chance reached down and pulled a baseball bat out from under the chair. Holding it loosely in his hand, he said, "It won't be hard to figure out who squealed if we get busted."

"I wouldn't—" I began.

"No, you're a pansy that follows all the rules," Mike said. "You don't smoke and you've probably never been drunk. Come on, admit it. I bet you don't even stay up past your bedtime."

I ignored him. "Give Billy a break," I said quietly to Curtis. "It's not easy being a little brother."

"He's not my little brother, so that's really not a problem."

I turned to open the door, then stopped. "Anyone got a cigarette?"

"Why? You want to try to prove something?" Mike asked with an evil grin.

"No," I snapped, "but I don't want to go home smelling like weed. One of you needs to blow cigarette smoke on me."

Chance smiled and tossed me a pack. "No way I'm going to let you tell anyone I blew you. Blow your-self."

I fumbled as I pulled out a cigarette. I stuck it in my pocket and tossed the pack back to Curtis, eager to get out of there.

"Here," Curtis said, throwing me his lighter. "Go ahead and light up. We'd hate to see you get smoke in your house. You know, the big one where the base commander lives?"

Jackass, I thought. I wasn't afraid of these losers, but I wasn't stupid, either. There were three of them, and I had no doubt that if one of them chose to jump me, the other two would join right in. But now I was stuck. They were watching me, smirking, making me feel worse than stupid.

I stuck the cigarette in my mouth and fumbled with the lighter. One of them snickered, but I didn't bother to look up to see who it was.

Luckily the lighter was cooperative and I got a flame on the second try. I let it go out.

"What's wrong?" Chance asked.

"It ain't that hard," Mike said. "Do you need a demonstration?"

I flicked the lighter again and raised it to the cigarette. My plan was just to suck some smoke into my mouth. But it didn't look like the tip was burning, so I inhaled to try to help it catch. I inhaled too hard.

Immediately my lungs began to burn. I started coughing, and the guys all burst into laughter. I concentrated on taking a few puffs into my mouth and blowing the smoke down the front of my shirt. The feel of the smoke rolling around in my mouth was odd but not unpleasant. On the third puff I inhaled too much again, setting off another bout of coughing. I threw the cigarette on the garage floor and stepped on it.

As I walked out the door, I said, "If I could smell the weed over those candles, I bet Vinson can too. You're gonna squeal on yourselves if you don't start airing this place out now."

I slammed the door behind me, cutting off their replies.

"Curtis?" Billy's voice wavered just a bit.

"No," I said, following the sound and flickering light of the TV to the living room. "Sorry, Billy, it's just me."

"You wanna stay and watch this with me?" he asked hopefully.

I shook my head. "Some other time," I said, observing the screaming severed head on the screen. "You like this movie?"

111

He opened his mouth, then shut it again and shook his head. "Not really."

"You know what I do when there's a movie I don't like?"

"What?"

"Turn it off and go to bed."

"But I ain't tired."

I shrugged. "Suit yourself. Me, I'd rather go to bed and then get up early for a bike ride or basketball game."

"You goin' on a bike ride tomorrow?"

I grinned. "Maybe." Billy yawned, and I laughed. "See ya later, Billy."

When I got to my front yard, I turned around and looked across the street. The house was still dark, but as I watched, a light turned on in an upstairs window. I was smiling when I opened my front door.

"Where the hell have you been this time?"

I blinked and took an involuntary step backwards. Mom was standing in the kitchen doorway, hands on her hips. She had never cursed at me, but even without that clue, I could tell that she was incredibly angry. Her face was flushed and her eyes were nearly shooting sparks.

"I was—"

"For someone who wants something from me, you seem awfully bent on getting in trouble."

"Mom—"

"I don't understand what's gotten into you, Stuart! You used to be a kind, respectful, responsible kid. Now all of a sudden you're wandering around at night past curfew, being defiant, and—" She broke off suddenly.

"What's that smell?" She took two quick steps toward me and said, "My God, you haven't been smoking, have you?"

"Mom, I just—"

"You *have* been smoking! Stuart Ballentyne! You're violating the athlete's code of conduct, not to mention breaking the law—"

"Yeah, and that's all that really matters, isn't it?" I exploded at her. "Following the rules and keeping the perfect image. The fact that smoking might *hurt* me means nothing to you!"

"Is that what you're trying to do?" she asked in disbelief. "Hurt yourself?"

"No! God, Mom, if you'd just give me a chance to explain…"

"Okay," she said, crossing her arms. "Explain."

"I—" I stopped and swallowed. I didn't know where to begin.

"Well, clearly, you need time to formulate your 'explanation.' Maybe you could think better up in your room."

I threw my hands in the air. "Fine. It's not like you're going to believe what I have to tell you, anyway. You've already made up your mind that I'm a lying delinquent. I'll go to my room and you can avoid talking to me, just like you avoid everything else."

"Stuart—"

I charged up the stairs, two at a time. Forget that I had stayed up, waiting for her to get home so I could apologize to her. She was the one who should be apologizing to me for dragging me up here in the first place.

3 September

On Monday morning, I woke up with a nasty taste in my mouth. I brushed my teeth twice and gargled, planning never to smoke again. Then I took a really, really long shower, finishing off all the hot water. I got dressed, then made use of the rest of my Labor Day morning by working on the first English essay of the year. When I got tired of that, I spent a long time on the computer, mostly writing e-mails.

Ray—
Hey! I forgot that we have a fall break here. I've
got a four-day weekend Oct. 18–22. Maybe I
could come visit then instead of spring break.

I looked at what I had typed, and then deleted the last line.

Maybe I could come visit in Oct. and spring
break. Swim season for the school doesn't start
until Nov. It really sucks up here. It'd be bad
even if things were normal, but they aren't.
Mom's yelling at people all the time. You should
have heard her when she found out that two of

the gate guards were busted for having dope in their dorm rooms. And nothing I do is right. If she's not yelling at me, then she's not talking to me. I went across the street for a few minutes last night, and she totally flipped out. I don't know what to do. It sucks with you not here. Anyway, let me know if I can come down in Oct. I'll start checking airfare.
Stu

I'd been hoping to catch Taylor on line. He wasn't logged on, but there was an e-mail from him waiting for me.

Stu—
Hey! Hope things have gotten better in Minot. Things have been crazy here since we found out about the move. Mom's really pissed because she just got a promotion and now has to quit her job. Theo's on a rampage because this is his senior year and he doesn't want to go. Randy cries all the time because he doesn't want to leave his friends. Dad's stressed because he has so much to do and everyone at home's unhappy. And I don't know what to think. I'm tired of DC—it's too crowded and smoky and everyone's always in a hurry. But Minot's going be a big change of pace. What's it like, really? Dad says we're going to live on base because town is too far away. So how far is the enlisted housing from the officer housing? Is the year-round swim team any good? Do cell phones work up there?

Tell me I'm going to like it. Lie if you have to!
e-ya later. Taylor

P.S. $5 says the Bears win Sunday night!

My fingers skimmed over the keyboard in reply:

Taylor—
Sounds like no one in your family wants to move
to Minot. At least my mom was excited about
coming here, so she tried to keep everything pos-
itive for me. I'm sure you'll like it. The base has
some problems, but I've found a few good things
too. The movie theater isn't too far behind on
releases, and sometimes they have free screen-
ings (that new Vince Hale movie about Vietnam is
coming in a couple of weeks). The youth center
actually has a fairly decent teen program with
lock-ins, snowmobiling, camping, and other trips.
I haven't started swim team yet, but Wyatt says
it's good. I thought I'd start swimming this week,
but Mom and I had a huge fight and I'm not sure
what I'm doing now. I'm worried about the little
kid across the street. His parents are gone a lot,
and even though his stepbrother's supposed to be
watching him, it's like he's home alone. In fact,
Billy might be better off alone rather than with
Curtis. I went over to help him last night, and
found Curtis and his buddies getting high in the
garage. The guy's pretty messed up. He'd scared
Billy half to death by turning off the power while
the poor kid was watching a horror movie. Curtis

said it was just a prank but to me it bordered on child abuse.

I don't know how well cell phones work up here—unfortunately, I'm one of the few people in the U.S. who doesn't have one!
BTW, you didn't say how soon you'll be moving up here. Let me know when you'll be getting here.
Oh, our address is 112 Chevy Chase, and our number is 727-5555.

e-ya later,
Stu

PS Ha! The Cowboys are going to thrash the Bears! I hope the golf course paid you well this summer, cause you're gonna lose all your money to me if you keep betting on the Bears!

I logged off and sat at my computer for a few minutes. Taylor had asked about enlisted housing and officer housing, just one of the differences we were able to ignore while exchanging e-mails from different bases. Unlike a long time ago, there really wasn't a problem for officers' kids to be friends with kids of enlisted members. But it could be a little awkward when one parent worked for another. Of course, the whole base worked for Mom, so pretty much everything was awkward for me here.

Although I tried to walk downstairs casually, I was painfully aware of the sound each footstep. I knew Mom would be listening for me.

She wasn't in the living room. I went into the kitchen, fixed myself a bowl of cereal and half a grapefruit, and took them to the dining room.

Mom was at the table, drinking coffee and reading the newspaper. I sat down and began eating. The silence stretched out. I wished I'd thought to turn the stereo on to drown out the sounds in the room. I flinched every time she turned a page or took a sip. The crunch of my cereal was practically deafening.

I had just pushed the bowl away and was pulling the grapefruit toward me when Mom folded the paper and took off her glasses. "We need to talk," she said.

"By 'talk' do you mean you're going to lecture me, or can we have a real conversation?"

Mom pursed her lips for a second then said, "I would like to have a conversation."

"Me too. I wanted to have one last night."

"So did I."

I leaned back in the chair. "Seemed more like a lecture to me."

Mom closed her eyes for a moment. "Maybe I was a little too upset and frightened to listen to what you wanted to say."

"You didn't sound frightened. You sounded really mad."

She spread her hands in front of her. "I guess the relief of seeing you walk in the door, smiling and unhurt, flipped my fear to anger."

I shook my head. "Why would you be scared?"

"Stuart, I came home close to midnight to find the TV and living room lights on and you were nowhere to be found! It didn't look like you'd planned to leave,

118

and I...I was scared," she said simply.

I noticed that although her hair was neatly brushed, she was still in her sweats, her eyes were bloodshot, and her face was pale. "I didn't mean to scare you, Mom. I hadn't planned on going anywhere. I wasn't at a party or anything like that."

"So where were you?"

"Billy—" I saw her blank look. "The younger Vinson kid, came over in a panic because Curtis was gone and the lights wouldn't work. I went over to help him out. I wasn't gone that long," I added. "That's why I left the TV on. I was coming right back."

Mom frowned. "So what was going on?"

"Curtis was playing a joke," I said. "He flipped the circuit breakers and hid while Billy was watching a scary movie."

"Not a very funny joke," Mom said.

I shrugged. "Ray did it to me once."

"He did not!" Mom was shocked. "You never told me!"

"Well, he didn't mess with the circuit breakers. But one night when we were staying up late watching a scary movie, he turned off the lights and hid." I grinned. "Of course, the minute I started looking for him, he jumped out and yelled. Scared the crap outta me."

Mom didn't grin back. "You should've said something to me."

"I was taught that unless someone was hurt or in danger of being hurt, if I told on someone then it was tattling."

"Yes, but if he really scared you, you should have told me."

"Mom, it was years ago. It's no big deal." Before she could continue, I said, "But I still don't get why you were so worried last night. We're in the middle of Minot Air Force Base. It's not like anything's going to happen."

Mom sighed. "As a general rule, yes, that's true. But people are people and just being in the Air Force doesn't mean a person's trustworthy. We don't have as many crimes as people do off base, but we still have them."

I thought about asking why we always left our doors unlocked in that case, but decided it wasn't worth it. "Anyway, I'm sorry. I was trying to help out a neighbor. You know, like you and dad taught me."

"So why did you come home smelling like smoke?"

"We found Curtis smoking in the garage," I said. "That's it. Honestly. I wasn't at a wild party or anything."

Mom watched me, and I knew she was trying to decide if she believed me or not. I was insulted that she had to think about it, but I turned my attention to the grapefruit instead of trying to convince her.

"I know that this move has been especially difficult," Mom began. I looked up and was surprised to see her eyes glistening. "But I don't think that—"

A crash came from the living room. We both jumped and Mom let out a little screech. Then we pushed back our chairs and ran to the front of the house.

The big picture window was shattered. The glass shards all over the living room floor caught and reflected the morning sunlight in a way that was almost pretty.

"What—" Mom put a hand to her forehead and

stared out the broken window. I followed her gaze, just in time to see the front door of the Vinsons' house slam shut. We could hear the slam just fine. "What happened?" Mom sounded dazed.

I took a step into the living room. She grabbed my arm. "Be careful!"

"I will," I said, shaking off her hand.

She grabbed for me again, but I stepped away. "Just a second."

It took four more steps to get to the baseball I had spotted next to the wall. I picked it up and carried it back to her.

Her face cleared. "Ah. I see." A smile flicked across her face.

"What did you think it was?"

She shook her head. "I'm jumping at shadows," she said. "I'm tired and stressed and I'm seeing problems where there aren't any."

"What do you mean?"

"Nothing," she said, shaking her head again. She tossed the ball and caught it lightly. "Do you think he ran inside to tell his parents?" she asked, staring out the window. "Or to hide?"

"Probably to hide," I said. "He's pretty scared of getting in trouble with his stepmother."

Mom frowned. "I hate to cause trouble in the family," she said, "but I'm afraid he'll have to face the consequences."

"Housing maintenance will replace the window, won't they?"

"Yes, but we'll have to pay for it," she said. "Remember the patio door?"

"Duh," I said, disgusted with myself. "How could I forget?" Back in Colorado, when I was eleven, we'd been in a unit that had a sliding glass door. A friend and I had been playing tag on a hot summer day, and I had thought the door was open. I discovered it wasn't by putting a huge spider web crack in it with my head.

Mom tossed the ball up one more time, then set it on the table by the front door. "I'll go get dressed and put some shoes on."

Part of me wanted to run across the street and tell Billy to come over and confess before Mom went over there. But the rest of me insisted that it wasn't my problem.

Still, when Mom came back downstairs a few minutes later, I followed her out the door and across the street. I stood in the driveway, a discreet distance away. I could see a baseball bat lying in the yard—the same bat Chance had been fondling the night before.

Curtis answered the door. "Hello."

I almost choked. Not only was Curtis's tone modest and respectful, but his shirt was tucked in and his long hair was neatly combed.

"Good morning," my mother said. "Is Captain Vinson or your mother home?"

"No, ma'am." Curtis shook his head. "They're not in."

"I see." She hesitated briefly, then held out the baseball. "Do you recognize this?"

Curtis reached for the ball, but at the last second, Mom pulled it back out of his reach.

"No, ma'am, that's not my baseball."

"That's not what I asked."

"It might be Billy's," Curtis said thoughtfully. "He thinks he's going to be a big-time ballplayer."

"I asked if you recognize this baseball."

A surly look crossed Curtis's face, but he got it under control with impressive speed. "I don't know for sure," he said. "It looks like any baseball to me."

"May I speak to Billy?"

"No."

For a moment, I didn't think I had heard him correctly. "Excuse me?" my mother said in disbelief.

"Ma'am, his father isn't here. I don't think I should let you speak to him until he gets back."

"Son—"

"Your son's behind you," Curtis snarled, all pretense of courtesy gone. "My name is Curtis Sweeny. I'm not your son, and I'm not one of your troops. I'm not even a dependent of one of your troops. We're done here." He stepped back and shut the door.

Mom stood there for a moment, simply staring at the closed door, then she turned and strode down the driveway. "Close your mouth," she said as she walked briskly past me.

I did, but before I turned to follow her back to the house, I glanced up. Billy was looking out the window. His hair was tousled and he looked confused. I would have sworn he'd just woken up.

* * *

I helped Mom clean up the broken glass, and then washed the breakfast dishes while she called housing

123

maintenance. I'd settled down with a book when she came upstairs and stuck her head in my room.

"Housing maintenance should be here in half an hour with a new window," she said.

I tried not to smirk. There were definite perks to being base commander. It was Labor Day morning and maintenance would be here within an hour. I knew full well anyone else would have been told to tape something over the window and wait till Tuesday.

"That's nice," I said.

"How long will your homework take?"

I shrugged. "I'm done."

"Okay. As soon as they've got the new window in, let's go into town."

"Why?"

"I thought we could look for some new shoes for you, go out to dinner, maybe catch a seven o'clock movie…" When I didn't say anything right away, she asked, "Do you have other plans?"

"No. I just…"

"What?"

"Nothing. No. I mean, yeah, that'll be fine." I could tell that wasn't the reaction she was looking for. I forced more enthusiasm into my voice. "That'd be great!"

She smiled, almost looking relieved. "Good."

The doorbell rang fifteen minutes later. I heard muffled voices, and then the sound of a high-powered vacuum. Mom and I had already vacuumed, but I guessed the maintenance guys wanted to make sure there weren't any glass fragments in the carpet. They'd probably vacuum the sofa cushions and everything, just to make sure they got it all. Gotta take good care of the base commander and her kid.

They were done pretty quickly. I grabbed my wallet and headed downstairs. Mom was on the phone. I could tell from the way she was focusing on a blank spot on the wall that it was something about work. Her responses were terse but not rude. I wandered out the front door, not caring to eavesdrop on a call I wouldn't understand anyway.

I sat down on the front porch. The Vinson house was still very quiet. I wondered where the captain and his wife had gone this morning. Or had they stayed out all night?

And what was with Curtis's nice-guy act? All the *ma'ams* had been almost rude in their patronizing tone, though I couldn't tell if Mom had caught that or not. But she'd certainly caught his attitude when he refused to get Billy. I wasn't sure if I'd ever seen anyone flat-out deny her like that.

I thought about Billy knocking the baseball across the street. He must have been really scared when he saw the ball heading for our living room window. I sat up straight. That was one heck of a distance for someone Billy's size. Not to say it was impossible, but it would be an impressive feat for him. Then I remembered seeing him through the upstairs window. He really had looked like he'd just woken up.

"Ready to go?"

I stood up and brushed off my pants. "Sure."

I walked to the car, trying to decide if I was going to tell Mom about Billy. Watching out for neighbors is part of her job, but she already had so much she was dealing with. What could she do about it anyway? I wasn't sure, and decided it'd be safer to ask her, just in case.

I had just opened my mouth to bring it up, when she caught me off guard.

"Hey, Stu? Think fast!"

I just got my hand up in time to block the keys from hitting me right on the nose. Dumbly, I stared at them on the ground, winking up at me in the sunlight.

"You don't want to drive?"

"Sure," I said, all thoughts of Billy and Curtis evaporating. I scooped up the keys. I hadn't driven for the last three weeks, and I hadn't driven on Highway 83 at all.

In the car, she didn't say anything as I adjusted the seat and mirrors and changed the radio station. She didn't say anything as I backed out of the driveway. Or as I turned down Tangley Drive. She didn't say a word as I drove out the base gate. The silence was getting downright creepy.

After I pulled on to Highway 83, heading south into town, I risked a glance at her. She didn't seem to be angry, but she was staring straight ahead and had her hands folded in her lap.

"Mom?"

"Mmmm?"

"You all right?"

"Yes. Just thinking." She sighed. "You handle the car well, Stu, and I know I can trust you. It's the other drivers and the road conditions that I don't trust."

"Mom, you can't protect me forever."

"I know, I know. You're growing up. But do you know how many people die on this stretch of highway every year?"

"Do you?" I countered, even though I really didn't want to hear about it.

"I don't have exact numbers, but I do know that it's a very dangerous section of road. They call that the ditch," she said, pointing to the median of the divided highway, "and Cardinal said that after the last snowstorm, there were more than *sixty* cars stuck in it between town and base."

"That's a lot of cars," I said.

"That's six cars every mile, Stu. And most of the drivers had lots of bad-weather experience."

"I don't have to drive when it's snowing."

"You don't? What if it starts snowing while you're at school? Or while you're at swim practice? The weather changes fast up here."

"Mom—"

"I know," she said again. "I know. You're a good, responsible kid and you've certainly earned my trust. And I think, if we can agree on the ground rules, you'll have permission to use this car after you get your license."

"Awesome, Mom!"

"Hold on," she warned. "You haven't heard the ground rules your father and I agreed on."

"No tickets," I said quickly. "Keep at least a 3.0 GPA and never ditch classes."

"Or practices," Mom said firmly. "The car is for going to school, practice, and home, in that order without any side trips. And you'll have to keep at least a 3.5—"

"What?" I squawked.

"—and no friends in the car, and no using the cell phone while you drive."

I snorted. "I don't have a cell phone."

"You're going to get one," Mom said.

I turned my head to look at her and the car swerved slightly. "Seriously?" I asked, straightening the car again.

As she loosened her grip on the dashboard, she said, "Since it's just you and me, and town is so far from base, you'll need one."

"Right." I stared at the road for a moment. We were almost to the first intersection, the one where you either went straight through the center of town, or took the bypass around it. "Where are we going?"

Mom checked her watch. "Let's start at the mall. Get off at the next exit."

"Okay."

After only an hour of shopping we were so loaded down with packages we had to take them out to the car. During our second hour, Mom bought me two pairs of sneakers, some khakis and jeans, two pairs of shorts, four shirts, a new football, two pairs of goggles, swim trunks, two CDs, and three DVDs.

I was stunned by the amount we bought. Even with the Labor Day sales, Mom had dropped a big chunk of change. I had enough money for the two CDs, but Mom insisted on buying everything, not just the clothes. I asked twice, just to make sure that it wasn't a loan.

"No," she said, laughing. "You and I both deserve a bit of a splurge, I think."

We stopped in at Eagle Cellular and looked at a few phones, but Mom wasn't happy with any of the contracts they were offering. "I think we can get a better deal," she told the salesperson who had been at her elbow from the moment we walked in, "Thank you anyway."

For dinner, instead of going to Dos Margaritas across the mall parking lot for a quick, inexpensive meal, she directed me to Bar Lazy J, the priciest steak house in town. When she ordered two appetizers, I couldn't take it any more.

"What's going on?" I didn't exactly yell, but the waiter turned back and gave me an uneasy look before deciding I wasn't talking to him.

"What?" Mom asked. She was frowning at me.

Fighting to keep my voice down, I said, "What is all this?"

"I told you I thought we needed a splurge. I didn't know it was going to bother you."

"Mom, this is bigger than every splurge we've ever done combined!"

"Stuart," Mom whispered, leaning forward conspiratorially, "I'm making a bigger paycheck than I ever have!"

"Not that much bigger," I said, shaking my head. "You've been a colonel for almost two years."

"It's just you and me now."

"But you've got Ray in college. And I'll be going in a couple of years too, unless you're planning to blow my college fund tonight." *And what about Dad, I thought. In the eyes of the military, Dad has been her dependent almost as long as I have.*

Mom smiled, but her eyes looked a little misty. "Ray's got his scholarship, and what that doesn't cover comes out of his college fund. And don't worry, your college fund is in great shape."

She returned to the menu. "Yum, filet mignon with sautéed mushrooms and onions. Ooh, and I can add a lobster tail too! Yep, that's what I'm having," she said in a flamboyant tone. "What about you?"

The dinner was great, and we both walked out feeling stuffed. But through all our joking conversations and laughter, I couldn't get rid of the nagging feeling that something wasn't quite right.

When I got home after practice on Tuesday, I dropped my bag by the front door. I could hear Mom talking upstairs. Figuring she was on the phone, I took a detour to the kitchen. I had eaten a snack before practice, but after two hours of swimming, I needed something to tide me over while I made dinner.

Mom's briefcase was on the counter, and three of her folders were next to it. The top one had "Legal Issues" printed in the middle. The only legal issue I could think of that Mom might be dealing with was divorce. Suddenly I didn't have an appetite.

When I got upstairs, I was surprised to hear her voice coming from Ray's—I mean, the spare—bedroom.

I didn't hear the man's voice until I was halfway across the threshold, or I wouldn't have gone in.

Captain Jonathan Cardinal jumped when he saw me. "Stuart," he said, flushing.

Mom turned quickly. She looked like she'd been caught too, but she recovered faster than he did. "Hi, kiddo. How was practice?"

"Fine," I said. "I didn't see Captain Cardinal's car out front."

"We drove over here together because we've got to get back right away."

"Back to work? At seven-thirty?"

"Yes. There's…something…" She couldn't seem to figure out what to say. "There's something…" She looked at Cardinal.

"There's something coming down the pipeline, Stu," he said in a patronizingly gentle tone, "and we've got to deal with a lot of things ASAP."

My loss of appetite was rapidly becoming a need to throw up.

Mom nodded, visibly pleased with her XO's answer. "Well, unless you have any other questions—"

"Actually I do," I said.

"I was talking to Captain Cardinal, honey," Mom said.

He answered her quickly. "No, ma'am. It's all pretty straightforward."

"What about *my* questions?" I asked.

"I'm sorry, Stu. They'll have to wait. I won't be back until late tonight. I'll explain everything tomorrow." Without waiting for my response she said to Cardinal, "Let's go."

"Mom!" I shouted as she turned to follow him out of the room. "What the hell were you two doing up here in the bedroom?"

Mom spun back around. "Watch your language, Stu!" She waited until Cardinal was on the stairs. "I don't like your new attitude," she snapped.

"I don't like what I'm seeing."

She took a step toward me, and it took everything I had not to step back. "You're not seeing anything,

Stuart." I flinched as she suddenly reached out to me, but she pulled my head down and kissed me on the forehead. "I'll explain everything as soon as I can. Good night," she whispered. "Sleep well."

She left me standing in the middle of the spare bed-room. I heard her go down the stairs, and after a few seconds the front door slammed. I heard the car start and saw the glare of the headlights splash across the wall before I found my voice.

"Sleep well?" I yelled. "*How?*"

5 September

Classes on Wednesday were a blur. I almost felt like I was coming down with something. I declined Jorge's offer of a ride home and took the bus. He looked at me oddly, but I didn't feel like explaining to him that I didn't want to talk to anyone and that I didn't want to go back to the house either. Riding the bus was the best way to put off both of those things.

I missed my brother. Ray would have known what to do, what questions to ask. He would've already worked it all out in his head.

I missed Dad. If he were here—well, if he were here none of this would be happening.

From the bus window I could see Mom's blue-and-white staff car parked in front of the house. I thought about staying on till the last stop and then walking back home from there, but I made myself get off.

"Stu?" a voice called from across the street.

I turned, grateful for an excuse not to go right inside. "Yeah, Billy? Jeez, what happened to you?"

His right arm was bandaged from his wrist to his elbow.

"Fell," he said.

"You fall a lot, don't you?"

He grinned. "'Cause I do the tough stuff. I fell when I was tryin' a front flip."

"Weren't you on a mat?"

"You don't ride a bike on a mat," he said, looking at me scornfully.

"You were trying a flip on your bike?" I asked in amazement. "Why?"

"To show Curtis."

"Show him what?"

"That I can keep up with him. He won't take me places unless I can keep up."

I took another look at the bandage. "Did you do that yourself?"

He shook his head. "Curtis took care of me."

"What did your parents say?"

Billy shrugged. "Nothin' yet. It just happened a little while ago."

"Make sure you tell your parents about it, okay?"

Billy looked troubled. "Dad's awful busy. And I don't wanna bother Mother Darla any more. She's still sore about your broken window."

"Why was she mad? It was an accident, right?"

"'Cause it costs money."

"Do you have to pay for the window?" I asked, feeling strangely guilty.

"Yeah," he said morosely. "I gotta pay for half of it."

That sounded like what my mom would have made me do. "Your dad's paying for the other half?"

"Yeah. He was gonna make Curtis pay for it, 'cause Curtis was s'posed to be watching me. Dad and Mother Darla had a big fight about it."

"Sorry. I know that's rough. How long have they been married?" I asked.

"They got married right before we moved," Billy said. "But she's been around longer'n that."

"So...you play baseball?" I asked, because Billy seemed uncomfortable.

"Sometimes."

He was lying, I could tell, and he still seemed uneasy. I tried another topic. "Where's Curtis now?"

Billy shrugged. "Don't know."

"Isn't he supposed to be watching you?"

Billy stood up straight. "I'm almost nine," he said. "I'm not a baby! I can take care of myself!"

I held up my hand. "I know, I know," I said. "I always felt the same way. But base regs are base regs. It's one thing for you to stay home by yourself for a couple of hours as a nine-year-old, but you can't be here alone all day. "

"Curtis'll be back before dinner," Billy said, sounding more confident than he looked.

"Okay," I said with a sigh. "I've got to get going."

"See ya!" Billy grinned and gave me a big wave with his good arm.

I walked into the house, shaking my head.

"Damn it, Dave!" Mom's voice was coming from the kitchen. "I know you don't think he should use the car, but you're not here! It's difficult!"

I set my backpack down and very slowly shut the front door. For a moment I couldn't make out what she was saying, but then her voice rose again.

"Maybe if you hadn't left, it would be easier to.... No, don't *you* start with *me!* I'm doing everything I can! I'm working *and* taking care of our son, not just running away.... Yes, I did say running away! You're

136

just using your mother as an excuse. I know she needs help, but I find it hard to believe that you can't work *something* out. I'm sure you could get her in an assisted living center or something and be here in a few days."

I tried not to make any noise as I edged toward the stairs.

"You're being incredibly selfish," she shouted. "I can't believe this!... *I* don't need you home, *Stuart* does!... You're letting us down, but that doesn't really matter, does it?" She laughed sharply and her voice dropped back to her old cold tone. "I knew I couldn't count on you.... Don't worry about it. Forget I even called. I've already made other arrangements!"

I heard a loud noise. It sounded like she'd slapped her hand down on the counter. Then I heard her footsteps. As she crossed in front of the door, still holding the phone to her ear, she caught sight of me and stopped. In a much calmer tone of voice she said, "I don't think this conversation is getting us any-where, Dave. Just get here as soon as you can." She wiped her cheeks like she'd been crying. "And Stuart just walked in the door.... Not right now. I'll have him call you later. Good-bye." She hung up the phone and stared at me. "How long have you been standing there?"

I shrugged miserably. "Long enough." I was upset that Dad had gone to Nevada, but I'd held on to the belief that he was there because he had to be there, not because he wanted to be away from us. Now, hearing the way she'd been talking to him...well, I wasn't sure there was any kind of hope left.

"What have I told you about eavesdropping?"

"That it's more informative than interrupting?"

"Stuart!"

"Okay, okay. You always say that eavesdroppers usually hear something they don't want to know," I said with a sigh. "But I think it's better to be informed," I added before she could say anything. "And it seems like eavesdropping is the only way to get information around here."

"And what kind of information did you get?" Mom asked, crossing her arms.

"That you don't respect Dad," I said flatly.

Her eyebrows shot up. "I beg your pardon?"

"Look, Mom. He stayed home to take care of us, and you never respected him for that. Now he's gone to take care of Gram and you don't respect him for that, either."

"That's not true..." Her voice was low, almost a whisper.

"Come on, Mom! I'm fifteen, I'm not stupid! You never considered him to be your equal."

She opened her mouth, and then snapped it shut again and pointed toward the dining room. We went separate ways, me through the living room and Mom through the kitchen, and took seats at the table across from each other. I was painfully aware of the two empty chairs.

"Your father worked very hard keeping our house going," Mom said. "If he hadn't stayed home, you and Ray would have been in a lot fewer activities. You'd probably still be struggling with math if you and Dad hadn't worked on it together every day of third grade."

138

I nodded.

"And Ray never would've made Eagle Scout. Your dad sacrificed a lot so that our family could *be* a family. It wasn't easy for him to give up his career, but he did. I have nothing but respect for your father."

"What about love?"

"I have love for him too." She swallowed. "And I always will."

"Didn't sound like it," I said.

"That's what you get for eavesdropping," she said tartly. "You only get part of the conversation."

I stared at her, waiting for an explanation.

"I will always love your father," she mumbled, looking away from me, "but that doesn't mean..." She shook her head. "Your father and I are trying to figure out a lot of things. And it's going to take a while to sort it all out." Clearing her throat, she said, "But you and I need to talk about something that must be dealt with now."

"Oh?"

"The reason I called your father in the first place..." Mom put her head in her hands, rubbed her eyes, then tossed her head back. "I wanted to get everything worked out before I hit you with this, but there simply isn't time. I have to go TDY...."

My mouth dropped open. "You're going on temporary duty?" I heard myself ask.

"We're being deployed right away—" She broke off suddenly. "Stuart? Are you okay?"

I sat there, feeling the blood drain out of my face. She couldn't possibly have said what I thought she had.

"Stu?" Mom reached across the table and put her hand over mine. I tried to pull away, but she held on.

Through numb lips, I stuttered, "You're being d-deployed? Where?"

She smiled sadly. "You know I can't tell you that."

"When are you leaving?"

"Tomorrow morning."

"*Tomorrow?*"

Mom had deployed many times before, but Dad had always been around. And it had never been on such short notice before. I knew she kept a packed bag—she was required to be ready at all times for immediate deployment—in her closet, but she'd never had to use it. We'd always known at least three weeks ahead of time, and even that had felt like short notice. An immediate deployment like this sounded really serious. And risky.

"For how long?"

"We don't know."

There was a buzzing building in my ears. I took a deep breath. "You can't go."

"Honey—"

I used the only argument that I thought might sway her. "But Mom, you're the base commander! You can't go!"

"I don't want to go, but..." She sighed. "I'm keeping Lt. Colonel Porter here to run the base. His wife's on bed rest and he should be here for the birth of his child."

"So you're *choosing* to go." Again. It was always her troops first.

Mom looked down at the table for a second, then back at me. "I'm making what I consider to be the best decision for my troops. They need a leader on this mission who won't be distracted. I couldn't send Porter when his wife is expecting their first child and is confined to her bed."

"And you obviously won't be distracted by the fact that you've left your youngest child home alone," I said.

"Hey!" She squeezed my hands. "I know I can trust you, I know you're self-reliant. And you know I'd never leave you home alone."

"You asked Dad to come home to babysit me?" I said, putting it all together. "The only reason you want him home is to babysit me. That's completely unfair!"

"It's practical," Mom countered. "But he shared your view."

"I don't need a babysitter," I muttered.

"Base regs say you do."

I glared at her. I was almost sixteen, but I was as confined by the base rules as Billy.

"So Cardinal's going to stay here," she said.

I closed my eyes. "That's why he was here yesterday."

"Yes."

"You knew this was coming but you didn't tell me?"

"I'm sorry, Stu. At first immediate deployment was just a rumor, only a possibility. I thought we might be here for another week or maybe even two. But things are heating up too fast."

"Why isn't Cardinal going?"

"I've asked him to stay. He'll be able to help Colonel Porter handle all the extra responsibilities. I've known Jonathan longer than I've known anyone else here. I can trust him."

I shook my head. "I don't want him here."

"It's not open for discussion, Stu. You have to have an adult staying with you."

"I could go stay with someone," I pointed out. "I could stay with the Porters."

"Pam's on bed rest," Mom reminded me. "She doesn't need anyone else around right now."

"With the Reyes?"

"They have four kids. And Juan is deploying too."

"But—"

"Jonathan doesn't have family depending on him and he's very responsible," Mom said. "He has agreed to stay here while I'm deployed. Don't look at him as a babysitter. Consider him a roommate."

The doorbell rang.

Mom pushed her chair back. "Here he is now."

I groaned and put my head down on the table.

"Don't be difficult, Stu. This is hard enough already," Mom said as she left the room.

I heard the front door open. "Mrs. Vinson!" Mom exclaimed. "What are you—"

From outside, a man's voice yelled, "Darla! Stop!"

I hurried to the front hall so I could see. This could get interesting.

Mrs. Vinson had on a tight shirt with a plunging neckline that revealed way too much of her chest. Her hands were on her hips, and her chin was thrust out almost as much as her chest was.

"You really think you're something, don't you?" she declared. "You're on one hell of a power trip."

Mom blinked.

"Darla!" Captain Vinson was cutting across our yard to the front porch. "Darla, stop it right now!"

"No way," Mrs. Vinson said. "I can't stand this cocky bitch." Her face was flushed and her eyes were red and puffy.

"Darla!" Captain Vinson shouted, almost moaning.

"Is there a problem, Mrs. Vinson?" Mom asked, folding her arms across her chest. Her words were polite but her tone was icy.

"No!" Captain Vinson panted as he reached our porch and put a hand on his wife's shoulder. "There's no problem, ma'am. So sorry to have—"

"There are so many problems, I don't know where to begin!" Mrs. Vinson cut in. "First, your snobby son decides to snub Curtis and tries to turn everyone against him."

"What?" Mom and I said together.

"Second, you blame Tim's son for breaking your window and expect him to pay for it, even though you make way more money than he does."

"The money wasn't—" Mom began, but Mrs. Vinson rolled right over her.

"And now, now you decide to send my husband away? Well, I won't have it. You go. You try leaving your family and see how it feels."

"Colonel Ballentyne, I'm so sorry," Vinson said, pulling ineffectually at his wife's arm. "Obviously she's real upset right now. I'll straighten everything out. I promise."

Mrs. Vinson tried to shake off his grip. Since she couldn't, she merely planted her feet and resisted his tugs. Short of putting her over his shoulder—which, even with his size and strength, I doubted he could do—I didn't see how he could get her to move.

"Mrs. Vinson," my mom said, "you do realize that

143

your husband is Captain Timothy Vinson? A captain in the United States Air Force? An officer who took an oath to uphold the constitution and defend the country?"

"Listen here—"

"No, you listen." My mother cut her off without even raising her voice. "I issue orders based on what is best for the country first, the unit second, and the individual troops third—in that order—because that is my duty. Not my job, Mrs. Vinson, but my *duty*. Your husband understands his duty and performs it well. It's time you evaluate your duty to him and find a way to support him."

Mrs. Vinson was gaping at Mom like a largemouth bass.

"Support him? I—"

"Darla, please," Vinson begged. "It's time to go."

"As for the window," Mom continued as if there had been no interruption, "it was never a matter of money. It was a matter of responsibility, again something that your husband understands and you seem to have difficulty accepting."

"Well, I never!"

"Clearly."

They stared at each other. The tension in the air made my hair stand on end. A fight was coming, I could just feel it. I was pretty sure Vinson could hold Darla back, but it might be a close call. I was starting to get nervous. But just then Cardinal's car pulled in the drive.

Captain Vinson swore under his breath. "Come on, Darla. Now!" He tugged on her arm again, and this

144

time she let him pull her away. They backed down the porch steps, and as they turned to walk back across the yard, Vinson looked over his shoulder. "Sorry, ma'am," he said.

"That woman can't go around like she's all high and mighty..." Darla's voice carried easily through the early evening air.

Vinson nodded at Cardinal as they passed him, but he and Darla didn't slow down. I didn't blame him. If he lost momentum getting his wife out of here, things would just start up again.

"What was that all about?" Captain Cardinal asked as he joined us on the porch.

Mom laughed weakly. "That was about a new Air Force spouse letting off some steam. I hate to ask you this, Jonathan, but—"

"Sure. I'll try to keep an eye on what's going on over there too."

"You'll be the only bachelor in the state looking after two families."

He smiled. "That's all right, ma'am. It'll look great on my dating profile: good with kids, even if they're not mine."

Mom frowned at him as she opened the front door and led us inside. "If you're resorting to a dating service, the singles world has really taken a turn for the worse."

"Why didn't you tell Mrs. Vinson that you *are* going?" I asked Mom. "Maybe then—"

"Nothing was going to make her feel better," Mom said. "She needs someone to be mad at and she picked me. I'm a close target. Besides, I'm sure that Captain

Vinson will tell her that I'm deploying too." She gestured to the dining room table. "Let's sit down for a minute. Jonathan, can I get you anything?"

"No, ma'am, I'm fine."

"You sure? Because I need a beer."

"Well, okay then. My father always told me never to let a lady drink alone."

She smiled and turned to the kitchen. "How about you, Stu?" she asked over her shoulder.

"Yeah, I'd love a beer."

"Ha ha."

"I'll take a Coke."

"Do you need to write that down, Jonathan?" she called from the kitchen. "No beers for Stu."

"I think I've got that, ma'am," he said, grinning. "And I'll keep him out of the tequila too. But rum's okay, right?"

"Maybe this isn't such a good idea," she said, but she was still smiling as she brought the three cans into the dining room. She put them on the table carefully, sat down next to me, and pulled out the folder she had tucked under her arm.

"So, no drinking," Captain Cardinal said. "That's a pretty easy one to remember."

"This folder will be in the top desk drawer in the office. You need to keep it there, because you'll both be using it. Jonathan, I'm leaving you with a health-care power of attorney for Stu," Mom said, pulling a paper out of the folder. "But Stuart, I'd really rather he not have to use it. Stay out of the hospital for me, okay?"

"Do I have to?" I said. "It might be more fun than staying here with him."

146

"If he does go to the hospital, can I leave him there awhile?" Cardinal asked.

Mom sighed and closed her eyes. "This is almost like leaving Stuart with Ray."

Cardinal laughed.

I breathed a sigh of relief. Mom's XO wasn't so bad after all. In fact, this could be great!

"I've let the school know that you can sign his permission slips and report cards," Mom continued, pulling out another piece of paper. "And here are his father's phone numbers. We're not sure when he'll be coming up. It could be next week, it could be longer. It depends on too many things to know right now. Stuart will obviously talk to him whenever he wants. But I'd like you to call him at least once a week, just to check in."

Cardinal nodded.

Then Mom pulled out a checkbook. It looked brand-new. "I've signed checks for the bills that I know will be coming up, like the phone and cable, and I've got an insurance payment due at the end of next month. I've written ten checks for the commissary. All you have to do is write in the amount, record it in the register, and keep track of the balance. I've also signed five blank checks—for emergency use only." Mom looked at both of us. "I'd prefer that these not get used. But most important, whatever you do, don't lose the checkbook. I don't want the account wiped out."

"Yes, ma'am," Cardinal and I said together.

"You should have written a few checks for Domino's Pizza," I said. "Oh, and for JR Rockers too.

147

I hear they've got great milkshakes and onion rings."

Mom looked at me for a second, then smiled. "I'll write a few more tonight, for Domino's and Rockers, so you won't be deprived of your junk food."

I tried not to look shocked.

"Okay, so no drinking or smoking for Stuart," Mom said to Cardinal. "No smoking for you in the house, and only responsible drinking." Mom looked down at her hands folded on the table. "I hate to put a crimp in your social life, Jonathan, but no overnight female guests. And that goes for you too, Stuart."

"Bummer," I said. "Guess I'll have to call all my girlfriends and cancel."

"I'm sorry, but that's the way it's got to be."

"I'm afraid that's a deal breaker, ma'am," Cardinal said suddenly. His face looked serious, but I could see a sparkle in his eyes. "I can't leave Molly."

"Molly?" I asked.

He winked at me. "My black lab."

"How could I have forgotten Molly?" Mom said. "Of course she comes with you. I meant no overnight female guests of the human variety."

"Understood," Cardinal said easily.

Mom gave him a relieved smile.

"We get to have a dog?" I asked. Cardinal grinned and nodded. This kept getting better. Cardinal was going to be an awesome roommate. "How long will you be gone?" I asked Mom.

"I told you, Stu, I don't know. It could be three days; it could be three weeks; it could even be three months. I just don't know."

"Come on," I said. "You mean to tell me you

haven't heard any kind of whispering about it looking like a short time or a long time? No hints at all?"

Frowning, she shook her head. "No hints. No ideas. They haven't even told me exactly where we're going yet."

"But you have a general idea."

"Anyone who's been watching the news would have a general idea," Mom said dryly.

"And you deploy in the morning." The reality of her leaving suddenly hit me.

"Yes."

"Can I stay home from school? To say good-bye?"

For a second I was afraid she'd say no, that I needed to be in class and that it would be easier to say our good-byes tonight, like we'd done in the past. But she surprised me. Again.

"I'd like that," Mom said softly. "Very much."

Later, after Cardinal left, Mom pulled the checkbook out of the folder again. "I set up this checking account yesterday," she said. "It's only got five thousand dollars in it. That should be more than enough for any emergencies that may come up while I'm gone. If you need more, call Dad and he can wire some to the account."

"So that's the only account Cardinal and I will have access to?"

"Like I said, I think Jonathan's a good guy, and I trust him, but I only worked with him for a few months in Barksdale. It's enough to make me wish the Macleans or the Sampsons were stationed here," she muttered, referring to our good friends from the Academy. "This is the debit card," she continued, pulling it out of the folder. "I put it in your name. The PIN is my birth date. You do know what that is, right?" she asked with a small smile.

"December...so it starts with twelve..." I could never remember her birthday.

"It's 12-06," Mom said with exasperation.

"Right."

"Make sure you write down whatever cash you take out of the account in the checkbook ledger," she said sternly. "And don't go crazy."

"What? No splurging?" I joked. Then I stopped short. "Hey. You knew about this over the weekend, didn't you?"

"I didn't want to worry you," she said.

"You could have at least warned me it was a possibility," I snapped, "instead of dropping it on me out of the blue."

"I wanted to get everything arranged first. I thought it would be easier this way."

"For you, maybe. Not for me."

"I'm sorry," she said. She put the checkbook down and hugged me. "I thought it would be easier for both of us."

"Does Ray know?"

"I've called him, but he wasn't in. I'll try again in a few minutes."

"This really sucks," I said.

"Yes," she agreed. "It certainly does." It was the first time I'd ever heard her say anything negative about the Air Force.

The next morning my alarm went off at five, much earlier than on a usual school day. Mom's two large duffel bags were waiting by the front door when I came down for breakfast. We ate together, but we didn't talk much. My throat was so tight I had trouble swallowing my food. I couldn't risk talking.

Cardinal rang the doorbell before we were done. We left the dishes on the table. I told Mom I'd clean up later. She let Cardinal in, and he carried his duffel and a garment bag upstairs. Then he went back out to his car and brought in a supply of dog food and a dog bed.

"Where's Molly?" I asked.

"I left her in my truck," he said. "I'll take her around back and let her explore the yard for now. We can bring her inside later this afternoon."

This time when he went back out, he took Mom's duffel bags. A few moments later, I heard barking from our backyard. I'd always wanted a dog, or even a cat, but Mom and Dad said it was too hard to move with pets. I didn't see why; a lot of military families had pets. But we never did.

Today it was hard to get excited about the dog, though. Having a dog around would be great, but it wasn't going to make up for my entire family being scattered all around the world.

"Ready to go?" Mom asked me. Her hair was slicked back into a bun at the base of her neck. She had simple gold studs in her ears and her wedding band on, the jewelry she usually chose to wear while in uniform. Her pressed flight suit was clean, crisp, and authoritative.

"No," I said. "I'm not ready."

She took a deep breath and then pulled me down to kiss me on the forehead.

"Did you talk to Ray?" I asked.

"No," she said. "I'll try one more time before we take off. It's not the kind of message I want to leave on a machine. You may have to tell him."

"Great."

"Ready?" Cardinal asked from the front door.

"Yes," we said together.

The parking lot was full of men and women in flight suits or uniforms taking care of last-minute details. Family members who had come to see off husbands or wives or mothers or fathers crowded behind the rope on one side of the lot, straining to keep loved ones in sight as long as they could.

I had been to deployments, and I knew there was usually a speech or two while the departing squadrons stood in formation. Not this morning. This was a short-notice deployment, and it was all business with no time for show and sentiment. There was anxiety in the air, fear and pride mixed with love and sorrow.

Military good-byes were always hard; not having a return date to focus on made it even harder. It was

September. Would they be back in time to take the youngest kids trick-or-treating? In time to carve the Thanksgiving turkey? To hang the Christmas lights? Or would we not see them again until next year?

Were some saying good-bye forever?

Being in the bombers was safer than being in the Army ground troops, but there was still risk. There was always risk in being deployed, but that was something you didn't dwell on. You couldn't.

Too soon it was time for the crews to board the buses that would transport them to their aircraft. Mom hugged me tight, pulling me down at an uncomfortable angle. But I didn't complain. When she took a step away from me, still cupping my cheek with her hand, I could see Mrs. Vinson glaring at us over her husband's shoulder. Neither Billy nor Curtis was there.

"I love you, Stu. I'm sorry about all this. I never intended—" Mom's breath caught and she stopped for a moment. "I'll be in touch as often as I can, okay? Don't be afraid to ask Jonathan for help. And you can call your dad at any time."

"Did you talk to Ray?"

"Only briefly," she said, visibly fighting the tears. "I told him you'd call and fill in the blanks."

"I can't fill in very many."

"Fill in what you can," she said simply. "That's the best we can ever do." She let go of me and stepped back. "I'll be home as soon as I can. I know you'll make me proud while I'm gone. I love you."

"Love you too, Mom," I said.

She turned on her heel and strode away.

"Fall in!" the cry echoed around me.

On all sides people were sniffling or sobbing as family members went to join their crews. When they'd all boarded the buses to take them out to the tarmac, Captain Cardinal materialized next to me.

"Come on," he said. "I know a great place to watch the takeoff."

Mutely I followed him to his truck. We drove part of the way behind the buses, and then when they turned for the tarmac, he headed toward the old air control tower. Inside, he led me up the stairs to an office on the second floor. A row of large windows overlooked the runway.

For more than an hour we watched the crews load their gear and perform preflight checks.

The B-52s, the big, heavy planes dubbed "flying fortresses," don't have landing gear only under their fuselage; they have additional gear under each massive wing. The huge bombers don't look like they should be able to take off, let alone fly, but they do. Since these planes were fully loaded, the noses would lift off first. Normally, when they're just running sorties and carrying minimal weight, they seem to take off nose-last, which is really weird looking but isn't nearly as hard to watch as the landing. When they land, they approach the strip nose-first until they're almost down, and just when you're sure they won't make it, the pilots "flare" the nose up ever so slightly and touch down on the tarmac.

Cardinal and I stood together in silence as the planes lined up in the correct order for takeoff. The twelve monstrous iron birds taxied to the end of the runway one after the other, ponderously gained speed, and lifted smoothly into the air. The last of the group was a supply plane, a C-5, loaded with support personnel and gear. It looked like a goose chasing a flock of cranes. The planes turned, banking sharply to the right while they were still fighting for altitude, and then disappeared one by one into the clouds.

Cardinal put his hand on my shoulder. "You want to go home?" he asked. "Or would you like me to drive you to school instead?"

"I'm going home," I said. "But I'd like to walk."

"You sure?" he asked, dropping his hand.

"Yeah. Nothing personal."

"Okay. Well, I'm going in to work. I should be home pretty early tonight, since the boss isn't in." He grinned.

"See you later." I didn't return his grin.

* * *

Mom's departure happened so fast that I wasn't immediately able to appreciate all of the repercussions. It seemed like I kept discovering problems that she had left unsolved.

It started when I called Ray that night.

"I can still come in October, right?" I asked after I told him what I didn't know about the deployment.

"I don't know. I don't see why you couldn't, but you'd better talk to Dad first." I was about to take a breath of relief when he added, "I guess I'm not coming for Thanksgiving."

"What? Why?"

"We don't know if she'll be home by then," he said. "I don't want to buy a ticket now and then not use it. But I can't wait until the last minute either. If I don't buy a ticket soon, I probably won't be able to get one, since we're talking about the busiest travel time of the year." He sighed. "I guess I'll look at tickets to Vegas instead."

"But Dad may not be there," I said.

"What do you mean?"

"Mom said he'd come up here as soon as he gets Gram settled."

"Well, yeah, but he hasn't found any place that can take her before Christmas."

"Why doesn't anybody tell me any of these things?" I yelled into the phone. "What about me?"

"You'll have to come to Vegas too," he said. "Better make a reservation soon, though."

"But what if Mom comes home earlier?" I asked. "What then? We leave her alone for Thanksgiving? And what about Christmas? Should we buy tickets for Christmas too?"

"How the hell do I know?" Ray snapped. "No one knows when she'll be home. I'd say plan as if she won't be. Otherwise you'll be stuck celebrating all the holidays by yourself up there in the frozen tundra."

"Have you talked to Dad about Thanksgiv—?"

"No," he said before I could finish. "Mom just told me this morning, remember? I haven't had time to figure anything out."

"You don't have to be such a jackass about it," I said. "I only found out last night."

"I gotta go," he said. "I've got a class."

"Okay," I said, "Let's—"

"See ya," he said, and the dial tone filled my ear.

The next morning, I woke up to whining. I rolled over and found Molly staring at me. She shoved her wet nose into my face and let out a muted bark. I looked at my alarm clock.

Five thirty.

"No way," I mumbled. The moment I closed my eyes I heard Molly's claws clicking across the floor to my open door. She whimpered.

"Go find your owner."

She danced back over to my bed and barked again, louder.

"You need out?"

She whirled around and ran out of my room.

I sighed and threw the covers back. Where was Cardinal? This was his pet. As I stepped into the hallway, I saw the light from under the spare-room door and heard the shower running.

Molly barked again from the back door.

"Coming," I called, trying not to trip down the stairs. It crossed my mind that maybe Mom and Dad had had good reasons for never getting a dog.

14 September

had survived the first week and thought things were settling down. Cardinal and I had managed most of the little things that Mom had failed to cover before she left: the newspaper subscription she'd ordered for the weekend that was coming daily instead, the voice mail that we couldn't access, the lawnmower that had died before she left and needed to be replaced, to name just a few. But when I was waiting for the bus on Friday morning, the biggest omission of all hit me.

Fourteen days, I thought. *Fourteen days until—*

OH CRAP!

How was I going to get my driver's license with Mom out of town? I wished I could call Captain Cardinal that second to see if he could take me, but I didn't have a cell phone—one more thing Mom hadn't had time to deal with before she left.

I failed my quiz in American lit, and because I wasn't paying attention in biology I couldn't answer when Mr. Knorr called on me. I dropped my tray at lunch. I felt slow and thick and couldn't think about anything else but how to get my license. All in all, I was sure the day couldn't get any worse.

And then I ran into Curtis. Or rather, he ran into me.

"Ballentyne!"

"Yeah?" I said tentatively.

"That's the new favorite swearword at our house. Ballentyne this, Ballentyne that."

"Thanks for letting me know," I said.

"So the party's at my house," he said, leaning against the locker next to mine.

"What?"

"Tonight. There's a party at my house. You know, to celebrate."

"Celebrate what?"

"The fact that Tim's gone."

"I don't think your mom is celebrating."

"Are you kidding? As soon as he took off, she headed to the nearest bar."

"That's sad," I blurted out before I could stop myself.

Curtis kept on talking as if he hadn't heard me. "So you can bring a six-pack or ten bucks."

"Is this your way of inviting me?"

"Well, yeah."

I stared at him. "Why?" I asked.

"So you won't rat us out," he said, looking at me like I was the biggest idiot on the planet. He pushed off the locker and started down the hallway. "Beer or bucks, anytime after school."

Wyatt appeared on the other side of my locker. "What was that all about?" he asked.

"Nothing," I said, putting the rest of my books away. "Hey, how's your stepmom?"

"All right, I guess," he said with a shrug. "She's not supposed to get out of bed, so it's kind of hard. Dad's gone a lot, working extra hours trying to keep up with the new job. I try to help out—you know, with the cooking and cleaning and stuff—but either it's not enough or I don't do it right. I catch her out of bed all the time. And I know Dad's going to blame me if anything happens."

"Have you told him she's getting out of bed?"

"Tell on Pam? Are you kidding me?" He looked at his watch. "We better go or we're going to be late for history."

"On it," I said, slamming my locker shut.

"Maybe after swim practice we can get Mrs. Reyes to stop for some pizzas."

"I'm not going tonight."

"Why?"

I shrugged. I was in a funk, and I really didn't care enough to try to get out of it.

"Dude, season's creepin' up fast."

"I know," I said. November would be here before I knew it, but it still felt like forever before Mom or Dad would be home.

***

When I got off the bus after school, I was surprised to see Cardinal's truck in the driveway. I figured he was enjoying the fact that Mom wasn't keeping him at the office until seven or eight each night.

"Hello?" I called as I went in the door.

"Out back!"

I set my backpack on the table as I walked to the back screen door. "What's up?" I asked, then saw the small black bundle in his arms. "What's that?"

He grinned. "I took the afternoon off to bring Molly some company."

"Company?" I asked, stepping outside.

"Yeah, I think Molly gets lonely staying home every day, so I called the breeder a couple of months ago to find out when they were going to have another litter." He set the pup down. "This is her sister."

The puppy ran over to me, wobbling a bit, and crashed into my shoe. I had to laugh. "So where's Molly?"

"Over there, sulking," Cardinal said, pointing to the far corner of the yard. "I didn't realize what a jealous girl she is."

The puppy pounced on my shoelace and gave it a determined tug. I sat down and she climbed into my lap, her tail going so fast it was almost a blur. She lifted her head, stretching her neck as far as she could, and began licking my face.

I laughed. "What's her name?"

"Dunno yet. Haven't come up with one."

She looked up at me, her dark brown eyes looking way too serious for her playful attitude.

"Molly, come here!" Cardinal called.

Molly lifted her head, looked right at him, and then put her head back on her paws, staring off to the corner of the yard.

"I didn't know dogs sulked."

"Yep," Cardinal said as he stood up. "They're worse than kids sometimes." He glanced at me. "No offense."

I smiled and waved it off. "None taken. I wasn't allowed to sulk anyway."

He walked across the yard to Molly, picking up a well-chewed knotted rope along the way. Molly didn't lift her head, but I saw her tail twitch.

Before Cardinal reached her, she bolted across the yard, a black comet chasing a tiny brown one.

"Get him!" I hollered to her. "Get that nasty prairie dog!"

"Dak rat." Cardinal chuckled, watching Molly scratch furiously at the fence where the rodent had escaped. "We call them dak rats."

We spent almost half an hour in the backyard before Cardinal finally gave up trying to get Molly to play with the pup. Molly would play with Cardinal, chasing after the knotted rope when he tossed it, playing tug-of-war when she brought it back, and wriggling happily when he patted her head. But as soon as he moved toward the porch—and me and the pup—Molly retreated to the far back corner of the yard.

Cardinal shook his head. "I don't get it," he said. "She likes other dogs. When I take her to the dog park, she's always very friendly. Maybe if we leave them alone out here together, she'll come around."

"You don't think Molly would hurt her?"

"I don't think she'll even let the pup get close," he said. "But if she does, no, I don't think she would hurt her." He held his hand out. I grasped it and he pulled me up. "What are your plans for the night?" he asked, moving toward the house.

"Nothing, really. Probably just watch a movie or something."

He nodded. "So I don't have to worry about you making curfew tonight?"

"Nah. What about you, Captain? Heading out?"

He stopped with his hand on the doorknob. "Please, oh, please, don't call me captain here. It's Friday night and I'm out of uniform, and I'd like to get away from my job, at least mentally!"

"I thought I *was* your job," I said.

"You're a favor to a friend," he replied, opening the door. "And a chance to be—well, I guess I'm too old to be your brother, so maybe it's a chance to be an uncle."

"And that's a burning desire of yours?"

"I'd rather be an uncle than a captain right now, that's what it is," he said firmly. "You can call me Jon or Jonathan, or if you must, just call me Cardinal, okay?"

"Okay."

"And yes, I am heading out tonight."

"Hot date?" I asked with a grin.

"A date. I'm not sure about the hot part yet."

"A blind date?"

He grimaced. "Yes. Another favor."

"You must like doing favors."

"I like to help out when I can," he said, heading up the stairs. "That's all."

I waited in the living room while my enchiladas reheated in the oven. Although the TV was on, I was really watching the Vinsons' house and the two strange cars parked out front. While I stood at the window, a Security Forces car pulled up. I immediately recognized the tall, skinny SF airman. Simon strode confidently across the Vinsons' yard carrying a couple of brown paper grocery bags and walked in the front door—without ringing the doorbell or knocking.

Cardinal came clattering down the stairs, tucking in his shirt. "Let the dogs in if they start whining too much," he said. "Or earlier if you want the company." He looked out the window. "What's going on over there?"

"Don't know. They just pulled up."

"I'd better check this out," he said, sounding resigned. "I'll be right back."

I followed him out the front door but stayed on the porch. Cardinal was almost at the curb when Simon came back out of the Vinsons' house. The brown bags were nowhere in sight, but he was fumbling with his wallet. He pulled up short when he saw us.

"Is there a problem?" Cardinal called. "Everything all right?"

"Oh, no. Everything's fine. We had a noise complaint. The kids have turned down the stereo now, so I just gave them a warning." Simon slipped the wallet behind him, and I assumed he was putting it in his pocket.

"Did you talk to a parent?" Cardinal asked.

"No, the parents aren't home right now. And it was only a noise complaint," Simon repeated. "They've already taken care of it, so it's really no problem. No point wrecking a kid's Friday night by telling the parents, right?"

Cardinal didn't say anything, but I could tell he wasn't pleased by the answer.

Simon opened the door to the patrol car. "Have a good evening, sir," he said.

"You too," Cardinal replied automatically.

As the patrol car pulled away, Cardinal turned to me. "You going to be all right tonight?"

"Fine," I said absentmindedly, staring at the Vinsons' front door.

"I'm sorry, Stu, I don't mean to be overbearing. I know you're perfectly capable of taking care of yourself. But I also know that your mother just left, and that maybe…maybe you'd rather have company."

"Company? That's what Molly and Midge are for, right?"

"Midge?"

"Yeah. I know you'll want to name her. But I was just thinking how she's sort of a midget Molly, so—"

Cardinal let out a great booming laugh, probably the first real laugh I had ever heard from him. "That's perfect!" he exclaimed. "Molly and Midge! I love it!"

I smiled. "Glad I could help."

He checked his watch. "I've got to get going or I'll be late. I left my cell phone number on the counter, in case anything stupid happens." He looked across the street. "And I mean *anything* stupid."

I shrugged. I wasn't planning to get involved in anything over there.

"I'll be back late," he said. "Don't wait up, roomie."

"No problem."

After dinner I went out to the backyard to see how Molly and Midge were doing. Molly came running to see me, but as soon as I touched the puppy, Molly ran back to her corner. I spent almost twenty minutes playing with Midge before I went back inside.

I was settling down to watch a movie when the

doorbell rang. I pulled the door open, sure that it would be Billy.

"Jorge!"

"Hey, Stu. Good choice skipping practice tonight. It was brutal."

"Should've listened to me," I said. "What's up?"

"I talked Wyatt into coming over here." He inclined his head toward the Vinsons' house. "Rumor has it there's a party across the street."

"Ten bucks or a six-pack," I said.

"What?"

"That's the cover."

Jorge's eyebrows shot up. "You knew about it and weren't going to invite us?"

"It's not my party," I said. "And I wasn't planning to go."

"Come on!" yelled a voice from the street.

I looked past Jorge. "Why is Wyatt waiting out there?"

"Told you," he said. "Practice was brutal. We flipped a coin to see who had to walk all the way up here to get you."

I laughed. "That's sad, man. That's really sad."

"Hey, slacker, you weren't there," he replied. "So you're not coming to the party?"

I thought it over for about five seconds.

"Let me get my shoes and some cash," I said. "I'll be right out."

* * *

Now there were eight cars in front of the Vinsons' house, two of them crammed into the single driveway and one partially hanging out into the street and others along the road. The cars must have been full of kids when they arrived, because the house seemed to be packed.

We paid our cover to Mike as we went in. He told us we could drink whatever we wanted and that all smoking had to be done in the garage or backyard.

"If you're looking for more than a nic fix, you're gonna have to see Chance and fork over more cash," he added.

Jorge looked confused, but Wyatt and I pushed him past Mike before he said anything stupid.

"What did he mean by 'more than a nic fix'?" Jorge asked when we were in the kitchen.

"If some idiot wants to smoke something other than a regular cigarette," Wyatt said in a low voice as I primed the keg and he got cups, "he has to pay for it."

"What do you think they've got?" Jorge asked, pitching his voice to match Wyatt's.

"Weed," I answered quietly, filling a cup and handing it over to Jorge. "And they've probably got some X too."

"Think they've got mushrooms?" Jorge asked.

I blinked.

"Who cares?" Wyatt snarled at him. "You're not seriously thinking about doing drugs, are you?"

Jorge shrugged uneasily. "I dunno. I've heard mushrooms are cool. I've never had the chance before..." He trailed off under Wyatt's glare.

"Don't be an ass," Wyatt snapped.

"What's the difference between drinking and doing

drugs, really?" Jorge asked. "Can you tell me what the big difference is?"

I took a sip of my beer, grimacing. Beer was okay, but I knew I wouldn't drink ten dollars' worth. I'd only paid the cover to be with my friends.

"C'mon, Jorge. Drugs are illegal!"

"So is drinking when you're not twenty-one," Jorge argued, "but we've all got cups in our hands."

Wyatt sort of pushed Jorge up against the counter. "No!" he growled. "It's not the same, and you will *not* do drugs. Not here, not now, and never when I'm around. Got it?"

For a moment I thought Jorge was going to shove back and fight. Then he just seemed to wilt. "Okay, Wyatt, okay. Jeez. I was just asking."

"Don't. Curiosity kills more than the cat when drugs are involved." Wyatt released Jorge and took a step back. He started to raise his cup but then stopped. "Let's go out to the living room," he said. "I think I saw some girls in there."

He dumped his beer down the sink, grabbed a can of Pepsi, and headed out of the kitchen.

I looked at Jorge. "What was that all about?"

"I don't know, dude, but it was serious." He looked at his own cup, glanced over at the sink, and then shrugged and chugged his beer. He refilled his cup before we left the kitchen, just a splash of soda and the rest whiskey.

Wyatt introduced us to the girls he'd just met and we sat down, joining their conversation.

For a long time we just hung out. The three girls stayed on the sofa, and we sat on the floor next to the coffee table. Other groups were scattered around the room, and I could hear people going up and down the stairs. People were drinking, laughing, and flirting, but no one in the living room was doing anything totally crazy.

I finished my beer but didn't bother to get another one. Jorge got up a few times, refilling his cup and getting drinks for the girls. He seemed interested in them, but then for some weird reason, he started talking about his girlfriend.

"What's her name?" Jaylene asked. She had short curly blonde hair and long earrings dangling just below her chin. Her eyes were bright blue, but I thought she'd gone a little heavy on the makeup.

"Tricia Hatz."

"Don't know her," Jaylene said. "What grade's she in?"

"Tricia is a sophomore, but she goes to Our Redeemer," Jorge explained.

"Why isn't she here?" Tania asked him. Her hair was the opposite of Jaylene's: nearly black and pulled back in a long ponytail that reached down to her waist. She was wearing a low-cut top and a short skirt. She looked great and I could tell she knew it.

"She lives in town," he said, "and she couldn't get a ride."

Tania looked skeptical, but she let it drop.

"They're showing a free movie next week," the girl named Lindsay said. "I don't usually like war movies, but since Vince Hale's going to be in it, I think I'll go." Lindsay was the one I liked best. She had blonde hair too, but it looked natural, especially compared to

Jaylene's. I'd seen her before on the bus in a seat a few rows back from my usual spot, and there were never empty seats close to her. Hearing that she liked Vince Hale gave me the slightest bit of hope. My friends in Barksdale had compared me more than once to Hale, though right now my red hair was longer than his, and my eyebrows weren't as bushy.

Jaylene nodded, curls bobbing. "Me too," she said. "And if it's too depressing, we can always leave. It's not like we're paying for it."

"The base paper said that you have to get tickets in advance, though," I said.

"Yeah, at the BX," Lindsay said, tucking her hair behind her ears. "But they don't cost anything."

"Oh. Do you want to—"

"Ballentyne! Yo, Ballentyne!"

I turned. Curtis was standing in the hall between the kitchen and living room, hollering.

"He's in here!" Jorge yelled helpfully.

"Is your babysitter still around?" Curtis asked, obviously checking out the girls on the sofa.

"What?"

"Your babysitter. The one that was at your house this evening."

"He's a family friend who's staying at our house, not a babysitter. And Jon's not home right now," I said. "He went out." It felt weird referring to Cardinal that way, but I didn't want it to sound like he was staying there to watch me.

"He gonna be home soon?"

I shrugged. "He's on a date. He'll be out late."

"You sure?"

"Dude, what does it matter?" Wyatt asked, irritated because Curtis had sprawled on the arm of the sofa, cutting him off from Jaylene.

"It matters, *dude,* because this Jon guy was asking Simon questions and now Simon doesn't want to come back," Curtis said, flipping open a cell phone.

"If this Simon's too chicken to come to a party—" Jorge began.

"Simon's our supplier, jackass. If he won't come back, this party's gonna suck real soon. Hey, bud, no worries," he said into the phone. "No one's home across the street. Yeah. See ya in five." He snapped the phone shut but didn't leave.

Instead, he reclined along the edge of the sofa. Idly he lifted one of Jaylene's curls with his pinky finger. She shifted away from him. "I thought it was going to suck," he said, "Simon having to work tonight. But it's actually better this way."

"What do you mean?" Tania asked.

"He's been by twice in his patrol car, so it looks like the cops are keeping an eye on us. No one's going to call anything in." He smiled, looking very pleased. "You girls having a good time?"

"Yes," they all said, nodding.

"Are you sure? Because there's more fun to be had in the garage, if you're interested." He reached for Jaylene's curl again. This time she jerked her head away.

"I think we're all comfortable here," Wyatt said, with a slight edge to his voice. "But don't let us keep you from that good time in the garage."

"Curtis?" a high, reedy voice called. "Curtis?"

Curtis rolled his eyes. "What?" he snapped.

Billy walked into the room, staggering a little. I hadn't expected him to be here tonight, and I was horrified to see that he looked like he hadn't just been at the house—he looked like he had been partying.

Billy glanced over at his stepbrother. "Curtis, Chance said—"

"Don't listen to Chance," Curtis said impatiently. "I've told you that before."

Billy started to turn unsteadily.

My fists clutched involuntarily. I'd never dreamed that a kid his age would be at a party like this. I'd just assumed that he was off somewhere with his stepmother. "Hey, Billy," I said. "Why don't you hang out here with us?"

He looked at me for a moment like he didn't know who I was, then he gave me a grin so big I thought it must hurt. "Stu! Stu! How ya doin', Stu?"

"I'm good," I said, trying to stay calm. "How are you?"

Wyatt caught Billy by the elbow when he tripped. "Easy, kid," he said gently, then he glared at Curtis. "What the hell do you think you're doing?"

Curtis smiled, though it didn't reach his eyes. "I'm throwing a party. Drinks all around."

"You're letting this little kid drink?" Jaylene asked in disbelief.

"He paid his cover."

I stood up so suddenly that I almost knocked Billy over. "Come on, Billy, let's go to my house."

He stared up at me, swaying slightly. His usually bright eyes looked glassy. He reeked of weed, and I prayed that it was just because he'd been out in the garage. I didn't trust myself to speak to Curtis.

"Is there a party at your house too, Stu?" Billy asked, almost falling down on the couch between Jaylene and Tania.

"No," I said with a smile. "Something even better. A new puppy."

Lindsay and Jaylene both stood up quickly.

"Ooh, I'd like to meet your puppy," Lindsay said.

"Me too," Jaylene said, helping Billy to his feet.

"Let's go," Wyatt agreed, standing at the same time Tania did.

Jorge looked up at us, his bleary eyes looking almost as bad as Billy's. "But we paid to drink," he said.

Wyatt reached down, grabbed him under the armpits, and pulled him up. "Yeah, but we're done drinking now."

Jorge shook his head. "I think I'll have one more."

"No," Wyatt said, steering him toward the front door. "You've had enough."

Lindsay held her hand out to Billy. "Come on," she said gently. "Let's go see the puppy."

He looked up at her shyly and took her hand, then let her guide him toward the front door.

"Ladies," Curtis said, "you don't need to leave." He looked at Wyatt and me. "You either," he added as an afterthought. "The party's just getting started."

"Thanks," I said, "but I need to go let the dogs in."

"Suit yourself." Curtis glared at Billy. "Hey, butt-head! You're not going anywhere. You gotta stay here."

"No," I said sharply.

Curtis raised his eyebrows. "I'm watching him, Ballentyne."

173

"You're doing a crappy job," Wyatt said. "The kid's coming with us."

"You like hangin' out with little boys?" Curtis said, wrinkling his nose.

Wyatt took a couple of quick steps toward him. I grabbed his arm and pulled him back. "Billy's staying at my house," I said to Curtis, "at least until the party's over."

Curtis stared at me with heavily lidded eyes. "Whatever." He rolled off the arm of the couch and stood up. "You losers were bringin' the party down anyway."

When we got out to the front porch, Lindsay, Billy, and Jaylene were in the middle of the yard waiting for us. Tania was standing in the driveway, using her cell phone. "Where's Jorge?" I asked.

Wyatt swore. He turned to go back in, but the door opened and Jorge came out carrying two plastic cups.

"Do you really have a p-puppy?" Billy asked as we joined the others.

"Yep," I said. He grabbed my hand, forming a chain between Lindsay and me.

She gave me a shy half smile over the top of Billy's head. "So where are we going?"

I pointed with my free hand. "Right there," I said.

"Long walk," Jaylene observed. "Don't know if I can make it."

"Allow me to assist you," Wyatt said, gallantly offering his arm. She laughed and placed her hand in the crook of his elbow.

We were in my yard before we realized that Tania and Jorge were hanging back a bit. She was giggling.

Wyatt ran back to them, ripped the cups out of their hands, and dumped the drinks in the gutter.

"Hey!" Tania exclaimed.

"Jeez, Wyatt, just because you don't want to drink doesn't mean—"

"You're done!" Wyatt yelled. "You've already had way too much!"

"What's your problem?" Jorge yelled back. "Why won't you let anyone have any fun?"

"If that's the kind of fun you want, maybe you ought to go back to the party," Wyatt snarled.

"Good idea," Jorge snapped. He spun on his heel, stumbled a few steps, and then lurched across the street.

"Jorge," I called. "Wait, man!"

He kept going. Tania looked at him, looked back at us, and shrugged. She followed Jorge.

"You all right?" I asked Wyatt.

He shook his head, looking far more upset than I would have expected. "Not really," he muttered. "Tell you later."

Suddenly Billy leaned over the porch railing and puked.

"Gross," Jaylene said, stepping away and covering her nose.

Lindsay put her hand on Billy's back and murmured something to him.

"Sorry," Billy said, still leaning over the railing.

"Hang on, Billy, I'll get you some water." I hurried into the house. Before I could get back to the porch, they'd brought Billy into the living room and set him down on the sofa. Someone had found a trash can and placed it between Billy's feet.

I gave him the glass of water and a couple of tissues. "I always need to blow my nose after," I told Billy. He smiled weakly.

"What grade are you in, Billy?" Lindsay asked.

"Third."

"Thought so. Who's your teacher?"

"Mr. Jacques."

"My brothers are in Mrs. Sunchild's class," she said. "Do you know Zach and Zander Danforth?"

"The twins?"

Lindsay nodded.

"Sure. Everyone knows them."

We sat in awkward silence for a minute or two. Billy took cautious sips of water and his color began to return to normal.

I heard scratching at the back door. "Want to meet Molly and Midge?" I asked Billy.

"I jus' wanna lie down," he said pitifully.

"Okay," I said. "I'll take you up—"

"We need to keep an eye on him," Wyatt said in an undertone.

"Want to stretch out on the couch?" I asked Billy.

"Um-hmm," he mumbled. He could barely keep his head up.

We got him settled on the couch, lying on his side with the trash can right beside his head. I repeatedly told him it was there, but I was still afraid he wouldn't remember when the time came. Jaylene carefully spread the blanket from the back of the couch over him.

"Well," Wyatt said. "I think he'll need to rest awhile."

"I'd still like to see the puppy," Lindsay said with a smile that made my stomach do a pleasant roll.

"This way," I told them. "We'll leave the door open so we can hear if Billy needs help."

* * *

When I opened the back door, Molly came bounding into the house, but I didn't see Midge anywhere. For a few seconds I was afraid something had happened to her. Then I heard a whimper.

"Midge?" I called.

"Over there," Jaylene said, pointing.

Midge was really whining now, almost squeaking. I followed the sounds until I found her stuck at the bottom of one of Mom's planter boxes. How she'd fallen in there, I had no idea. I picked her up and got a thorough face-licking as a thank-you.

"So tell us," Jaylene was saying as I handed Midge to Lindsay, "why'd you go off on Jorge like that?"

"It's nothing," Wyatt said.

"Baloney," Jaylene said bluntly.

"Total crap," I agreed. "You were pretty upset."

"He needs someone to clue him in," Wyatt said. "Believe me, I know what I'm talking about."

"But why—?"

"I told you, I don't want to talk about it."

"Come on," Jaylene said. "You can tell us."

Wyatt sighed and rubbed his hand through his short-cropped hair. "When I was five, my mom's youngest brother came to live with us. He was way too much for my grandparents to handle. As it turned out,

177

he was too much for my parents to handle too."

I thought I heard a rustling in the bushes behind me, but I didn't see anything when I turned to look.

"Myles was sixteen when he moved in," Wyatt continued, "and I thought he was so cool. I wanted to be just like him. Of course, he wanted nothing to do with a dweeby five-year-old. But I tagged around whenever he let me, which wasn't often."

Wyatt took a deep breath. "He went out a lot, you know, especially at night. Mom and Dad fought about it all the time. Dad wanted to make him follow the house rules; Mom said he was just being a teenage boy. Then Myles stopped going to school. And things started disappearing around the house."

He slumped down in a lawn chair and looked away from us. We didn't say anything. We could tell that he was reliving some bad memories.

Wyatt's voice was raspy as he continued. "One morning I went to get Myles. I wanted to ask him if he'd play catch with me, even though he usually said no. The first thing I noticed when I opened his bedroom door was the stench, but I didn't realize.... I went all the way in his room, right up to his bed."

Wyatt stopped, though not for long. When he began again, his voice was unsteady. "His eyes were wide open and he wasn't moving. I ran and got my parents, but it was too late. Myles had overdosed on heroin and he was dead. I kept thinking about his eyes, staring straight at me, and his...his..." Wyatt bent forward, letting his head rest in his hands.

We all watched him silently, not knowing what to say.

"Way to make a first impression, eh?" Wyatt said, turning back to us.

"Hey, dude!" We all jumped at the voice and looked toward the bushes. Jorge emerged from behind a big shrub. "Why didn't you just tell me that before?"

"I never talk about it," Wyatt said. "Usually I just tell people that my uncle died, but the rest of it.... I don't even know why I decided to tell you guys. I just…"

"It must have been awful," Lindsay said.

"It was," Wyatt said. "Nothing was the same after that night. My mom was a wreck. And it pretty much destroyed my parents' marriage. She felt so guilty about what had happened to Myles that she just kind of lost it. She's still a mess. Dad hates it when I go to visit her because he never knows what she might do or say. I don't like it that much myself."

"So why go?" Jaylene asked.

"She's my mom."

"God, that bites." Jorge held out his hand and Wyatt shook it. "I'm really sorry, dude."

"No worries, mate," Wyatt said, copping an Australian accent with an odd little laugh. "Now you know how I ended up with a stepmother who's only eight years older than I am! But Pam's actually pretty cool."

Jaylene looked over at Jorge. "So why didn't you stay at the party? And where's Tania?"

"They let her back in," he said. "They didn't try to charge her the cover again."

"They wanted you to pay again?" Lindsay asked him. She was still holding Midge, who appeared to have fallen asleep in her arms. Lucky dog.

Jorge nodded. "Mike was being a real dickhead about it too."

"Come on," I said. "Let's go inside."

* * *

Wyatt checked on Billy and then joined us at the dining room table. "He's out like a rock, but he's going to feel like hell in the morning." He nodded toward the living room. "What's the big dog's name?"

"Molly," I told him.

"She's curled up on the floor in front of the couch, kind of watching him."

Lindsay set Midge down. "Maybe she'll go hang out there too," she said.

The puppy scampered off, sniffing happily.

"Do you think Curtis talked him into getting drunk?" Jaylene asked, looking toward the living room and shaking her head. "I can't believe a brother would do that."

"I'd freak if anyone let my brothers drink," Lindsay said. "It borders on child abuse."

"It *is* abuse," Wyatt said. "We ought to call the cops."

"Billy's asleep on my couch," I pointed out. "It'd look like we were the ones who got him trashed."

"And how do we know Curtis *made* him drink?" Jorge asked. "Maybe Billy was sneaking around, drinking on the sly."

"Do you really believe that?"

"No," he said. "But Curtis could claim it was all Billy's idea."

"We could report a wild party at Curtis's," Jaylene suggested.

"We're the only ones who left," I reminded her. "They'll know who ratted them out."

"Who cares?" Wyatt said. "It's not like we're going to want to hang out with them after this, right?"

Everyone but me nodded in agreement.

"Easy for you to say. You don't have to live across the street from them."

"Besides," Jorge added, "what if we call the cops and his buddy Simon shows up?"

"His supplier?" Wyatt asked. "What's he got to do with it?"

"When I was trying to get back in," Jorge said, "an SF car pulled up and I just about peed my pants. But it turned out to be Curtis's buddy Simon."

"Seriously?"

"Yeah," I said. "I've seen him around here before."

"Crap," Wyatt said.

I thought about calling Cardinal, but I decided against it. I told myself I didn't want to wreck his date, and I hoped maybe he'd get home while there were still cars lining the street and decide to check it out for himself.

We raided the kitchen and came up with microwave popcorn, a bag of potato chips, and a jug of lemonade. Wyatt sent me looking for a deck of cards, and we played a game called BS that had us all in hysterics. I wasn't the only one who was holding my sides, aching from the laughter but unable to stop. It felt good to really laugh.

Billy woke once and threw up again, but he managed

to get to the trash can, which Wyatt promptly took outside to clean. After that, Billy slept so soundly that we could hear him snoring.

At quarter till twelve, Lindsay put her cards down. "I've got to go," she said. "If I miss curfew, my parents will turn me into a pumpkin."

"I've gotta go too," Jaylene said.

"You're not driving, are you?" I asked.

"No. We walked over from the other side of the elementary school," Lindsay said. "My dad's a tech sergeant."

"The other side of the school is pretty far," I said. "We'll walk you home."

"Jorge and I will do it," Wyatt said. "You should stay with Billy."

"Right," I said, disappointed. I didn't admit that the prospect of walking Lindsay home had made me forget about Billy for a second.

"You'll need to wake him up every couple of hours, just to make sure he's not slipping into a coma or anything. Want me to come back and help you out?"

"That's all right, Wyatt," I said. "I can handle it."

"You sure?"

"Yeah." We wandered out to the front porch. I wasn't ready to say good-bye to Lindsay yet. "What about the movie next weekend?" I asked. "Who wants to go?" I figured it would be easier to suggest it to the whole group instead of asking Lindsay on a date.

"I'm up for that!" Lindsay said with a smile.

"Me too," Jaylene and Jorge said together.

"Okay," Wyatt said. "I think I can afford it."

"Oooh," Jaylene teased, elbowing him. "Big spender!"

"Who's going to pick up the tickets?" Wyatt asked.

"I can go," Lindsay said. "But there's a four-ticket limit, and there are five of us."

"I'll go with you," I said quickly.

"Thanks. I guess we should ask Tania if she wants to go."

"What about Tricia, Jorge?" Jaylene asked, giving him a mischievous look.

"I'll ask her," he said. "If it's a group thing, her parents might let her come."

"So we'll meet in front of the theater next Friday?" Wyatt suggested.

"Yeah," Lindsay said, and then she turned to me. "Want to go get the tickets Monday after school?"

"That'd be great."

Jaylene looked at Lindsay. "What about Tania?"

"We can't leave her at that party," Lindsay said.

"A lot of the cars are gone now," Wyatt said, inadvertently crushing my hopes that Cardinal would come home and call the cops on Curtis. "We can probably just stick our heads in the door and get her attention."

"It'll cost you ten bucks," Jorge said gloomily.

"No, it won't," Wyatt said. "Let's go."

I stayed on the front porch while they went back to Curtis's. It looked like Wyatt was right, because they weren't over there for more than a minute or two before I saw all five of them walking down the sidewalk. Well, four were walking. One was stumbling and leaning on someone. That had to be Tania.

I went back inside and cleaned off the table. The phone rang and I answered it quickly, hoping it'd be Mom.

"Hi, Stu." Cardinal's voice sounded harassed.

"Hey," I said. "Everything okay?"

He laughed. "I'm the one who's supposed to be asking that, but as it happens, I've got a small problem. I just had to bring my date to the hospital."

"Oh? What's wrong?"

"She seems to be having a pretty bad allergic reaction to something. I don't want to leave her here alone. Are you okay?"

I looked at Billy. He was still sleeping. "Yeah, I'm fine."

"I don't know how long I'll be—"

"Don't worry about it," I said.

"You're home for the night, right?"

"Right."

"Okay. I'll be there as soon as I can. Don't wait up."

"Hope your date feels better soon."

"Thanks."

I hung up.

After letting the dogs out one more time (Molly determinedly ignored Midge's nips at her heels), I woke Billy up and made him go to the bathroom.

"How are you feeling?" I asked him.

"Sick," he said. "Do I hafta go home?"

"Nope." I was sure that by now Curtis was too wasted to miss him. "You're on our couch tonight."

"Thanks, Stu," he said, burrowing under the blanket again. Upstairs, I found another blanket for Billy and pulled the comforter off my bed. I figured I might as well just make a night of it in the living room.

Relaxing in the recliner, I flipped through the TV channels. I found a *Die Hard* marathon on the Action Channel and decided that would be the easiest way to keep myself awake.

***

"Stuart?" Cardinal's face came into focus. I blinked up at him in confusion. My back hurt and I had a terrible taste in my mouth. I should have brushed my teeth after all the sour cream and onion chips.

"What's going on?"

"Hmm?" I wasn't awake yet. There was a warm weight on my lap and it took me a few moments to figure out it was Midge. I vaguely remembered picking her up to stop her whining.

"Who's that?" Cardinal pointed at the couch.

"What time is it?" I asked.

"Almost three. Who is that?"

"Billy."

"Who?"

"Billy Vinson," I said, yawning, "from across the street. Curtis had a party, so I let Billy hang out here. He wasn't feeling very well."

Cardinal looked out the window. "Looks like the party's over," he said. "Cops are there."

I snorted, sure it was Simon.

"Why'd you crash down here?" Cardinal asked.

"Keeping Billy company," I said. I wanted to get up and check on him, but I didn't want to make Cardinal any more suspicious than he already was. "Is your date okay?"

He shrugged. "Seems to be. Of course now she wants to take *me* out as a thank-you for looking after her…"

"And you were thinking this was a one-date thing?"

"Exactly."

"Must be rough."

Grinning, he said, "Yeah, it's hard when the ladies find you irresistible."

Sunday afternoon, Cardinal and I took Molly and Midge out for a walk. Well, he walked Molly. I kind of tugged Midge along. She was really fighting the leash.

"She'll get it soon," Cardinal promised. "Especially if you walk her more than once a day."

"Me?"

"Er, well...yes. That is, if you don't mind. Things are going to be hectic at work for a while, and I won't have a whole lot of time to spend training Midge."

When I didn't say anything right away, he asked, "You do like her, don't you?"

"Well, yeah," I said. "But I've got swim team and school. Plus I've never had a dog before. I don't have a clue how to train one."

"I'll help," he assured me quickly. "I know you're busy too, but you could walk her after school, before you go swimming, right?"

"Most days," I said. We turned back onto our block, Midge still straining at her leash.

"We'll just—" He broke off suddenly and swore.

I looked up. "What?"

"Just something I've got to do that I'd rather avoid," he muttered.

"Huh?"

"Mrs. Vinson!" Cardinal yelled.

We were on the sidewalk two houses down from the Vinsons'. She put her hand on the hood of her car and waited while Cardinal trotted up to her. Molly kept an easy pace with him. Midge suddenly decided she didn't want to be away from Molly and bolted after them on her fat puppy legs. I could have stopped her, but I was curious, so I jogged next to her.

"Is everything all right?" Cardinal asked Mrs. Vinson.

"Of course," she said. "Why wouldn't it be?"

"I saw a Security Forces car in front of your house a couple of times Friday night, and I wondered—"

"There's no call to be watching my house," she said icily. "Everything is just fine."

"I wasn't watching your—"

"You must have been," she countered. "Else how would you have seen them?"

"Look," Cardinal tried in an earnest tone, "I know things are hard on the spouses and children when there's a deployment. I'm just trying—"

"It seems like you're trying to cause trouble," Mrs. Vinson snapped. "Trying to make it look like Curtis's done something wrong."

Cardinal frowned. "I didn't say anything about your son, ma'am. I assumed you were home that night and I—"

She cut him off again. "You know where I go on Friday nights. I've seen you at Sneaky Pete's often enough. If you're trying to apologize, this is hardly the way to do it."

Cardinal's neck flushed a deep red. "Mrs. Vinson, I'm not trying to cause trouble—"

"Nosy neighbors always cause trouble," Mrs. Vinson tried to interrupt again, but this time Cardinal kept talking.

"—I'm trying to *prevent* trouble. If there wasn't anything wrong, that's a great relief. If you need help with anything while your husband's deployed, just let me know. I'm staying across the street with Stuart and I'd be happy to help any way I can."

Mrs. Vinson glared at me. "Curtis and I are doing just fine," she said. "We don't need any help."

"What about Billy?" I interjected.

"He's fine too," she said dismissively.

"Is he feeling better?" I pressed. "You know, he was pretty sick Friday night."

"And how would you know that?" Her eyes narrowed suspiciously. "Billy and Curtis stayed home to watch a movie. Now, I'm late for an appointment. Excuse me." She swung into her car and gunned the engine. As she peeled out, we jumped clear of the driveway, pulling the dogs with us.

Cardinal looked at me. "She didn't even know Billy spent the night at your house?"

I shrugged.

"Crap. If this gets any worse, I'll have to call family advocacy."

"What?"

"I'd say she's being pretty neglectful of Billy. Since Captain Vinson's not here to look after his son, then it looks like we'll have to do it for him." He sighed. "I hate messing in other people's business."

Me too, I thought. "It's just a part of Air Force life, right?"

"Yeah. But that doesn't make it easy."

I was glad I hadn't told him that Billy was drunk. It would have only upset him more, and he would have been forced to do something. He had enough to deal with already.

Back in my room, I logged on and was surprised to find an e-mail from Dad.

Stuart—

I tried to call you earlier, but you were out. I have good news and bad news. The good news is that I am back among the civilized and have Internet access. I will try to be better about keeping in touch with you.

The bad news is that Gram is in the hospital with pneumonia. This may make it harder. Just bringing up the idea of an assisted-livng home is enough to send her into a rage. Let me tell you, Stu, it's no fun getting old. Gram has enjoyed having me around, at least that's what she says, and I don't want to upset her when she's so sick. I really hate it, but this means that I won't be able to get up there in time for your birthday. Sorry, pal.

I hope everything is going well up there. Your mom said that Captain Cardinal is a good guy. Keep your chin up, and call whenever you want.

Love,
Dad

After school, I rooted through the kitchen cabinets, looking for something to eat. The apple I was holding with my teeth just wasn't going to be enough.

I had made it to practice on Monday and Tuesday, and I wasn't looking forward to tonight. Jorge had warned that coach's preferred method was to increase yardage and decrease rests each day of the week, ending with true torture sessions on Fridays. Saturday morning practices, he told me, were the best ones, because she let us play water polo for the last half hour. Of course, there was a flip side: We'd have to leave base around five thirty in the morning to get there for the six o'clock start.

I pulled out a box of Mom's granola bars. They didn't look especially appealing, but I decided they'd be better for me than Cheetos or Pringles. Cardinal seemed to think the commissary began and ended at the junk food aisle.

I swore when I heard the doorbell ring, just managing to catch the apple as it fell out of my mouth. I juggled it and the granola bars as I dashed to the front door. I'd been sure that I had another ten minutes before Mrs. Reyes would be pulling up. Thankfully my swimming bag was already packed and waiting in the living room.

"Sorry, Jorge," I said as I opened the front door. "I'm almost—"

It wasn't Jorge on the porch.

"Hey, Stu!" Billy said.

"Hey. What's up?"

"Wanna play catch?"

"Um, I'm sorry, but I can't."

"Oh," he said. "Okay."

I waited, but he didn't move. "I've got to go somewhere soon," I added.

Immediately he perked up. "Can I come?"

"I've got swim practice."

His face fell. "Okay," he said listlessly.

"Is everything all right?"

He shrugged.

I looked across the street. Mrs. Vinson's car wasn't in the driveway, but a beat-up Chevy with a busted headlight was. "Is Curtis home?"

"Yeah."

I got the sense that he didn't want to say more—but that something was on his mind. Unfortunately, at the moment I really didn't have the time to find out what it was. "Look, I gotta go," I said. "My ride's going to be here in just a minute."

"Okay," he said.

"See ya later."

"Okay," he said again. But he didn't move.

"Really, Billy, I've gotta go."

"I know." Still he stood there.

Sighing, I slowly and gently eased the door shut. I didn't know what else to do.

Back in the kitchen, I poured a tall glass of milk to wash down the dry granola bars.

The doorbell rang again. I glanced at the clock. Five minutes had passed; it was still too early for Jorge to be here. I gritted my teeth and ignored the bell.

I was taking the last swig of milk when the doorbell rang again. I put the glass in the sink and tossed the apple core into the trash, and then headed to the front door.

I yanked open the door. "Billy, I told you—" I broke off. No one was on the porch, but I saw a girl about halfway down the driveway.

"Lindsay?"

She spun around, her blonde ponytail whipping across her cheeks. "Oh, hey," she said. "Sorry I rang the doorbell twice. I wasn't sure it worked the first time. I'm really not a stalker or anything."

"It's all right," I said. "What's up?"

"Sorry it didn't work out to go get the tickets on Monday."

"Me too," I said. I was looking forward to going to the movie.

"I thought I'd go over and pick up the tickets now. Want to come?"

I only hesitated for a second. "Sure. Let me make a quick phone call first, though, okay?"

She bobbed her head and I held the door open.

"Have a seat," I said, gesturing to the living room. "I'll be right back."

I darted to the phone and dialed Jorge's number. No one answered. Before I could call Wyatt, a car honked in the driveway.

193

"Crap," I muttered.

I trotted down the short hall to the front door.

"Were you expecting someone?" Lindsay asked.

"Wait here a sec," I said, leaving the front door open behind me and hurrying to the car.

Jorge rolled down the window. "Where's your bag?"

"I'm not going tonight," I said quickly. "I just tried to call, but you'd already left." I leaned down and looked past him to his mom. "I'm really sorry, Mrs. Reyes. I'll make sure I call earlier next time."

She pursed her lips in that way that all mothers seem to do. "What's wrong?"

"I'm not feeling well."

"Do you need to call the clinic?"

"No," I said, brushing aside the guilt. "I'm sure I'm just getting a cold." She looked skeptical, so I hurried to add, "If it gets bad, I promise I'll call the doctor."

"How about chicken noodle soup?" Mrs. Reyes asked. "It's good for fighting colds."

"We've got some Campbell's in the house. I'll have it for dinner. See you guys tomorrow. Sorry I didn't call in time," I said to Mrs. Reyes again. I stepped back from the car. As they pulled out, Wyatt pantomimed holding a phone and I nodded.

Lindsay was standing in the entryway when I went back inside. "Is there a problem?" she asked.

"No!" I said quickly. I glanced out the window to be sure the car was gone. "Absolutely no problem. Ready to go?"

She smiled and we headed out.

At first our conversation was slow and awkward, but by the time we got to the corner, we had relaxed

194

a little. In a few minutes we were talking and laughing like we had been Friday night.

"I'm just a couple of weeks from getting my license," I said, trying to sound casual. "Maybe the next time we go to a movie I'll be able to drive us."

"Are you getting a car?"

"No, but I'll have one to use."

"Me too. I don't turn sixteen for another three months, though. The waiting is killing me."

She told me that Jaylene was going to the movie but that Tania didn't want to come. "She's not into war movies," she said. "Are Wyatt and Jorge still coming?"

"Yeah," I said, although I was sure they'd forgotten. We hadn't talked about it since the party.

"How about Jorge's girlfriend?"

"I think so," I said, figuring it was a safe answer.

"Have you met her?"

"No." There was something about her smile that made me ask, "Why?"

"Jaylene doesn't think she's real."

"What?"

"Hey, Stu!"

I groaned as I turned around. "Hi, Billy."

"Where y'all goin'?" he asked, bringing his scooter to a stop.

"Taking a walk," I said.

"You said you had practice!"

I glanced at Lindsay and felt the burn creep up my neck and onto my face. I absolutely hated blushing in front of girls. "I decided not to go."

"I forgot you had swim practice," Lindsay said.

"Why didn't you just tell me? We could have gone to the BX later."

"It's no big deal," I said. "I—"

"You goin' to the BX?" Billy broke in. "Cool! Can I come too?"

"No!" I snapped at the same time Lindsay said "Sure."

We looked at each other. Her big brown eyes looked confused.

"Do you have any money?" I asked Billy.

He laughed. "I never have money. I just like to look at the toys."

"Fine," I said in surrender. "But scoot ahead of us. I don't want you rolling up on the back of my heels."

"I wouldn't do that!" Billy said. "But since I go faster, I'll go in front."

As he pushed out ahead of us, I suddenly felt a pang of sympathy for Ray. I distinctly remembered all those times I tagged along with him when he didn't want me to. Was it too late to apologize?

"He seems like a good kid," Lindsay said.

"Yeah."

"But he also seems lonely."

"Uh-huh."

"Too bad he doesn't live closer to us. He could hang out with Zach and Zander."

"You'd end up with three brothers instead of two," I muttered.

"At least that would give him someone his own age to play with." She frowned. "Have you told anyone what happened the night of the party?"

"Who would I tell?"

"What about his mother?"

"It's his stepmother, and I don't think she'd care. I could try to say something to Curtis."

"I don't think talking to him will do much good."

"I don't know what else to do," I said. "There's no use reporting him. Like we discussed on Friday night, nothing's clear-cut."

Once again the conversation sputtered. I got the feeling she was disappointed in me, but really, what was I supposed to do? They were my neighbors but I hardly knew them. I didn't want to interfere in their business. I could have told Cardinal the little bit I knew, but I didn't want to dump more in his lap. He was stressed enough already. This past week he'd left for work every morning before I woke up, and he was hardly ever home until after I got back from swim team.

At the BX, Billy put his scooter in the bike rack and headed inside without us. Lindsay and I went directly to the customer service desk.

"How many tickets did we decide we need?"

"Jaylene, me, you, Wyatt, Jorge, his girlfriend." She held up a finger for each name. "That's six, right?"

"Sounds good," I said. "So we'll each get three?"

"Um, maybe I'll just get two and you get four. So you cover the guys and what's-her-name."

I tried not to grin. "I think Jorge said his girlfriend's name is Tricia."

"Yeah. The mysterious Tricia."

We got the tickets and I was about to suggest that we go get a soda when Lindsay's cell phone rang. "Hello?... Oh, hey, Jay.... No way! I'm here too!... Seriously!... At customer service, getting tickets for the movie.... A shoe sale? No way!... Hang on, I'll be right there!"

She snapped the phone shut and turned to me with sparkling eyes.

"Let me guess...a shoe sale?"

"Do you mind?" she said. "Jaylene says they've got the exact pair of Two Lips I've been looking for."

"Sure," I said, although I had no idea what two lips had to do with shoes.

I tagged along to the shoe section of the BX, where I was taught about the Two Lips shoe brand. After Lindsay and Jaylene picked out their shoes, we stopped by the music section. When they headed toward the women's clothing racks, I realized I was in over my head. But I couldn't think of a way to bow out gracefully.

"Oh," Jaylene said as she pulled out another shirt. "I'm meeting Tania at Rockers for dinner. Wanna come?"

"That'd be awesome," Lindsay said. "My dad's working late and my mom's taking the boys to flag-football practice."

"Stu?" Jaylene asked, still holding the shirt up to her chest and viewing it critically in the mirror. "Join us for dinner?"

"Thanks, but I've gotta run," I said. "I told Cardinal I'd eat with him tonight. It's the only night this week that he'll be home early enough." I had no idea if that was true, but as much as I wanted to have dinner with Lindsay, I didn't want to have dinner with Lindsay *and* Jaylene *and* Tania.

"See you at the movies?" I said to both of them.

"Yeah," Jaylene said, putting the shirt back and pulling yet another from the rack.

"You're going to go get Billy, right?" Lindsay said.

"Um, yeah, of course," I said. I looked around the racks of female clothing.

"I bet you'll find him in the toy aisle."

"Right," I said, nodding. "Well, I'll go get him and then head home. See you Friday."

Jaylene was still preoccupied with her reflection and the new shirt. Lindsay looked right into my eyes and smiled. "I'm looking forward to it."

Maybe the afternoon wasn't such a loss after all.

I did, in fact, go to the toy aisle and look for Billy, but he wasn't there. Relieved, I walked out of the BX only to find him sitting next to the bike rack, waiting for me.

What do you mean, you don't believe she's real?" Jorge demanded of Jaylene. "Are you calling me a liar?"

With a half-smile, half-frown, Jaylene gave him a shrug.

Jorge turned to Wyatt. "Come on, man, back me up here. You've met Tricia."

"Nope."

"What? Come on!" Jorge sputtered. "She set you up with her friend! You know she's real!"

"I've never actually *seen* her," Wyatt insisted. "You talked me into letting her set me up with her friend. Then Tricia got sick the night of our double date and you guys didn't go, remember? And it turned into the single blind date from hell."

Jaylene, Lindsay, and I all burst out laughing. We'd gotten in line for the movie twenty minutes early so we could get good seats. The fact that it meant more time to talk with the girls was an added bonus.

When I saw Jaylene, I realized she was wearing one of the shirts she'd looked at while we were at the BX. "New threads look good," I said.

"New threads? You stuck in the '70s?" she asked, but from the way she smiled, I could tell she was pleased at the compliment.

Lindsay cleared her throat and held out her foot.

"And the shoes look awesome," I added quickly. "If you step out of one, I'll search the kingdom to find the girl it fits."

"Dude, you already know who it fits," Jorge said, looking at me like I was totally out of it.

"Dude, he's calling her a Cinderella," Wyatt said. "But wait a minute. In that case, he'd be the handsome prince, so it loses all credibility right there."

I shot a lighthearted punch to his shoulder, which he promptly returned.

I made an exaggerated face and held onto my shoulder. "Ow! You know I'm sore!"

"That's your own fault," Wyatt said. "You're the one who skipped practice this week."

"What happened?" Lindsay asked.

"He got an extra five minutes of hard sprints every day for the rest of the week."

"What's a hard sprint?" Jaylene asked.

Jorge jumped in. "A fifty-yard swim followed by fifty push-ups."

"Ouch," Jaylene said.

"Mmmm. But totally worth it," I said, smiling down at Lindsay. I thought she blushed a little, but I couldn't be sure in the dim light.

She changed the topic fast. "How's Billy?" she asked.

"Who?" Jorge asked.

"You know, the little guy who got sick last week," Wyatt explained.

"Yeah, how is he?" Jaylene asked. "Did you talk to Curtis?"

"I haven't seen Curtis at all this week," I said. "But

201

Cardinal tried to talk to his stepmother on Sunday."

"Who's Cardinal?" Jaylene asked.

Briefly I told her about him, and then gave them all a description of his unsuccessful conversation with Mrs. Vinson.

Wyatt shook his head. "What a witch. I hope you can talk some sense into Curtis. If his mom's going to be like that, turning him in won't do any good."

"If his mom's like that, do you really think *he's* going to be very different?" I retorted.

"At least there's a chance," Wyatt insisted. "Is Billy okay?"

"He was fine Wednesday," I said, looking at Lindsay. She nodded.

"Uh-oh," Jorge said suddenly, straightening up. "Don't look now, Stu."

I closed my eyes, afraid that if I turned around I'd find Billy, my own personal parasite, right behind me.

"Stuart!"

I looked back. "Cardinal!" I tried to match his enthusiastic tone, but I'm sure the surprise showed in my voice. He was with a group of friends, but he was walking up with a very pretty, very petite, very busty blonde. "Um, I didn't know you were going to be here."

"Hey," he said, looking a little sheepish. "You didn't happen to pick up any extra tickets, did you? Our group is one short."

I laughed. "As a matter of fact, I do have one extra ticket. What's it worth to you?"

"Come on, Stu. The tickets were free," he said.

"Yeah, but they were limited. It's all about supply and demand."

"You're right," the blonde said to Cardinal. "He *is* smart."

Cardinal gave me an exaggerated grimace. "What do you want? No curfew tonight? Or do I buy pizza tomorrow night?"

"How about both?"

He opened his mouth, then shut it with a snap when the blonde giggled. "You should never offer more than you can deliver, Jon," she said.

"Deal," Cardinal said. As I held the ticket out to him, he grabbed my wrist and pulled me close. "I'll give you an extra hour tonight," he said in a whisper, "but it's your mother's curfew rule and I can't just drop it."

I grinned at him. He groaned, took the ticket, and led his date back to join their group.

Lindsay said, "Not bad for a babysitter."

"Not bad at all," Jaylene agreed.

"He's a *roommate*," I said. "Just there to meet base regs. And he's way too old for you two."

The theater doors opened and we all filed in. The girls went ahead to save us seats, and we stood in line to get popcorn and drinks.

"I can't believe you didn't have my back," Jorge groused to Wyatt. "You know Tricia's real!"

Wyatt sighed. "I just said I haven't met her. I didn't say she wasn't real." He gave me a push on the shoulder. "But what's real is the way Lindsay has the hots for you! Man, she won't even look at me!"

"Or me," Jorge said. "Although that's probably because she knows I already have a girlfriend."

"Oh please!" Wyatt and I said at the same time.

* * *

"I don't know," Lindsay said as we walked out of the theater. "I guess it was good, but you have to admit it was kind of a downer."

I raised my eyebrows. "War is usually a downer."

"Well, yeah, but—"

"But you were looking for an uplifting war movie?" Jorge asked.

Before Lindsay could think of a comeback, taps began playing over the PA system, letting us know it was ten o'clock. We must have been between two loudspeakers, because there was an eerie echo throughout the mournful song. A vision came into my mind: an empty table set for one, with nothing but a slice of lemon and some salt on the plate. I felt goose bumps rising along my arms. We all stood in silence until the music stopped.

"So you were looking for an uplifting war movie?" Jorge prompted Lindsay when we started walking again.

"Well, no..." Lindsay was getting flustered.

Jaylene came to her rescue. "She was looking for a movie that had at least partial male nudity," she said, "just like I was. I mean, you guys got a strip-club scene that was at least ten minutes long, and we girls got what? A sixty-second snippet of Vince Hale without a shirt in the doctor's office?"

"Sounds about right to me," Wyatt said. "A perfect movie."

"Besides," Jorge added with a leer, "if you girls need chest shots to make it a successful night..."

Wyatt grinned and then whipped off his shirt about two seconds after Jorge.

"Come on, Stu!" Jaylene crowed. "Take it off!"

"No, thanks," I said. "I'll wait till there's worthy competition."

"We won't know until you show us," Jaylene said, waggling her eyebrows while I ducked Jorge's attempt to get me in a headlock.

Lindsay looped her arm through my elbow. "I don't think you can get into Rockers without a shirt," she said. "And anyway, that's where Stu's taking me to get a chocolate shake and French fries."

I looked down at her for a second, fighting the butterflies. "Yeah," I said. "That's right."

Wyatt tugged his shirt back on and offered his arm to Jaylene. "Shall we?" he asked in a totally snobby voice.

She lifted her chin as she took his arm, "Of course, darrllink," she said, sounding absurd.

Jorge sighed, pulled his shirt on, and offered his arm to the air. "Let's go, then," he said, leading us off with his invisible girl.

23 September

This really sucks!" I tried to relax my hand. I'd been gripping the phone so hard it hurt.

"I'm sorry, Stu," Dad said. "I can't leave for at least two more weeks, probably three."

"Three weeks? Mom might be home by then!"

"If your Mom's back first, then she'll take you to get your license."

"But for all we know, that could be after Christmas, maybe even after New Year's!"

"I'll be there as soon as I can, Stu."

"Why don't you fly out this weekend?"

He chuckled. "It's nice to know you miss me so much that you'll invite me out when you need something. But I can't come this weekend. Gram's in the hospital, remember?"

I switched the phone to my other ear and changed tactics. "Can't you send power of attorney or something for Cardinal? So he can take me?"

"No!" he said. "I'm not giving some complete stranger power of attorney over my son!"

"Oh that's brilliant," I retorted. "You'll let a complete stranger come live with me—"

"As a temporary roommate," he said sternly. "Not as your guardian."

"But—"

"Look, Stu, I know it's important to you to get your license on your birthday, but in the long run it's really not that big a deal."

"You let Ray miss class to do it! You took him as soon as the DMV office opened!"

"This is a totally different situation and—"

"It sucks!"

"You've already made that clear. Too many times."

I flopped on the couch and clenched my jaw. I could feel the anger pulsing through me.

"How's school?"

"Who cares?"

"I do," he snapped. "And if you want *any* chance of getting your license, you'd better care a whole lot. If you let your grades slip—"

"They're fine. I'm doing everything I'm supposed to do, just the way I'm supposed to do it." And I was heartily sick of it.

"Stu, I know this isn't easy on you—" he began.

"You keep saying that, but you're not doing jack to make it any easier!"

He was quiet for a moment. Then he said, "Maybe it's time for you to quit asking everyone else to help you out."

Great, I thought. Out loud I said, "I've gotta go."

"Yeah, I should run too."

"Talk to you later."

"I'll call you on Friday," he said. "And I mailed your gift last week. It should be there by tomorrow,

Tuesday at the latest, but you can't open it till your birthday. Drop me an e-mail and let me know when it arrives, okay?"

"Sure," I muttered.

I didn't want some box of junk. I just wanted my license.

* * *

Cardinal was inspecting the refrigerator. "We're gonna need to go shopping soon," he informed me.

"Hope it can wait till Tuesday," I said, joining him to stare at the relatively bare shelves.

"Why?"

"Commissary's closed on Mondays."

"Really?"

I turned to stare at him. "How long have you been in the Air Force?"

"Five years," he said. "But I don't do much grocery shopping."

"You eat out all the time?"

"More than I should," he admitted, pulling open the freezer door. "Aha! Someone planned ahead!" He set a frozen casserole in a Tupperware container on the counter.

"Nope," I said. "That's left over from the welcoming wives."

"Still, it looks like our best bet." He put the container in the microwave and got it going, then leaned against the counter. "One of the perks of being a single Air Force officer is having a bit more disposable income. So, yeah, I eat out more than most people. When I was

208

married, Renee did all of the shopping and cooking."

"You were married?"

"For a little while," he said. "By the time I got orders out of Barksdale, she'd decided she couldn't hack the Air Force lifestyle. She—"

The doorbell rang and Molly and Midge made a tremendous racket as they skittered, barking, across the hardwood floor toward the front door.

"Hush, Molly!" Cardinal yelled. "Settle down!"

Lieutenant Colonel Porter was on our front porch, holding another casserole dish.

"Good evening, sir," Cardinal said.

"Good evening, Jonathan," Porter said. "I sent out an e-mail on Friday, asking for volunteers to bring you meals during the deployment."

"Why?" Cardinal asked.

"Two young bachelors on your own? Colonel Ballentyne was afraid your diet would be a little short on vegetables, and frankly, I agree with her."

"We'll just grab a few bags of salad at the commissary on Tuesday," Cardinal said. "That should take care of our veggie needs."

"You need to have real meals, not just salads."

"I'm insulted!" Cardinal said, laughing. "I can cook!"

"He's going to need more than your fireball chili," Porter said.

"I can cook," I said. "I can take care of myself."

"Yeah," Cardinal said, crossing his arms and nodding. "Me too!"

Porter sighed in a much put-upon way. "I've only got enough volunteers to bring two meals a week, so you *will* need to cook for yourselves a few days. But this is to get you started. Chicken-rice-and-broccoli casserole. Meat, grain, and vegetable in one convenient dish."

"I hope you didn't make poor Pam get out of bed to cook for us!"

Porter looked offended. "I'll have you know I made this myself." He paused for a moment. "I was already making one for us anyway. It's one of the few dishes I do know how to cook."

I started to laugh.

"Maybe you ought to add yourself to the e-mail list," Cardinal said. "Stu and I will volunteer to bring you some chili on Thursday."

Lieutenant Colonel Porter stared at Cardinal for a moment, then said, "Excuse me, Stuart, but I need to talk to Captain Cardinal."

"Sure." I held my hands out for the casserole dish. "I'll go serve it up." Just then the microwave chose to beep.

"Guess we can't have popcorn for dinner after all," Cardinal said. He winked at me and then pulled the door shut behind him as he stepped out on the porch with the lieutenant colonel.

When Cardinal joined me a few minutes later, I was setting the plates on the dining room table.

"Smells good," Cardinal said, rubbing his hands together. "Maybe he *can* cook."

"I put his in the fridge," I said. "This is what you were defrosting."

He frowned. "Looks like chicken-rice-and-broccoli casserole."

"It is," I sighed. "It's the Minot meal of choice

when someone's sick or moving in. We already got four of them; Porter's makes five."

"Okay. Then we can take broccoli off our grocery list."

"Are you in trouble?" I asked him.

"No," he said, grabbing a soda from the fridge. "Why would you say that?"

"Porter didn't look too happy."

Cardinal shrugged. "I like to joke around more than he thinks is appropriate. He's a bit...uptight. Not that you need to repeat that to anyone."

"I won't."

"But he's also a little stressed. There's been, as you know, a lot of vandalism in the last month, and he doesn't think the Security Forces are doing enough to try to catch the kids. And this weekend four young SF airmen got busted in town for underage drinking and one of them got a DUI. So he's been leaning on the SF commander, who, quite frankly, doesn't appreciate being told how to do his job."

"It looks kinda bad when the cops are getting DUIs, huh?" Briefly I thought about mentioning Curtis's friend Simon, but I talked myself out of it. After all, I hadn't actually *seen* Simon do anything other than talk to Curtis and go into his house. Curtis had said that Simon was his supplier, but supplier of what? And I didn't even know Simon's squadron or last name. It wouldn't make any sense to get the SF commander spun up even more about something that might or might not be going on.

"DUIs don't look good no matter who's getting them," Cardinal said. "But, yeah, you kind of hope that the cops will obey as well as uphold the law. I understand why Porter's stressed. SF isn't ordinarily his business, but when you're acting base commander, everything's your business."

"And on top of all that, his boss's kid is staying with a footloose captain, which is almost as bad as staying alone."

"Hey!"

"I'm joking, Cardinal, I'm joking. I'd rather have you here as a roommate than be staying with the Porters or Reyeses. You're cool."

"I think that's why Colonel Porter is concerned."

"Don't worry. If he asks, I'll tell him you're such a strict SOB that you've got me doing calisthenics every morning." I picked up a forkful of casserole. "And I'll tell him you've got me on a rice, chicken, and broccoli diet."

Wyatt, Jorge, and I were waiting at our stop for the bus on Tuesday morning when a beat-up old Trans Am pulled into the Vinsons' driveway and began honking.

"Hope no one on this street wanted to sleep past six thirty this morning," Jorge grumbled.

"Oh, this way everyone'll be up in time to enjoy hearing all of reveille," Wyatt said.

Curtis came running out the front door and bolted toward the car without shutting the door behind him. He was halfway in the car when Mrs. Vinson appeared in the doorway, wearing a much-too-short purple robe belted at the waist.

"Curtis!" she practically screamed. "Get your lazy ass back in here!"

In reply, Curtis slammed the car door and the Trans Am backed out, just missing a passing sedan.

As the Trans Am rounded the corner, Mrs. Vinson turned and saw all of us. She sneered, gave her belt a yank, and disappeared back in the house.

"Have you talked to Curtis yet?" Wyatt asked me.

"That's the first time I've seen him since the night of the party," I replied.

"We need to talk to him," Wyatt said, staring

thoughtfully in the direction that the Trans Am had gone.

"I don't think it'll help," I said. I didn't know why Wyatt was so stuck on talking to Curtis.

"Good luck finding him," Jorge snorted. "I don't think he really goes to school."

"Then why would he leave home so early?"

"Duh!" He jerked his thumb toward the Vinsons' house. "So she *thinks* he's going."

Wyatt shook his head. "Maybe we should just call the cops."

"And say what?" Jorge asked. "That we think Curtis got his little brother drunk? How do we prove something like that? We didn't actually see anything."

"We know he at least allowed it to happen," Wyatt murmured. "It doesn't seem right to let him get away with it."

"I know," I said. "I'll try to talk to him as soon as I get the chance. But Billy's doing okay right now."

Wyatt looked at me but didn't say anything.

On the bus, I slid into the seat behind Jorge and Wyatt, half listening as they compared answers for the American lit worksheet.

"I swear she said Mark Twain was something other than the dude's name," Wyatt argued. "What else did she say it means, Stu?"

"I don't remember," I said.

He and Jorge began flipping through their books. I stared out the window, trying to figure out what to do about Billy and Curtis. I didn't want to be in conflict with the family, not when they lived across the street from me. Besides, I was just a kid. If something really serious was going on, surely someone else should take care of it.

When I woke up Friday morning, I lay perfectly still in bed, listening. The house was silent, just like it had been yesterday and the day before that. Before we moved to Minot, I had never woken to a silent house. Dad was always up first, banging around the kitchen, and Mom turned on the radio as soon as she got up. Ray rarely slept later than I did. It was particularly noisy on birthdays, when the rest of the family would barge in early, singing "Happy Birthday" at the top of their lungs.

I listened to the silence a few more minutes, then I rolled out of bed and opened the drapes.

As I stared out the window, I realized that the promised cold front had come through: the trees and grass had been painted with frost crystals. The windshields of the cars parked along the street were a sparkly white. *Maybe I should give myself a present and take my birthday off,* I thought. But I had an English paper due and a quiz in science. It'd be too big of a hassle to miss school.

Just as I was ready to leave, I remembered my essay for English still sitting in the tray on the printer. I dropped my pack by the front door, ran back upstairs, and grabbed the paper. I needed a stapler. It wasn't in the desk where it belonged. I finally found it in the junk drawer in the kitchen. As I dropped it back in the drawer, I saw the keys.

The keys to Mom's car. Just sitting there.

The phone rang and I jumped.

"Hurry, man," Wyatt said when I picked up. "The bus has just turned the corner."

"I'm—" I'm...what? I'm the good kid who always does what he's told, always follows the rules? I looked down at the car keys in the drawer. Maybe it was time to try something new, let go a little bit. "I'm not coming to school today," I said. "I don't feel all that great. Talk to you later."

"Sure," Wyatt said. "See you."

I looked out the front window. Down at the end of the block I could see Wyatt and Jorge get on the bus. As it pulled away, I felt a moment of panic, a need to grab my bag and run after the bus as it rumbled down the street. What was I doing?

Fifteen minutes later, when I got behind the wheel, I forgot all about that. I had the keys in my hand, and I was the only one in the car. No one to remind me of the speed limit or when to change lanes or when to start braking. Freedom. Total, complete freedom without anyone telling me what to do.

Complete, lonely freedom.

I took a deep breath and pressed the garage-door opener. After the door was totally up, I inserted the key in the ignition and turned it. The motor started smoothly. I adjusted my mirrors and waited a moment or two to let the car warm up. I put the car in reverse and backed out cautiously, looking both ways before I pulled onto the street.

My heart was pounding in my throat as I drove through base housing. I kept telling myself that I was driving a totally ordinary, plain car and that no one would recognize me—but I still felt like everyone had to be staring at me. I passed one SF car, and I checked the speedometer. Not too fast. Not too slow. By the time I drove through the gates, I had to focus on breathing slowly so I wouldn't hyperventilate.

When I pulled onto the highway, I relaxed a little. I had done it, and there was no turning back now. But after a few minutes, a wave of doubt washed over me. Why was I doing this? Just so I could drive on my birthday? *It doesn't matter,* I reassured myself. *No one else is going to know.* But what if it started to snow? What if I got pulled over for a random check returning to base and had to show the license I didn't have?

Why was I doing this?

Because today, for once, it was just about me. Me all alone in Minot, doing my own thing.

* * *

When I got to class, I told Wyatt and Jorge that I hadn't felt well when I got up, but had decided at the last minute to ask Cardinal to drive me to school. They didn't question me. My heart was still racing and I was sweating. I probably did look ill.

I thought I'd calm down during class, but I kept worrying about Mom's car. I wondered if the people parked next to me would be careful when opening

217

their doors. I hoped the person on the other side wouldn't clip the car when they backed out. I alternated between believing I'd forgotten to lock the car and thinking I'd locked the keys inside. I checked my pockets three different times in science class to be sure the keys were there.

During lunch, I had to fight the impulse to go out and check on the car. At one point I almost decided to just take the car home early.

After my last class, I detoured into the library to get a new book to read, but mainly to hide until the buses and most of the student cars were gone. My plan worked beautifully. By the time I headed out to the parking lot, more than three-fourths of the cars were gone. A thick blanket of fog hovered above the town, and the air had a cold sting to it.

I took two quick steps outside, feeling good, feeling free, sure that I would get the car home and no one would ever know what I had done. I had done it by myself, for me. On the third step, the ground fell out from under me. Literally.

All of a sudden, I was lying awkwardly on my backpack. I hadn't noticed that the sidewalk and streets were coated with a fine sheet of ice.

Gingerly I got to my feet and made my way to the car, nearly falling twice more. If I could have thought of a way to leave the car there and get home without anyone knowing it, I would have.

"Ballentyne!"

I nearly scratched the key across the door as I pulled it out of the lock. Curtis and a guy I didn't recognize were crossing the parking lot.

"I didn't know you had wheels!"

I faked a smile and waved. I wasn't about to try to explain anything to Curtis. I got in the car and pulled the door shut, cutting off whatever he was saying.

The car started smoothly, and for a moment I sat and listened to the hum of the motor, holding the steering wheel and thinking I could go anywhere I wanted. But I didn't have anywhere to go—or anyone to go with.

I backed out carefully. The car slid through both stop signs in the parking lot, in spite of the antilock brakes. The main roads seemed to allow a little more traction, but I was terrified of losing control and crashing. By the time I went through the last traffic light and was heading north on Highway 83, I had a pounding headache and my hands hurt from gripping the wheel so tightly.

Mom's dire warnings kept running through my head, almost as if she were sitting next to me instead of half a world away. I was grateful that the highway was practically deserted. I hoped no one would try to pass me. I sure wasn't going to be passing anyone else.

Claiming the right lane as my own, I drove nearly twenty miles below the speed limit. Gradually, though, I gained confidence, and my foot got heavier on the pedal. Soon I was cruising at the speed limit, and most of the tension in my shoulders was fading.

More at ease, I turned on the radio. Mom had it set on some news program. I reached over to change the station. All I got was static. I glanced at the radio, trying to find the right preset button. I looked back at the road just in time to see a large dog dart right in front of me.

I slammed both feet on the brake pedal. The car began to fishtail. Suddenly I was in the left lane. I yanked on the wheel to get back in the right lane, praying that a car wasn't coming up behind me.

For a moment, as the car briefly headed straight in the right lane, I thought I had pulled it off. But a sudden gust of wind slammed the side of the car, nearly jerking the steering wheel out of my hands. I felt a tug as the right wheels slipped off the pavement and slid across the shoulder.

Fortunately, by this time I had slowed down a lot. But when the tires hit the soft dirt beyond the shoulder, the car came to an abrupt and painful stop. I was lucky the airbags didn't deploy. The motor was still running.

I don't know how long I sat there, still gripping the steering wheel, panting as if I had just finished the hundred butterfly. Finally, though, I convinced myself that the car had indeed stopped and wasn't on the verge of rolling into the field.

I glanced in the rearview mirror. No cars in sight.

I took my left foot off the brake pedal, and then eased the right one off. The car didn't move. Tentatively I put my right foot back on the gas pedal and slowly increased the pressure. When I heard and felt the tires spinning, I let off the gas. Sighing, I put the car in park and turned off the engine. I checked the rearview mirror again before I got out, but all I saw was the same desolate view of the highway. The air had a bitter bite to it, and I zipped up my jacket.

The wheels on the driver's side of the car appeared to be fine. But on the passenger side, the ground had given way under the front tire, and it hung uselessly in the air.

"Crap, crap, crap, crap, CRAP!" I shouted. How was I supposed to get the car out of this? I'd been prepared to give the car a push, or to throw one of the floor mats under the tires for traction. But this—*this* would require towing. Maybe I could walk home, call a towing company, and walk back to meet the tow truck. But what if the state patrol came along before I got back?

In the distance, I could see car headlights. Maybe I should try to hitch a ride out to base.

As the vehicle approached, I realized that it was a pickup and not a car. I stepped partway out on the highway and waved my arm up and down. The truck's headlights flashed on and off several times and I sighed with relief.

But when it got closer, I had second thoughts. This could be anyone—a pervert, a murderer, or an officer in Mom's direct chain of command. At the time, I didn't know which one would be worse.

And the truck didn't seem to be slowing down. For a brief moment I thought it was going to run me over. I stepped back against the car as the truck passed me. It slowed, then came to a stop well beyond the car. Before I could begin to walk toward it, it began to back up.

I'd already decided that rather than get in that black pickup with the red pin-striping, I would ask the driver to call a tow-truck company for me instead.

Even if it was going to take a couple of hours longer, that would be better than ending up the victim of some maniac.

The passenger door swung open. "Ballentyne! Now I know why they don't let you drive! You suck at it!" Curtis was holding a Super Big Gulp in one hand and a cigarette in the other.

"Thanks," I said sarcastically. "Have you got a cell phone?"

"Nope. Battery's dead," he said.

As the driver's door opened, I realized that this truck had been in front of Curtis's the night of the party. "We got a towrope, though," the husky driver said. He was wearing a T-shirt with the sleeves ripped off and jeans with holes in the knees. I couldn't understand why he wasn't freezing.

Instead of pulling the rope out of the truck bed, he just leaned back against the tailgate, considering me. "How much can you pay?"

"What?"

"Towing ain't free," he said. "It's a big business, 'specially around here. In the winter, this stretch makes me more money than a job plowing roads would. Usually get seventy-five dollars a pop."

I looked helplessly at Curtis. He gave me an evil grin as he stubbed out the cigarette. "Maybe you can cut him a deal, Rice," Curtis said.

"I don't know," Rice drawled. "Business is business and all. I suppose, though, I could come down to seventy." He looked up at the iron gray sky. "You know, official tow-truck drivers are required to file a report with the cops if a car's off the road."

I pulled my wallet out and opened it wide in full view. "All I've got is thirty dollars."

"That ain't even half," Rice said with disgust.

"Do you take IOUs?" I asked desperately. "I can get Curtis the rest."

"And why would you pay Curtis when it's my truck and line? You think that little thief would get the money to me?"

"Nice," Curtis said, but he was still grinning. "I've got forty on me," he said. "Ballentyne can be in my debt instead."

Something about the way he said it made my skin crawl, but I didn't have much of a choice. Only two more cars had passed us, and they were long gone. I didn't know how long I'd have to wait for someone else to stop, and I sure didn't want a towing company reporting my mistake to the cops.

I handed my thirty dollars to Rice and watched as he crawled under the front of Mom's car and hooked the rope to it.

"Should I get in the car?" I asked him.

"Naw. Just put it in neutral and then stay out of the way."

I did as he said, although I really wanted to stay in the car, out of the wind and out of the sight of Curtis's condescending glare.

Seconds later, all four wheels were on solid ground again.

"Thanks," I said after Rice finished unhooking the rope.

Rice grunted in reply and walked to the front of the truck.

"Give me a lift home?" Curtis said suddenly, sticking another cigarette in his mouth.

"What?"

"Rice lives in town," he said. "Save him a trip since he saved your tail."

"Um, sure," I said uneasily.

He darted to the passenger side of the pickup and grabbed an old backpack. Rice must have said something, because Curtis was laughing as he shut the door. He walked toward me, in no hurry.

"You can't smoke in the car," I said.

He rolled his eyes. "I won't light up," he said. "Wouldn't want to smell up mommy's car, now, would we?"

We watched as Rice turned his truck around, going down into the median ditch and then gunning the engine to get back up the other side, spraying dirt and grass all over the highway. He honked as he headed back to town.

In silence, Curtis and I got into Mom's car. I started the engine and pulled back onto the pavement, keeping my eyes focused straight ahead. I tried to concentrate on driving, but my brain was buzzing with jumbled thoughts. I was still worried about being caught, still afraid that I might have damaged the underside of the car, and generally miserable about being alone with Curtis. Every time I talked to him, I liked him a little less, even when he was acting friendly or being helpful.

Thinking about Curtis led my thoughts to Billy, and then to my promise to talk to Curtis. I was too stressed to figure out a polite start to the conversation.

"Why don't you like Billy?" I blurted out.

"Why do you like him so much?" he countered, the unlit cigarette hanging from his lip.

"He just wants friends."

"There's a reason he doesn't have friends. He's a little snot."

"You don't need to be so rough on him."

He snorted. "I'm not rough on him."

"You shouldn't have let him stay at the party the other night," I said.

"First you complain that I'm not nice enough to him and then you complain about including him." He pulled the cigarette out of his mouth and used it to point at me. "Make up your damn mind."

"You could have killed him."

"Just gave him a couple drinks."

"Yeah, and too much alcohol can kill you."

"Really?"

In spite of his patronizing tone, I plowed on. "He's a little guy. No matter how much he wants to be big, he's still little. Just a couple of drinks could give him alcohol poisoning."

"It won't happen again," Curtis said in a falsely sincere voice. "I'll be much more careful, because I sure don't want to hurt Billy or upset you." He made a gagging noise and then put the cigarette back in his mouth.

I didn't know what else to say. Telling him it was abuse wasn't going to do any good; making threats or mentioning Social Services would probably make things worse.

I slowed down as I approached the entrance to the base and turned on the blinker.

"Going to have to mark you down for not keeping your hands in the proper position on the wheel," Curtis said. "How'd you slide off the road, anyway? You drive slower than my granny."

"Got your ID?" I asked, ignoring his jibe. We were pulling up to the gate, and I was terrified the guard would sense something was wrong.

The SF checked our IDs, then said, "Driving conditions on base are red. We really don't want anyone driving if it's not absolutely necessary."

"I'm going straight home, sir," I said. Curtis stifled a laugh, but fortunately the SF didn't seem to hear. He handed our IDs back and quickly retreated to the warmth of the guard shack.

Once we were through the gate, I felt an odd combination of anxiety and safety. I was almost home, but on base the chances of seeing someone who knew me had greatly increased. Panic wouldn't help, so I looked for a distraction.

"How do you know Simon?" I asked.

"We've partied together a few times."

"He's a little old to be hanging out with you, isn't he?"

"This from the guy who hangs out with an eight-year-old."

"I mean—"

"Simon's only nineteen," Curtis said. "And he's totally cool. He enlisted on his birthday."

It was weird to think that a guy only a few years older than I was could be going around carrying a gun and charged with protecting both the people and the weapons of the base.

I hit the garage door opener and pulled into the driveway.

Curtis looked at me. "What? You're not taking me home?"

"I think you can handle walking across the street," I said. Maybe I should have tried to be polite, but my nerves were shot.

"Nice," he said, swinging out of the car and almost immediately lighting up. "This is why people don't help each other out anymore. No gratitude."

"Take your smoke out of the garage. Please." As he shouldered his backpack, I added, "I'll bring you the forty dollars in the next day or two."

He didn't turn around, just lifted his hand in acknowledgment. He was stepping off my curb when the front door of his house flew open and Billy popped out.

"Hey, Curtis! Wanna play Halo with me?"

Curtis looked over his shoulder at me. "Yeah. Sure." And it would have been touching, heartwarming even, if he hadn't then shot his arm out, catching Billy under the shoulder blade and sending him sprawling in the front yard. "Watch out, butthead."

Billy almost bounced up off the fading green lawn, still grinning as he reached over to rub his shoulder. They disappeared into their house and I went into mine.

***

I logged on and was pleased to see an e-mail from Ray, then disappointed to find just a quick note:

To: StuForceOne
From: RGBallentyne
Subject: Birthday

Happy birthday, bro! I'm out tonight, so I'll call tomorrow around lunch.

Ray
PS—Dad said you can still come out next month. Got your tickets yet?

My note back to him was just as short:

Dad was supposed to buy my tickets yesterday.

I thought about e-mailing Taylor, but I couldn't think of anything to say. I sat there, staring at a blank e-mail window. There was no one to tell who would understand. I had never felt so lonely.

"Stuart!"

I must have jumped nearly a foot in the air.

"Stuart Ballentyne!"

"Coming!" I called as I logged off. My heart was pounding. Cardinal never yelled like that. Half the time I didn't know he was home from work until he came out of his room, already out of his uniform.

I was sure he'd found out about the car somehow. I hadn't gotten away with anything after all. No one would ever trust me again.

"Stuart!"

"I'm here," I said, rounding the corner into the dining room. I stopped short in complete shock.

There on the table was a big bouquet of helium balloons, a large pizza box with the smell of pepperoni and sausage drifting from it, the package that Dad had sent, and a large cake decorated to look like a swimming pool with lane lines and the words, "Happy Birthday, Stuart!"

Cardinal was standing in the corner of the room, grinning like an idiot.

"Wow."

"Your mom ordered the cake before she left and asked me to pick up the pizza."

"What about the balloons?"

"Those are from me," he said, looking a little sheepish. "It's not much, but—"

"They're great," I said.

"I know it's not the same as getting your license, but—"

"It's great," I repeated, feeling almost lightheaded with relief. "Really." I stared at the huge pizza box. "Who's coming over?"

Cardinal looked confused. "You want to invite some people?"

"You think we can eat all this ourselves?"

"I think we ought to give it a try!"

***

Cardinal went into the kitchen and wrapped up the last two slices of pizza while I opened and read the cards from Ray and my grandmother. Then I grabbed the package from Dad and sighed. Nothing in this box would make up for the situation we were in.

"Bring me a knife, will you?"

"Scissors?" he offered.

"Sure."

I cut open the box and lifted the card out, planning to open it first. But when I saw what was in the box, I frowned.

Nestled in the packing paper were a collar, a leash, a bowl, and a Frisbee. A Pet City gift card was in the bowl.

Cardinal came out of the kitchen, carrying Midge. She had a big floppy red ribbon around her neck and she was gnawing at it, trying to get it off.

"Sorry I lied about the pup," he said, handing her over to me. "Your mom mentioned she was going to get you one for your birthday, and I knew about the new litter. I brought her here early instead of leaving her with the breeders. So you could bond with her."

"She's mine? Really?"

"Really." Cardinal reached out and pulled on her ear. He smiled when the puppy turned her attention from the ribbon to his hand.

"That's why you let me name her," I said.

"Yeah, but now you know she'll be with you and not Molly. If you don't want to call her Midge, you could still train her to answer to a new name."

"I like Midge," I said, rubbing the short fur on her nose between her eyes. "You sure you don't want her?"

He winked. "Between you and me, pal, I can only handle one bitch at a time."

When I took Midge out for a walk the next day, I put her new collar on—but even tightened all the way, it was too big for her. She was getting better about walking with me instead of being tugged along, but she was a long way from learning how to heel.

I still couldn't quite grasp the fact that I finally had my own dog.

I couldn't help thinking that Mom had an ulterior motive. She'd gone to the trouble to order the cake and make arrangements with Cardinal about Midge, but she hadn't done anything about my driver's license or cell phone. Why?

I figured it was simple: She'd given me something that would tie me down more instead of giving me the freedom I wanted.

Billy came barreling up to me. "Hey, Stu! Can I walk her?"

Midge lunged against the leash, straining to get to him.

"Sit!" I caught up with her and pushed down on her haunches. "Sit, Midge! Sit!"

Billy knelt down, laughing as Midge basically

climbed on top of him to lick his face. "Ow!" he said suddenly. "Careful, Midge!" He pushed her away and stood up. A deep purple bruise covered almost half of his right cheek.

"What'd you do this time?" I asked him.

"Hit a tree branch while I was ridin' my bike," he said cheerfully. "Can I walk her?"

"Only if you tell me the truth," I said. "What happened to your face?"

"I told you—"

"If you hit a branch, you'd have some scratches too," I said. "So come clean."

Billy hesitated for a moment, and I really thought he was going to tell me that Curtis had hit him. "I ain't lyin', Stu," he said. "But if you don't want me to walk her, that's okay."

"Here." I handed him the leash. He was having a rough enough time without me harassing him too.

I walked while Billy skipped. Midge danced forward and backward on the leash.

Retreat sounded. I hadn't realized it was already 4:30. Cardinal had told me that they would stop sounding retreat from November till April because they didn't want people having to stand at attention out in Minot's dangerously cold weather. But I still had another month of stopping for the anthem whenever I was outside in the afternoon and listening for taps at ten.

I reached over and turned Billy so we were facing a house that was flying a large American flag. We stood patiently, hands over our hearts. A car went past us, and I glanced up. I was surprised it didn't stop for the anthem. Even if their windows were up and their music was loud, it was pretty clear that's why we had stopped.

"When're they comin' home, Stu?" Billy asked as soon as the music stopped.

"Nobody knows," I said, starting to walk again. Mom had sent me a birthday e-mail, but it didn't have much news. She'd said the mission was going well, but she hadn't mentioned when it might end. And I didn't expect a phone call unless it was an emergency. I figured that things were pretty crazy wherever the troops were.

"I miss my dad."

"I know. I miss my mom too. But when you're in the Air Force, you're blue."

"Huh?"

"You know, like in the Air Force slogan. You 'cross into the blue.'"

"Huh?"

"Never mind," I said, shaking my head. "Where are Curtis and your mo—Mother Darla?"

He shrugged. "Dunno."

"Curtis didn't tell you where he was going?"

"Nope." A strange look crossed his face.

"You sure?"

He looked up at me. "Why so many questions, Stu?"

"Just curious. He took you biking, though?"

"Sorta."

"Sort of?"

"He took me out there, but then he didn't do any bikin'. He just told me what to do."

"Where'd he take you?"

"Out that way," he said, waving vaguely to the other side of the base. "Whoa, Midge, whoa!" The puppy was going nuts on the leash. "What's got into her?"

"Dak rat," I said, pointing into the yard. "She wants to chase it."

"Should I let her go get it?"

"No!" I snapped before I could think about it.

Billy cringed.

I spoke again, more gently. "We'd better not let her off the leash. She's hard enough to catch in the backyard when she doesn't want to come in." Midge was even worse about coming when called than she was about heeling.

"Okay." He didn't seem at all upset. "Can we go over by North Plains?"

"Um…" I hadn't planned on walking Midge that far.

"The best playground's over there," he said. "It's only three more blocks."

"All right then," I said. "We can go over to your school playground."

Billy gave a little skip. "I can show ya how I can swing and then flip right off the bar!"

"Great," I said. Knowing my luck he would break his arm and I'd get in trouble for not watching him carefully.

Something woke me early Sunday morning. When I opened my eyes, I could tell it was still dark outside. I groaned and burrowed back under the blankets.

The doorbell rang twice in rapid succession. Molly barked, but I didn't hear Midge. I rolled over and looked at my alarm clock. It was two-thirty. I was too tired and sleepy to get up.

The doorbell rang again. This time Molly and Midge both barked, and then Midge started whining. Now that she was awake, she thought she needed to go out.

I rolled out of bed and followed Molly and Midge to the stairs. The doorbell rang, this time a long one, like the person was just leaning on the button. I wondered who could be at our door in the middle of the night.

"Coming!" I heard Cardinal shout in irritation.

"Got it," I shouted back, though I knew if it was anything serious, like a death in the squadron or something, then Cardinal would have to deal with it. But I didn't understand why the person on the other side of the door couldn't have called first. Then Cardinal would've had his butt out of bed and I could've kept sleeping.

The bell rang again just as I flipped on the porch light. I pulled the door open just a few inches, staying behind it since I was only wearing my boxers. "What?" I demanded.

When I saw Billy's pale, tear-streaked face looking up at me, I blinked.

"Stu, can I sleep over?"

I stared at him, trying to make sense of this.

"What's going on?" Cardinal asked, coming down the stairs behind me. He was in boxers too, but he'd taken the time to put on a T-shirt. I opened the door a little more. "Billy?" Cardinal said in surprise. "What's wrong?"

"Can I sleep over?" Billy repeated in a small, sad voice.

"Sleep over? What's wrong?" Cardinal asked again, and I suddenly had a vision of standing here for hours, repeating our questions in a sleepy stupor, and never being able to get back to bed.

"Sure," I said, pulling the door open. Midge immediately bolted out the door.

"I'm sorry, Stu," Billy said listlessly. "I'll get her."

Fortunately Midge had just gone out to pee, so Billy grabbed her by the collar while she was still squatting. He carried her inside, holding her close to his chest. She licked the tears off his face. He walked directly to the living room couch and sat down, still clinging to the pup.

Cardinal followed him and turned on a lamp near the couch.

"I'll go get the blankets," I said, yawning so big I thought I'd crack my jaw.

When I came back into the living room, Cardinal was sitting in the recliner watching Billy, who was staring ahead in stoic silence.

Midge saw me and wriggled out of Billy's grasp to trot across the couch cushions toward me.

"No, Midge!" I said sharply. "Get down!" I picked her up and set her on the floor.

As I spread the blankets out over the couch, I casually asked Billy, "Is Curtis watching another scary movie?"

He shook his head.

"Is he having a party?" I asked, although the house across the street was dark and quiet.

Again he shook his head.

"Did you have a bad dream?" I asked, because I couldn't think of anything else.

"No," he said, his voice full of scorn. "I ain't scared 'bout some stupid dreams."

"It's okay," Cardinal said. "Everybody has nightmares sometimes. I do."

Billy ignored him.

"Will you tell me what happened?" I asked him gently, sitting on the couch next to him.

"No." The moment he spoke his eyes began to well with tears again.

"That's all right," I said. "We can talk about it later. Will you be okay down here by yourself?"

He nodded.

I stood up and waited for almost a minute before Cardinal finally sighed and stood up.

"Sleep well, Billy," he said. "I was going to make Stuart some flapjacks and sausage tomorrow for breakfast. That sound good?"

Billy grinned, and the change in his face was almost startling. "Better than good," he said. "That sounds great!"

We left the room and I picked up Midge at the foot of the stairs so she wouldn't clatter all the way up.

"You got Mrs. Vinson's number?" Cardinal asked in a low tone.

"No. Don't you have it on the recall roster?"

"No. We have Vinson's cell phone number, but he took his cell with him. I'd have to go to the office to get his home number."

"Oh."

"Guess I ought to put a few more clothes on," Cardinal muttered behind me.

"Why?"

"Gotta go see what's going on," he said, "and let them know he's here so they don't panic tomorrow morning when they realize he's gone."

"No one's going to panic." I stopped short of saying that nobody cared. "I'd be surprised if anyone's home."

"What? You can't be serious!"

I shrugged. "They leave him alone a lot."

"There's something wrong going on over there. Do you have any idea what it could be?"

"Same thing that's going on over here," I said, swallowing another yawn. "Billy's dad deployed and he was left behind. But nobody volunteered to watch Billy."

"His stepmother did."

"I don't think she sees it that way."

"I need to know what's going on," he said, continuing down the hall, "before I file a report."

I settled Midge on her towels and climbed back

into bed. I was still awake when Cardinal crept down the stairs and went out the front door, but I never heard him come home.

* * *

The next time I woke, the sun was out. Neither of the dogs was in my room. It wasn't hard to guess where they were, though. The smell of sausage filled the house.

I threw on a pair of sweatpants and a T-shirt and headed downstairs. I heard Billy's high-pitched laughter before I reached the bottom.

"Smells good, Cardinal," I said. "You've been holding out on me. You could've been making this for dinner instead of making me eat broccoli casserole every night."

"But it doesn't fulfill the veggie need," he called from the dining room.

"I can suffer through without veggies," I said, "if those 'jacks taste as good as they smell."

"They do!" Billy's voice sang out. "They're awesome!"

I did a double take as I entered the dining room. Billy had a stack of at least six flapjacks in front of him, with a tower of whipped cream on top. He was holding our biggest coffee mug, which had another whipped cream mountain melting happily down the sides.

"Where'd we get whipped cream?" I asked.

"Shoppette," Cardinal said casually. "I made a run over there this morning."

"Want some hot choc'late, Stu?" Billy asked, setting down his mug.

239

"Sure," I said, knowing that had come from the Shoppette too. "When'd you decide to grow a mustache?"

Billy giggled and wiped the whipped cream off his face with the back of his arm. Cardinal pushed a napkin across the table to him.

"You need anything?" I asked Cardinal as I headed back into the kitchen.

He scooted his chair back. "I think I'll cook up a few more 'jacks," he said. "You gonna need more, Billy?"

"No thanks," Billy said around his mouthful of flapjacks.

In the kitchen, Cardinal asked me if I could help him keep an eye on Billy for the day.

"I guess," I said. "What'd you find out last night?"

"Nothing," he said grimly. "No one answered the door. I called family advocacy this morning, and they're sending someone over in a little while."

"On a Sunday morning?"

"The day of the week doesn't matter when you're trying to keep a kid safe."

The doorbell rang and both dogs ran for the door, barking and sliding the whole way.

"Keep him company for a few minutes while I talk to the social worker," Cardinal said.

I carried my mug of hot chocolate into the dining room.

"Din'cha want whipped cream?" Billy asked. "It's better that way."

"No thanks," I said.

"You called who?" A woman's voice suddenly yelled from the front room. I flinched, and poor Billy almost

240

sank right under the table. Midge came scuttling from the living room, tail tucked firmly between her legs.

"I gotta go now," Billy whispered. "Mother Darla's here."

"Finish your flapjacks," I said, trying to sound upbeat. "There's no hurry."

"I don't care what you thought, you had no right—" Mother Darla sounded pissed.

I couldn't make out Cardinal's words, but his firm tone sounded a lot calmer than her shrill outburst.

"Billy!" she yelled.

I smiled, trying to reassure him, and pointed to his plate. He set his fork down and shook his head, looking terrified.

"He was not unattended. Curtis was home all night!" I heard a thump and I wondered if she had stamped her foot or hit the door in frustration. "Billy, you come here right now!"

He stood up, and I could see that he was shaking. "I'll come with you," I said.

The poor kid tried to smile.

Mrs. Vinson was quite a sight. She was wearing shiny, tight black pants that I think might have been leather, and boots with spiked heels. Her white blouse was startling in contrast, but it was wrinkled and had a pale brown stain on the front. Her hair was a mess, and the smeared mascara stood out ghoulishly on her pale face. In short, she looked like she'd slept in her clothes, and not very soundly.

"I rang your doorbell several times last night and nobody answered," Cardinal said, keeping his tone moderate.

"Curtis is a very sound sleeper."

"I don't believe he was there. Billy didn't seem to think so."

Mrs. Vinson turned her piercing gaze to Billy. "Did you go into his room?"

Billy shook his head. "No, ma'am. Curtis don't like me to go in there."

Cardinal and I exchanged a look. We thought Billy had checked the house. And he never *said* he was alone. It put a hole about the size of a B-52 in the story.

Mrs. Vinson looked back at Cardinal with her head cocked to one side. "My son says he was home all night. Don't you dare accuse him of lying without proof! Let's go, Billy."

"I think Billy should stay here until you calm down," Cardinal said.

"He's my stepson. You can't keep him here, and you can't stop me from taking him home, where he belongs." She snapped her fingers. "Come, Billy. Let's go. You've caused enough trouble."

Billy took a few steps forward, but stopped next to Cardinal. "I'm sorry, Mother Darla."

Cardinal put his hand on Billy's shoulder. "The social worker will be here soon."

"Well, I hope you have a good visit with him."

"He's coming to talk to Billy."

"You'd better call and tell him you made a mistake," she said.

"I will tell him what I know," he replied evenly, "and what I think, and then I will suggest that he go talk to you and Billy."

"Well, I'm not talking to him!" Mrs. Vinson was

beginning to sound hysterical. "And Billy, you are grounded for causing all this!"

"You can't hide him from family advocacy," Cardinal said.

"I'll sue you for harassment." She turned and stepped off the porch. She wobbled slightly, whether from her stiletto boots or some other cause, I wasn't sure. "Billy!" she shouted again. "Your father's going to hear about this!"

Billy looked up at Cardinal. "Thanks for the flapjacks," he muttered, though he looked so green I was afraid he might throw them up in our front yard.

We watched them cross the street. She marched straight toward their house, her heels clacking on the pavement, and you could almost see the anger radiating off of her in waves. Billy followed meekly, making no attempt to catch up or talk to her. When they got to the front door, she threw it open and stood to the side. As he walked past her, she leaned forward and said something. Billy quick-stepped over the threshold and she slammed the door behind them.

Cardinal slowly shut our door and turned to look at me. "Why do I think this is going to get ugly?"

"Going to get ugly?" I asked him. "You mean it isn't already?"

* * *

After I finished my breakfast, I retreated to my room and sent thank-you e-mails out to Ray, Mom, and Dad. There was a message from Mom saying she was sorry that she hadn't been able to call on my birthday, but that she would try to call later this week. She also said she hoped they might be able to come home before Thanksgiving. She made a point, though, of telling me not to mention a possible return date to anyone.

The house felt empty when I got downstairs. "Cardinal?" I called. Then I heard barking. I found him out in the front yard with Molly and Midge.

"Hey," I said. "I thought family advocacy would have been here by now."

He nodded toward the Vinsons' house. "He just went in."

"When did he get here?"

"Maybe fifteen minutes ago."

"I didn't hear the doorbell."

"I was waiting out here with the dogs," he said, throwing the ball for Molly, who charged after it. "I wanted to watch and make sure she didn't try to bolt."

"He's already talked to you?"

"Yep," he said with a sigh. "He told me before he went over to talk to Mrs. Vinson that without physical proof of abuse or neglect, there's not much he can do, other than suggest counseling. And right now, it's just my word against hers that Billy was left alone last night."

I sat on the porch and watched Cardinal throw the ball for Molly. Midge chased her, never getting more than halfway to the ball before Molly was already running back with the prize in her mouth. After a dozen tries, Midge decided she'd had enough, and she came over to chew on my shoes. I pulled her up into my lap and she closed her eyes almost immediately.

The Vinsons' front door opened and the social

worker came out, heading for his car. He shrugged and waved to Cardinal.

"Isn't he coming over here?" I asked. "Isn't he going to tell you what—"

"It's not our business anymore," Cardinal said, sounding tired and disgusted. "He thanked me for telling him what I knew, and then he told me that I wouldn't be involved anymore. Rights of privacy and all that."

I watched the guy get in his car. Maybe I should have talked with him too. Would my information have changed anything? I didn't have any physical proof that Curtis had abused Billy. Any alcohol in Billy's system would have been long gone by now, and he had stories for every single bruise and cut he had. As a little kid, I always had tons of bruises and cuts too. Even now, after a game of hoops or touch football, I was likely to come away a little beat-up.

I stayed silent as the social worker drove away.

I was sure I couldn't make a difference.

H2Oxcelr8r: u really like this lindsay girl?
StuForceOne: she's easy 2 talk 2.
H2Oxcelr8r: and cute?
StuForceOne: no—hot! <g>
H2Oxcelr8r: so minot's getting better?
StuForceOne: don't know if i'd go that far—but yeah, it's not 2 bad. a little dull, maybe, but not 2 bad.
H2Oxcelr8r: ur mom coming home soon?
StuForceOne: don't know.
H2Oxcelr8r: dad?
StuForceOne: don't know. gram keeps going up and down. at least cardinal's cool. how's ur situation?
H2Oxcelr8r: still waiting 4 orders. we're not leaving 15 oct anymore. maybe 15 nov.
StuForceOne: hurry up and wait, huh?
H2Oxcelr8r: SOP for the air force.
StuForceOne: i think it's SOP for government in general.
H2Oxcelr8r: i've got a big meet this weekend and—sorry, gotta run.
StuForceOne: bye.

So Taylor wasn't coming to Minot soon. I had to admit it was almost a relief. I'd been in a funk all week, and I wasn't up for showing someone else around the base. I had too much on my mind already. I was worried about Mom and Billy—I didn't need to worry about meeting my online friend for the first time.

And somehow the whole adventure of driving the car to school and getting stuck out on the highway had left me with a nagging guilt I couldn't shake off. I threw myself into school and swimming all week, staying at the library instead of going home after school, getting to practice early and working every set as hard as I could. The only time I really talked to my friends was on the bus on the way to school. Lindsay, Jaylene, and Tania had taken to saving seats for Wyatt, Jorge, and me each morning.

Since I felt the need to punish myself, workouts were the perfect solution. Coach wasn't content with brutal sets in the water. He gave us brutal dry-land sets too. For four consecutive practices, our last set was twenty-five push-ups, a 75-meter sprint, lunges around the side of the pool back to the starting blocks, twenty-five crunches, another 50 sprint, twenty-five jumping jacks, a 25 sprint, and an easy 50 to catch our breath before starting all over again. Ten times. I could hardly walk when we were done.

The week felt like a year.

5 October

On Friday Jorge told us that he had plans with Tricia in town that night. He tried to get all of us to go too, so we could see that his girlfriend was real. But we couldn't all fit in Mrs. Reyes's car, and no one wanted to ask their parents to drive us to town and back.

Cardinal had said he'd be out for the evening, so I invited Wyatt, Jaylene, and Lindsay to come hang out at my house. Almost as soon as I got back from our killer practice, Wyatt called to say that he couldn't come because his stepmother had gone into labor. When Jaylene found out Wyatt couldn't come, she backed out too. She said she didn't want to be a third wheel.

A few minutes later Lindsay called to say she couldn't make it either. "I'm sorry," she said, "but my parents are really strict. I can't go out unless it's with a group."

"Maybe tomorrow night?" I suggested.

"Maybe," she said. "I'll call you later."

"Okay," I said. "Talk to you then."

So once again I was home alone on a Friday night, getting ready to watch a movie. In a way, it was kind of a relief. The practices had gotten harder each day, just like Wyatt had said they would, and I was wiped out.

I didn't understand exactly how wiped I was, though, until I suddenly jerked awake. Blinking, I stared at the TV screen, discovering I had no idea who two of the characters on the screen were.

Then I heard a tapping at the window, and I realized that was what had woken me. When I looked over my shoulder, I leapt off the couch, heart hammering painfully in my chest. I stood there crouching like I was waiting for an attack before I recognized that the pale face floating in the window was Curtis. He was wearing all black and the rest of his body blended in with the dark. The clock said it was nearly midnight. The DVD player must have started playing the disc again, maybe even a third time.

"You ever hear of a doorbell?" I asked irritably when I opened the front door.

"You ever hear of having a life?" He was practically dancing. "Man, it's Friday night and you've been crashed out for hours!"

I glanced over to his house. The familiar beat-up Trans Am was parked in the driveway. "You've been watching me?" I'd have to make sure I shut the curtains from now on.

"Billy wanted to come play with you," he said, taking a drag on his cigarette and rolling his eyes. "I told him he had to let you sleep."

"Then why are you here?"

"I need—"

"The money," I said suddenly. "Sorry, I completely spaced it. Hang on."

"Forget the money," he said with a violent wave of

249

his hand that sent smoke swirling into the house. "I just need a favor."

"What?" I asked suspiciously.

"A ride."

Again I glanced across the street. "Why can't your buddy take you?"

"He's passed out," Curtis said with a series of shrugs. "We started drinking during lunch today."

"I'm sorry, Curtis," I said, as sincerely as I could. "I really am, but I can't."

"Why not?"

For a second I stared at him. "I just can't."

He blew a stream of smoke right at me and rolled up on his toes, looking down at me. "Why not?"

Trying not to cough, I asked, "Why can't you?"

"Lost my license," he said. "Bad news to get a DUI when you're fifteen and then another one a month later. If I get caught behind the wheel before I turn eighteen, I go to juvie." He was speaking so fast I could hardly understand him. "So I need a ride."

"I'm sorry," I repeated. "But I don't have a license either."

He looked at me, clearly not believing. "You get busted for something?"

"No—" I faltered. "I mean—"

"Look, I just need a ride to the dorms." He took three steps to one side and then four back. It was like he couldn't stand still. "It'll take five minutes, tops."

"It'd only take you ten minutes to walk there," I said.

"I need a ride. No one will know."

"But—"

"Fine!" he said in exasperation. "I'll drive! Just give me your damn keys!"

"Excuse me?"

"No one will look twice at your mommy mobile. Ty's Trans gets the wrong kind of attention."

"Curtis—"

"Stuart, I'm not going to ask again." And suddenly he *was* standing still, and his voice was steel and his eyes were piercing. "One way or another, I need a ride to the dorms."

"Wait here," I said. "I'll go get the keys." My plan was to shut and lock the door, and then call Cardinal. But Curtis stepped inside before I could shut the door.

"I'll come with you," he said.

"Where's Billy now?" I asked, stalling for time.

Curtis did that weird series of shrugs again. "Last I saw he was chasing leprechauns in the basement."

"What?" I straightened up.

"He's tripping, and I think it's a bad one."

Suddenly I felt cold all over. "You gave him drugs?"

"He wouldn't get out of my face," Curtis said, tossing his cigarette into the kitchen sink. "He was entertaining for a while, but then it got old. We locked him in the basement."

"Locked him in?" I said, stunned. "God! What are you, some kind of a monster? He's got to be terrified."

I turned, but he grabbed my arm, squeezing with surprising strength for someone who looked so scrawny. "He's contained and he's not going any-where. I'll let him out as soon as we get back."

His eyes were wild, and I couldn't see any pity or emotion in them. I was Billy's only chance.

"Okay," I said, shrugging off his arm. "As soon as we get back, though, you have to let him out."

"Of course," he said with an evil grin. "Let's go."

On the way to the dorms, I drove over the speed limit, hoping to draw attention. Getting caught speeding seemed like a really good idea. But as is usually the case, if you're looking for the police, they're someplace else.

We reached the dorms without incident. Curtis reached over and pulled the keys out of the ignition, then jumped out of the car. "Come on."

"No."

He bounced on his feet, trying to stare me down. "Come on!"

I wanted to go back and check on Billy, but I sure as hell couldn't leave Curtis with the car keys. I was stuck. I got out and slammed the door.

The dorm was locked. Curtis swore under his breath and pounded his fist against the brick wall. But in a few seconds, someone came out and Curtis caught the door. He slipped in, not bothering to hold it open for me. I grabbed the edge of the door before it shut and hurried after him up to the second floor.

Curtis knocked twice. Then he pulled something out of his pocket and jimmied the lock.

"What are you doing?"

"Shut up!" he hissed, yanking me into the room after him. "This'll just take a minute."

He began rifling through the room. I looked around and saw a phone on the desk. I inched toward it, hoping Curtis was too busy to notice.

"Yes!" he crowed as he pulled a shoebox out of a

dresser drawer. "Found it!" He swung around, looking for me. "What are you doing?"

I shrugged.

"Check the hallway."

I opened the door and stepped out, looking reflexively in both directions. The hall was completely empty, and I didn't know if I was disappointed or relieved. I didn't have time to think about it because Curtis ran past me and jogged toward the stairs.

He had my mother's keys, so I had to keep up.

We had just reached the bottom of the stairs when Simon came through the front door. Curtis hid the shoebox behind his back.

"You looking for me?" Simon asked.

"Nope," Curtis said. "We were just heading home."

Simon glanced warily at me, then said to Curtis, "Thought we were going to make a deal."

"That was an hour ago," Curtis replied. "Deal's off."

"You owe me money," Simon said.

"Watch what you say," Curtis said. "You don't want Ballentyne hearing too much."

Simon glared at me and then looked back at Curtis. "I want my money."

"And I wanted to make a deal. Maybe next time you won't be late. Come on, Stu. Let's go."

He grabbed my arm and we pushed past Simon together. I knew he was using my body to keep the box out of view, but I didn't care. I could feel time pressing down on me, time when Billy was drugged and alone, time that should be spent getting him help.

Once we were outside, Curtis tossed me the keys, and I dropped them. I bent to pick them up, and as I stood, I looked back at the dorm. The front door had closed behind us, and the night was quiet.

Curtis bounded across the parking lot, and I sprinted after him. We reached my mom's car at the same time and scrambled into it.

"Go go go go go!" Curtis pounded on the dashboard.

I laid rubber as I pulled out.

Curtis was laughing hysterically when I turned on to the main drag. "Look at you go, Stu!" he cried. "Speeding away and you still turn on the blinker!"

I growled deep in my throat, unable to say anything. My mind was spinning so fast I wondered if Curtis had somehow managed to slip me some weird drug.

I flew home, blowing through stop signs, squealing tires on the turns, forgetting the blinker. The five-minute drive was only going to take one and a half if I could manage it. I didn't care about me or Curtis or Simon; I wanted to get to Billy. This was all my fault. If I hadn't taken the car to school on my birthday, Curtis wouldn't have thought to ask me for a ride. If I had said something about Curtis's treatment of Billy before, if I had talked to Cardinal or the social worker earlier, if I had—

Out of the corner of my eye, I saw a small black shape dart out in the road. I slammed both feet on the brakes, knowing it was too late, knowing I would feel the thump of a little furry body under the tires.

And then I saw the boy running after the puppy, and all I could do was close my eyes in the split second before impact.

The thud seemed too dull to be real. It almost sounded like someone had hit the hood of the car with a fist. The car was still skidding, screeching to a stop, but I knew it was too late. The thud may have been dull, but it was very, very real.

I opened my eyes, but all I could see was the dark street stretching out in front of me, quiet houses on either side with darkened windows as families dreamed in safety, oblivious to what had just happened. Curtis flung open his door. He almost fell as he hurried to get out. I thought he was heading the same direction I was until I realized that he had the shoebox tucked under his arm and was dashing toward his house.

I ran to the front of the car, terrified of what I would see.

I was looking for a body, but I didn't see one. I was looking for blood, but I didn't see any. I dropped to my hands and knees, convinced that I would find him pinned under the car, but there was nothing but skid marks under the tires.

"Stu?"

In disbelief, I looked to my right. The voice had come from Billy, lying in a very unnatural position, half on the sidewalk, half in his yard. I allowed myself to hope. *I hit the brakes hard. I was slowing down when I hit him…maybe….* I crawled over to him, looking for blood, unable to believe I didn't see any.

"Billy, are you okay?"

He swallowed, but that was the only movement he made. "I'm sorry," he said.

"No, no, no," I said, feeling tears stream down my

face. "Oh, no, Billy, don't be sorry! You didn't do anything!"

"I let Midge out."

"It's okay," I said. Even though I couldn't see any blood, I was afraid to touch him. What if he was bleeding internally or had some other injury I couldn't see? But I reached out and put my hand on his. "Where does it hurt, Billy?"

His eyes drifted shut.

"Billy! Billy!" My voice was getting shrill. "Don't go to sleep, Billy! Stay with me!"

He opened his eyes and gave me a puzzled look. "Why're you yelling at me, Stu?"

"Can you move?" I asked him in desperation. "Can you move at all?"

The street was still too quiet. Where was the ambulance? Where were the cops? Surely Curtis had called someone by now.

"Help!" I shouted. "Help! Somebody call 911! Help! 911!"

"You're yellin' again," Billy mumbled.

"Yeah," I said, glad that he was talking. "I am shouting. And I'm going to do it some more."

"Please don't," he said. "It makes my head hurt."

"It does? Does anything else hurt? Can you squeeze my hand?" I was talking too fast, and I wasn't giving him any time to answer my questions, but I couldn't seem to help it. "Maybe you shouldn't move, Billy. Just stay still. Is it your leg?" It hurt me just to look at his right leg, twisted around under him so his foot was pointing the wrong direction. "Help!" I yelled again. Mom's car was still in the middle of the street, both front doors flung wide open, headlights on. How could no one notice? Why wasn't anyone coming out to see what was wrong?

A car came careening around the corner, tires screaming in protest. I looked up, hoping to see the flashing lights of an ambulance, or at least a Security Forces car coming to help. Instead, the single-head-lighted Chevy flew past my mother's car, taking the driver's side door with it, and fishtailed wildly as it turned in to the Vinsons' driveway, hitting the back of the Trans Am and ramming it into the garage door.

Simon popped out of the driver's door and ran to the Vinsons' porch. He didn't waste time with the front door, though; he smashed right through the window next to it.

He hadn't seen me and Billy, hadn't even looked in this direction, but that didn't mean he wouldn't see us on his way out. And I knew that would be bad.

I couldn't believe no one had heard the commotion, couldn't believe there wasn't anyone opening their front door to see what was going on. Didn't anyone care?

"Billy," I said, swallowing bitter tears, "I've got to go—"

"No!" His eyes shot open, looking huge in his pale face. "Don't leave me, Stu! Please don't leave me alone!"

"Billy, I've got to get help. I've got to—"

"No," he begged, "Please! I'm so scared."

"Me too," I said before I could stop myself. "And that's why I've got to make a phone call. I'll be right back, I swear."

But the Vinsons' front door suddenly exploded open and Simon barreled toward his car. I stayed hunkered down next to Billy.

Simon took a flying leap and ran over the crumpled hood of his Chevy, looking like a stunt man from a bad movie. As he pulled the car door closed behind him, he glanced over toward Billy and me. I swear our eyes locked for a second, but he didn't do anything more than put his car in gear and back out of the driveway. How he missed ramming the front of Mom's car, I had no idea, but he was gone before I could think about it.

Billy moaned a little. His eyes had drifted closed again and his breathing seemed more rapid to me.

"I'll be right back, Billy," I whispered.

He moaned again, but didn't open his eyes.

As I stood up, headlights came around the corner, sweeping in a normal, controlled way. "Hang on, Billy," I said excitedly. "Someone's coming! Just hang on!" I dropped back to my knees and took his hand again, waving like crazy with my other arm.

My heart almost stopped when I saw the SF car pull up behind Mom's car, but then I remembered that Simon had already left.

I waved again and yelled for help as the flashers turned on. The SFs both jumped out of their car with weapons drawn. For one panicked moment I was sure I was going to get shot. But then they both reholstered their weapons. One of them spoke into his radio, and the other one ran toward me. Panic was replaced with hope. The hope that Billy would be all right.

"What happened?" the SF asked as she dropped to one knee next to me.

"I…I…I hit him," I said, feeling tears on my cheek again. "He ran out and I couldn't stop in time."

"Call for an ambulance!" she yelled to her partner. "A kid was hit."

"Billy," I said. "His name is Billy Vinson." I didn't want him to be just "a kid."

I kept talking to Billy, trying to get him to answer me. He kept repeating that he was sorry, kept asking about Midge. I couldn't believe that he was more worried about the puppy than about himself. The fact that Curtis hadn't come back out of the house was something I didn't let myself think about.

"Who's Midge?" the female SF asked.

"Stu's puppy," Billy moaned.

Another set of headlights splashed around the corner and headed toward us.

"That should be our backup," she said, sounding anxious.

"What's wrong?" a familiar voice called, and I felt the relief roll through my entire being.

"Cardinal!" I yelled. "I…I hit Billy!"

His truck jerked to a stop and he jumped out, leaving it right next to the cop's. He came around and took charge. The young SFs seemed relieved to have him there.

He sent me to fetch blankets from our house and when I came back, the male SF was pulling Cardinal's truck into our driveway. The female SF was working with Cardinal.

They had moved Billy's arms and the leg that didn't seem injured so he was lying more or less in a straight line. When the SF touched the twisted leg, Billy shrieked in pain, so the cop stopped and left it where it was, laying the blanket over him.

"Just try to keep him calm, Stu," Cardinal said. "We don't want him going into shock."

I knelt down near Billy's head and kept talking to him. He tried to respond, but his voice seemed weaker.

The ambulance arrived with a Security Forces escort, of course. SF didn't stop an ambulance to check the driver's ID before it came on base, but they didn't let it go anywhere alone, either.

Cardinal had tended to Billy calmly and efficiently and without any questions. He told the paramedics all he knew, and when I added that I thought Billy was on drugs of some kind, he actually bent over at the waist as if he'd been sucker punched. But as soon as the paramedics loaded Billy in the ambulance and drove away escorted by the first SF car, Cardinal and the other two SF guys were all over me, bombarding me with questions.

"Please," I begged, "can't we do this later? Billy doesn't want to be alone!"

"We'll go to the hospital as soon as you tell us what happened," Cardinal said, and I knew from his tone that there would be no arguing.

I tried to explain what had happened, but there was too much and it came out in a jumbled mess. I kept looking over at Curtis's house, willing him to come out, to pretend to give a damn about the little boy he had drugged. But the house stayed dark and silent. I couldn't tell them Simon's last name, but I was able to remember his room number. The two cops exchanged a look. I was too tired and frazzled to try to understand it.

Another SF car came, and I had to repeat the story yet again, this time a little more coherently. The officers took photos of Mom's car, drew some lines on the street, measured the skid marks, and then drove Mom's car into our driveway. They tossed the door unceremoniously onto the yard.

Finally Cardinal gave the cops his name, rank, unit, cell phone number, and my phone number. He promised them that I would be home all day tomorrow, available for questions, but told them that we urgently needed to go to the hospital and see about Billy. As we pulled out of the driveway, the cops were walking up to Curtis's door.

"I'm sorry," I said to Cardinal as we left base housing. He didn't say anything. I saw a muscle in his jaw twitch.

"I'm sorry," I said again as we turned on to Highway 83. "I really—"

"You really should stop talking," he said, cutting me off.

We completed the rest of the twenty-minute drive in silence. An ambulance with flashers on flew by, heading north, toward the base. Closer to town we could see more flashers, and Cardinal slowed down in the left lane as we passed two state troopers and an overturned car with a single headlight still shining.

6 October

mergency waiting rooms are awful places. They don't even pretend to be warm and reassuring. They're cold, stark, and bare, as if they're trying to get you ready for a life without the person you brought in. At three-thirty in the morning, they're almost unbearable.

Cardinal was standing a few feet away from me, talking on the phone. I had lost track of all the phone calls he had made. He'd called Colonel Porter first, even though I'd told him that Mrs. Porter was having her baby, probably somewhere in this hospital. He'd called my father, the Security Forces commander, family advocacy, and who knows how many others.

When we first got to the hospital, it had taken Cardinal fifteen minutes to convince someone to give him information about Billy. We weren't family, and just being his neighbor wasn't enough. Finally, mostly because the hospital had been unable to reach anyone else, one of the doctors had agreed to talk to Cardinal. But he'd refused to let us see Billy.

Now I wanted to explain everything to Cardinal, to try and apologize, but he wouldn't even look at me. Once, between his many calls, I almost got up the nerve to say something. When I saw the muscle in his jaw twitching again, though, I decided to wait.

I sat and let the thoughts rush through my mind.

I had to believe Billy was going to live. I clung to the fact that he'd been talking earlier, and I tried not to think about internal bleeding and all the other terrible things that could be wrong with him.

It slowly dawned on me that Billy wasn't the only one who had been hurt tonight.

The overturned car on the highway must have been Simon's.

Cardinal—I wondered if he'd get blamed for any of this. It could mean big trouble for him. For all I knew, it could mean the end of his Air Force career.

I worried about what had happened to Midge; I hadn't had a chance to look for her before we'd headed here.

I couldn't bear to think about my mom and dad.

A siren announced the arrival of another ambulance. I looked up as the automatic doors opened wide, allowing the attendants to roll the gurney in. I watched mostly out of curiosity, but I found myself suddenly on my feet.

The bruised and bloody face was all I could see, but it was enough. "Curtis!" I shouted. It looked as if someone had beaten him up pretty badly.

As they wheeled the gurney past him, Cardinal turned from his phone call and stared. He put his hand to his forehead and I could almost see the last of his calm strength draining out of him.

I slumped back in the chair and watched the nurses wheel Curtis in through the other set of doors. I made out a few words of medical speak that reminded me of the chatter on TV doctor shows. Cardinal tried to follow them in, but the security guard blocked his way.

He walked back to the row of chairs and sat down next to me.

Another ambulance pulled up outside the glass doors, but this one didn't have its flashers or siren on. Briefly I wondered just how many ambulances there were in Minot. The paramedics unloaded a gurney and wheeled it through the doors. This patient was completely covered with a sheet, and there was no medical chatter as they sped past us.

When the swinging doors closed behind them, Cardinal and I were sitting in the hospital waiting room together. And we were completely alone.

StuForceOne: so billy's going 2 b okay, but he'll be in a cast 4 a while.

H2Oxcelr8r: that's bad but it could have been a lot worse.

StuForceOne: the dr. looked at me like i was a bug he wanted to squish when i told him i thought billy was on mushrooms.

H2Oxcelr8r: curtis *should* be squished.

StuForceOne: he practically was. when simon went into the house looking for his stash, he stabbed curtis 2x in the stomach and broke his nose. i don't know how many stitches he had 2 get.

H2Oxcelr8r: i don't feel sorry 4 him. so how r u?

StuForceOne: OK, i guess.

I looked at my last message. Was I okay?

Under Cardinal's orders, I'd gone back to school right away. He took me in each day, and Mrs. Reyes brought me directly home after swimming practice. She waited in the driveway to make sure I went into the house. I then called Cardinal to tell him I was home. I walked the dogs, cleaned the house, and did the laundry. I cooked dinner every night, and then did the dishes before going to my room to do homework.

And still I had too much time to think. When I wasn't busy, I tortured myself by reliving the last month.

Every time I tried to apologize to Cardinal, he cut me off. But he did tell me about the things I needed to know.

The Vinsons' house was empty. Tuesday morning a tow truck had removed the Trans Am from the driveway (Cardinal didn't know what had happened to Chance, its owner), and that afternoon housing maintenance had come to fix the broken window and busted-in garage. Curtis was still in the hospital. For the first three days the doctors weren't sure if he would survive. Simon had died that night; he hadn't been wearing his seat belt when he rolled his Chevy off Highway 83.

Billy had been released from the hospital on Wednesday, which was the day that Captain Vinson returned. Billy's leg would be in a cast for a while. The doctors were hopeful that there wouldn't be any lasting damage from the drugs.

Things were bad, but I knew they could have been much worse.

H2Oxcelr8r: is ur mom home yet?
StuForceOne: no.

But I had talked to her, several times. I'd had to hold the phone away from my ear for most of the first conversation to keep her from blowing out my eardrum. I'd never heard her yell like that before, and it scared me. For the first time I was almost glad she was deployed; maybe it would give her time to cool down before she got ahold of me.

Dad had only had twenty-four hours to calm down. He flew up the day after what I now call "the incident." He hugged me hard when he got to the house, but the hug was followed by a lot of yelling and glaring. The first thing he did was cancel my trip to visit Ray and stick me with the bill for the nonrefundable ticket. I was, of course, grounded indefinitely. Dad hadn't had a chance to hand out any more punishments, though, because two days later he had to return to Nevada when Gram fell and broke her hip. Cardinal moved in again and I was back in limbo, waiting for my fate to be decided.

I don't know why any of that mattered now. There wasn't much they could do that would make me feel worse than I already felt.

    H2Oxcelr8r: what about billy's dad?
    StuForceOne: they brought him home early so billy wouldn't have 2 go 2 foster care.
    H2Oxcelr8r: foster care? what about the mother?
    StuForceOne: u'll never believe it.
    H2Oxcelr8r: try me.

When Curtis came out of surgery, he told the cops that his mom had left on the second of October. They found a note on the fridge that confirmed his story. Mrs. Vinson had left Billy and Curtis money to cover food and other necessities for the five or six days she'd expected to be gone. I told Taylor the short version.

StuForceOne: of course, curtis had already blown it all on drugs and booze. the fridge was bare.

H2Oxcelr8r: where'd she go?

StuForceOne: u'll never believe it.

H2Oxcelr8r: i'm waiting.

StuForceOne: she said she was going 2 audition for the new world pop star show.

H2Oxcelr8r: ur right. i don't believe it.

Apparently Mother Darla had convinced herself that her success at Sneaky Pete's karaoke bar meant she had talent. She'd driven over to Minneapolis to audition. Cardinal said she hadn't answered her cell phone when Curtis called. When the cops put out an APB for her car, they found it abandoned in the parking lot of a motel not far from the North Dakota–Minnesota border. They still hadn't located her.

H2Oxcelr8r: this sounds worse than a soap opera.

StuForceOne: u have no idea.

H2Oxcelr8r: i'm afraid 2 ask, but what about curtis?

I typed back that Curtis was still in the hospital, recovering. Rumors were flying around school. One of the most popular tales was that his real dad was going to come get him and put him into military school. Where that one started, I had no idea, but I kind of liked the irony. I did know from Cardinal that someone had contacted Curtis's dad and asked him to come get his son. Curtis had a slew of charges against him, as did Mrs. Vinson. Curtis would make his court appearance when he was able. Mrs. Vinson would have to be found before she could be tried.

StuForceOne: i'm sick of drama.

H2Oxcelr8r: i don't blame u but i think u've got more coming ur way.

StuForceOne: i know i do. i have my own court date early next month.

Although feeling miserable about hitting Billy was a terrible punishment, it hadn't been enough for the authorities. They'd written me up for driving without a license, excessive speed, failure to yield, and reckless endangerment. Because all of my infractions occurred on base and were vehicle related, they kept me under base jurisdiction. I was really, really grateful that I wouldn't end up in the juvenile detention center like Curtis probably would. My base driving privileges had been revoked until we left Minot. According to my parents, however, I wouldn't be allowed to get my license until I turned twenty-one anyway.

But in a way I wished the base had turned my case over to the local cops, because Cardinal told me that as a result of what I'd done, he and my mother would get a letter of reprimand in their files. I could only hope this wouldn't be a stumbling block for Mom's next promotion.

StuForceOne: it's going to take me a while to earn enough cash to pay to fix the car door.

H2Oxcelr8r: what about insurance?

StuForceOne: amazingly, simon did have insurance but i get 2 pay my parents anyway, on "principle."

H2Oxcelr8r: so ur parents r pretty ticked.

StuForceOne: u r good at understatement.

H2Oxcelr8r: it's a natural talent.

I could have used some of that talent for under-statement, because the reality of everything that had happened kept overwhelming me. I couldn't believe that the one time I'd taken a real risk to help Billy, I was the one who'd ended up hurting him. If I'd just stepped up to begin with, if I'd called the cops or even Cardinal during Curtis's party, or if I'd told Mom my concerns before she left, maybe everything would have turned out all right.

But understatement wasn't an option now. Bad things *had* happened, and dealing with the fallout was what I had to do now. I had to meet it head on.

StuForceOne: cardinal and i had to talk to family advocacy.
H2Oxcelr8r: good thing he had already talked to them. did they listen more closely this time?
StuForceOne: sort of.
H2Oxcelr8r: what do you mean?

Cardinal and I sat across from the two social work-ers, JoAnn and Ben, at a big table in a hospital confer-ence room. Cardinal talked first, explaining why he'd called family advocacy in early October and making it clear that he wasn't aware of any follow-up. Then he told them what he'd seen the night of the incident, which wasn't very much.

"Can you tell us more about what happened?" JoAnn asked me.

"Yeah, but I ought to start before that." I went back to the beginning, when Curtis and Billy had come over to ask me to go ATVing and Curtis had pushed Billy around. Then I told them about the scary movie night.

"Did any of this bother you?" Ben asked.

"Well, yeah, but I didn't know what to do."

JoAnn and Ben just looked at me, waiting for me to continue. I sighed and ran through everything I thought was relevant: Curtis's party, Billy's condition the night of the party.

"That's why Billy was sleeping over?" Cardinal interrupted.

I nodded.

He leaned back in his chair and let his head hang forward for a moment. He sat up straight again, a pained expression on his face. I couldn't tell if he was angry or sad. "I should never become a parent," he said. "I had no idea Billy was drunk that night."

"You don't usually expect an eight-year-old to be drunk," I said.

The look Cardinal shot me made me wish I'd kept my mouth shut. "But I would have expected you to tell me," he said.

"I know. I wish I had." I swallowed hard and tried to explain about the night of "the incident." I told them what Curtis had said and how I had decided to give him a ride. I filled in the scene at the dorm and the ride back. "I was speeding," I said, "because I wanted to get back to Billy as fast as I could."

"You said he was locked in the basement?" JoAnn asked.

"That's what Curtis told me."

"So how did he get out?"

"I have no idea."

"Let me get this straight," Ben said. "Curtis told you that Billy was not only locked in the basement, but also that he'd taken drugs? And you decided to drive Curtis somewhere and leave Billy there alone?"

"You don't understand how worked up Curtis was about getting to the dorms. I told him no, but he was hopped up on something. I didn't know what he might do, and…and I was afraid of him. The only way I could see to help Billy was to do what Curtis said. I didn't want to let him take Mom's car because I was sure he'd wreck it." The terrible irony of it all washed over me again.

I couldn't look at any of them as I tried to explain. Thinking back, it seemed stupid that I'd let Curtis intimidate me that much.

Ben looked down at his notes. "It sounds like you've spent a fair amount of time with Curtis."

"Not that much," I said. "He's not my friend or anything."

"What about Billy?" JoAnn asked.

"I hung around with him a little. He wanted to be my friend, and he's a good kid." I swallowed again and looked at the table.

"I'm sorry," Cardinal said. "If I had known any of this—"

"You made the first report, Captain Cardinal. We know you acted on the information you had."

The table blurred in front of me.

H2Oxcelr8r: gotta tell u, Minot's not sounding great.
StuForceOne: u'll do fine here, as long as u stay away from me.
H2Oxcelr8r: no way. i'm ur friend, stu.

Wyatt and Jorge had been awkward around me at first. It seemed like they didn't know what to say. Rumors about me were almost as common as the speculations about Curtis. Wyatt asked me point-blank about the rumors and I gladly set him straight, hoping he would pass the truth on. It was scary to know some people were saying I was a drug dealer or an addict.

By the middle of the week, though, things eased up a little, at least on the surface. I felt as awful as before, but I wasn't being avoided like the plague every single place I went. On Friday, Cardinal let me go with Mrs. Reyes and Jorge to meet Wyatt's new little sister.

Lindsay's reaction was the hardest for me to deal with. She quit riding the school bus and was avoiding me at school. After leaving six messages for her, I finally asked Jaylene if she knew what was going on.

"Lindsay's parents told her to stay away from you," Jaylene said.

I leaned against my locker. "What?"

"Her parents are really strict. They just started letting Lindsay go on group dates this summer. When they heard you were driving under the influence, they freaked out."

"But that's not fair. I admit I was driving fast to try to help Billy, but I *wasn't* driving under the influence. I wasn't even drinking. Come on, Jaylene, couldn't you call her for me? I just want one chance to talk to her."

"I don't think that's a good idea," Jaylene said. "If she wants to talk to you, she'll let you know. She has twin brothers who are in Billy's grade," Jaylene reminded me. "She's really bothered by everything that happened."

StuForceOne: when r u moving?

H2Oxcelr8r: looks like 2 november.

StuForceOne: pretty soon.

H2Oxcelr8r: i'm nervous. haven't moved in a long time.

StuForceOne: looking forward to meeting you.

H2Oxcelr8r: me 2.

closed the garage, hoping it was the last time I would have to rake leaves for a while. A taxi pulled up and stopped across the street. I watched from the driveway as two people got out of the back.

I didn't recognize the man, and it took me a minute to realize the other person was Curtis. His hair was cut so short it looked like he'd shaved his head. Curtis slouched toward the front door. The man leaned down to the passenger window and said something to the driver, then followed Curtis into the house as the taxi drove away.

The phone was ringing in our house when I walked inside, and the answering machine clicked on just as I picked up.

"Hello?" My answer was drowned out by my own voice saying, "Hi, we're not in right now—" I shut the machine off. "Hello?" I repeated.

"Just checking," Cardinal said.

"I was out raking the yard," I explained. "Finished up a couple of minutes ago."

"Good," he said. "I should be back within an hour."

"Okay. Hey, did you know Curtis was back?"

"What?"

"He just went into his house with some guy," I said. "Is he allowed to be there?"

Cardinal sighed and I could picture him rubbing his hand over his bristly flattop. "I don't know...I'll call Vinson and check."

I went out to the front porch and sat on the steps, enjoying the last of the Indian summer warmth and trying to watch the Vinson house without being obvious. Molly and Midge were sprawled in the grass in front of me. When we'd come home from the hospital that night, Cardinal had found Midge cowering in the backyard. She'd been jumpy and clingy for the first couple of days, but she'd recovered quickly. I held onto the hope that she'd remember enough never to run out in the street again.

Our phone rang again, and I ran inside. It was Cardinal. Vinson knew that Curtis and his father were coming by to pick up his stuff, but he thought it would be a good idea if I kept an eye on things.

I returned to my post on the front steps. I was beginning to think that Curtis wasn't ever going to come back out of the house when the taxi came back. It stopped in the same place and honked the horn twice. Almost immediately the front door opened and Curtis's father came out carrying two large bags. Curtis, obviously still weak after his stay in the hospital, struggled out with another bag and a backpack.

Curtis's father knocked on the trunk and the driver popped it open. While his dad loaded the bags, Curtis glanced once in my direction, then looked away.

His face looked haunted, beaten down. I wondered if that was because of what Simon had done to him or because no one had heard from his mother or maybe even because of how badly Billy had been hurt. Maybe it was a combination of all of it. Or, I thought, maybe he was just going through withdrawal.

As the taxi pulled away, I gave Curtis one last wave. In the Air Force, you never know when you'll see someone again someday at another base.

But I was sure I'd never see Curtis again.

* * *

When Cardinal walked into the house, he nodded to me and went upstairs to change. I waited in the kitchen until I heard him come back down to the living room. He let out a sigh as he sat down and unfolded the newspaper. I let about five minutes go by before I got up the courage to confront him.

"Can we talk?" I asked, sitting on the edge of the sofa.

He put the newspaper down. "Is there a problem?"

"You haven't let me apologize," I said. "And you haven't told me how mad you are. And I hate that you hardly look at me."

"You have apologized, Stu. Repeatedly."

"So tell me how to make things right."

"There are some things that you can't make right."

"So tell me off. Yell at me. Do something! Take Midge away."

"Would any of that make you feel better?" he asked.

I didn't answer.

"Do you think yelling at you would make me feel better?"

I shrugged helplessly.

Closing his eyes, he said, "There are some things you can't make right. You just have to accept the consequences and move on."

"But there has to be a way to get beyond this!" I insisted.

"Time," he said simply. "It'll take some time for me to get over my anger and disappointment. But it's going to be hard to get to a place where I can trust you again."

I swallowed hard. "I know. I don't blame you for that. But I wish..."

"You wish what?"

"I wish we could be friends again," I mumbled.

He sighed. "Maybe that was my mistake, Stu. Maybe if I'd tried to be more of a guardian and less of a friend, none of this would have happened. As it turned out, I failed on both counts."

"None of this is your fault!" I burst out. "It's all mine!"

"No, Stu. If I'd been a better friend, you would have confided in me. If I'd been a better guardian, I would have kept closer tabs on you. I did a half-assed job at both, and it backfired on us." He picked up the paper. "I'm not making that mistake again. Until your mom or dad gets here, I'm your guardian. I can't be your friend right now."

"But maybe—"

"Look, Stu. You're a good kid. I know you didn't intend for things to end up like they did," Cardinal said. "When all this is over, I'm sure we can be friends again. I just wish..."

My throat ached when I tried to speak. "Yeah," I croaked. "Me too."

Captain Vinson resigned his commission the week after he returned to base. He told Lt. Colonel Porter that he couldn't be a single dad and be ready to deploy at the same time.

I saw Billy smile more in the two weeks his dad was home than I'd ever seen him smile before. Even his limp seemed happy.

We had a half-day off for teacher planning, and I knew the elementary kids didn't. I walked over to the Vinsons' house. The front door was wide open. "Hello?" I hollered through the screen.

"Upstairs," Vinson boomed back.

I found the captain sorting through a large pile of clothes.

"Stuart," he said, obviously surprised to see me.

I fought the urge to run back down the stairs.

"Captain Vinson," I began, "I wanted to…um…apologize. I'm so sorry. I'd give anything if I could go back and change things." But then I didn't know what else to say. I wanted to give him a chance to yell at me. I wanted him to tell me that I should have found a way to stop Curtis, that I should never have been driving the car that hit Billy…

His lips compressed into a thin line, and I wasn't sure

he would say anything at all. Then, in the Southern drawl that I hoped Billy would never lose, he said, "Billy told me you were a good friend to him. He said you helped him a lot while I was gone. In fact, he said he wished you were his brother instead of Curtis." He sighed. "You woulda been a better choice, that's for sure."

That made me feel even worse. "I should've spoken up sooner. I should've—"

"You did the best you could. I don't blame you for anything, son."

"But I—"

"Stuart," he said, his voice cracking just a bit. "This...this has been tough on everyone. Don't beat yourself up. Don't second-guess every choice you made. You were there when he needed you."

"But I wasn't—"

"I'm sorry. I have a lot of work to do now." He turned his back on me.

"Please, Captain Vinson. Can I ask you one question?" I said. "I'd like to give Billy something—"

"That's fine."

"No, I need to make sure it's okay with you if I give Midge to Billy."

He turned to face me. "What's a Midge?"

"Midge is my—a puppy," I said. "She's a black lab, and Billy has—"

"No, Stu. It's nice and all, but right now I don't think—"

"Please, Captain Vinson, he really loves her. And I'd like him to take at least one good thing with him when he leaves Minot."

He considered me carefully. "A puppy's a big responsibility."

"That's right, sir, but Billy's been helping me train her. They're great buddies. She's gonna be a great dog," I said. "And she deserves to be with the boy who needs her most."

"I don't know," he said.

I sensed it wasn't the time to push, so I stayed quiet.

"We're moving to the TLF soon and pets aren't allowed there."

"I'll watch her while you're at the TLF," I said quickly.

"Aw, what the heck." He smiled. "The kid's been hankerin' for a puppy for two years now, and I won't be traveling in my new job. If you're sure—"

"Yeah, Captain Vinson, I'm sure."

"All right then," he said. "That'd make Billy really happy. Lord knows he could use a little cheering up. What'd you say the dog's name is?"

"Midge. She won't be a midget for long, but somehow the name just seems to fit."

"Got it. Thanks, Stu."

"Can I tell Billy this afternoon?"

"That'd be fine," he said.

"I'm sorry," I said again, but he was already back to the pile of clothes, sorting out what to toss and what to keep.

29 October

I'd made a large Welcome Home sign for Mom. I felt about six years old coloring the poster board with crayons and Magic Markers, but I figured it couldn't hurt. I had the house spotless, the refrigerator fully stocked with the fixings for her favorite meals, and straight A's on my midterm reports. I'd done everything I could think of to try to make up for what had happened, but I knew it wouldn't be enough.

Cardinal had said he'd be by to pick me up at two. The B-52s were scheduled to arrive at four. I hadn't argued with him about the timing; whether I waited at home or in his office made no difference to me. When the doorbell rang at one-thirty, I thought it was Cardinal coming by early.

Wondering if he had lost his key, I opened the door. Arms grabbed me in a big hug before I realized what was happening. "Dad?" I said. "What are you doing here?"

He held me at arm's length and scowled at me for a moment. "I'm here to get you back in line," he said sternly. But then he broke into a grin. "I've missed you!" And he hugged me again.

I laughed and pounded him on the back. "I've missed you too! I can't believe you're here!"

"So are you going to let me in?"

I stepped back so he could come through the door. "How long are you staying?"

"Two weeks. There was a sudden opening in a nursing home for Gram—not her first choice, but she's agreed to give it a two-week trial."

"And then?"

"If she likes it, I'll find a real estate agent I trust to sell the house. I'll probably have to go back a couple of times to settle things, and I told Gram I'd come visit her every three months at least. I promised to bring a grandson each time too."

"Yes sir," I said.

"We've got a lot to talk about," he said.

"Yes sir."

He hugged me again. "I should have been here sooner."

"I shouldn't have caused you and Mom so much worry."

"Your mom and I will always worry, Stuart. It's called being a parent."

"You remembered that Mom's coming home today, right?" I said cautiously.

"I know," he said, wandering into the living room. "That's why I'm here."

"You've been talking with her?"

"I could hardly just show up, Stu," he said. "Yes, we've been talking."

I had to hear him say it. "You're moving back?"

"We'll see," he said. "Your mom and I have had some time apart to think about a lot of things. Now we'll take some time to talk and think together, and then…"

"And then?"

He shrugged. "We can't do anything more than try it out and see what happens." He looked down at the Welcome Home poster propped against the wall. "Do you have any more paper? I'd like to make one too."

And so, when Mom led her crew in, Dad and I were standing together, waving two homemade signs, shouting happily in the crowded hangar where half the base had gathered to welcome home our heroes.

I got up extra early and was making breakfast when Mom came downstairs. Her first night back had been great, mostly because she and Dad said right up front that for the moment we were going to enjoy being together again and save the serious talk for later.

Now was later.

The French toast I'd made was staying warm in the oven, the coffee was ready, and I was busy scrambling eggs.

"Smells good," she said, leaning against the island.

"Hopefully it'll taste good too," I said, pouring her a cup of coffee. It had been a long time since I'd helped her make French toast, and I wasn't sure I'd done it right. I was hoping the thought would count more than the taste.

She wrapped her hands around the mug. "So, things here have been interesting."

"Very."

"You know what I've been wondering for the last three weeks?"

"How to kill me and get away with it?"

"Maybe that would have been a better use of my time." She smiled to let me know that she was joking. "No, you and I have discussed taking responsibility for our actions and facing consequences for our decisions and all that over the phone. What I've been wondering is how you could have let your brother down like that."

I stopped stirring the eggs and looked over at her. "My brother? What? How did I let Ray down?"

"Not Ray. Billy."

I dropped the spatula into the pan. "Billy?"

"Yes. Don't you know after all these years that what I told you is true? That the Air Force is our family?"

I groaned and turned back to the eggs. "Look, Mom. I didn't mean to let Billy down—"

"Not just Billy," Mom interrupted. "Your Air Force family."

"Mmm, smells good," Dad said, coming into the kitchen. He smiled at Mom and put his hand on her shoulder. "Have you started the inquisition without me?"

"Yes," I said.

"No," Mom said.

"As if we needed further proof that we don't all perceive things the same way," Dad muttered, shaking his head and reaching in the pan to steal a bite of egg.

"Dave, what's the Air Force to you?"

Dad looked at Mom. "Is this a trick question?"

"Stuart doesn't realize that the Air Force is one big family."

"Of course he does," Dad said. "He knows that we all look out for each other."

"That's just being neighbors," I said. "That's not being family."

"It's being close neighbors," Mom said, "or distant

286

relatives. How many times have we asked a neighbor to be the emergency contact for your school within two days of meeting them? How many times have we left our door unlocked and asked a neighbor to put packages inside the front door when we're gone, trusting that they'll treat our home as their own? How many times have we sat down for Thanksgiving dinner with neighbors we've known less than a month? The point is, we all look out for each other. We have to. Why weren't you looking out for Billy? You knew something was going on. You knew before I left."

"You knew too," I countered.

"I only knew what you'd told me," she said, "and that was hardly everything."

"I was afraid…" I began, but I couldn't continue.

"Afraid of what?" Dad asked as he served the eggs onto plates.

I bent down and opened the oven door to check on the French toast, and also to keep them from seeing the tears in my eyes. "Afraid of interfering," I said. "Afraid of getting too involved in someone else's problems."

"Didn't you end up pretty involved?"

I nodded, still facing the oven.

"That's because you've got a good heart, Stu," Dad said. "You can't shut people out."

"Perhaps if you'd 'interfered,' as you put it, a little earlier, you wouldn't have gotten as involved as you did," Mom added.

It was a lot easier to look back and see all the things I should have done differently. I took the toast out of the oven and served everyone's plate.

As we began to eat, I told them, "I'm so glad you're home."

"So am I," Mom said.

"Me too." Dad gave her a big smile.

"And remember the old saying, Stuart," Mom added. "'Home is where the heart is.'"

"And for us, that means home is where the Air Force sends us," Dad said, putting his hand over Mom's.

They ate their eggs and French toast; I pushed the food around on my plate. "How's Cardinal?"

"He's doing okay," Mom said.

"Is he going to get kicked out?"

She shook her head. "I'll have to include the letter of reprimand in his file, but it was really my fault for putting him in a difficult situation. His OPRs will still be good, and by the time he meets the board for major, he'll be at his next station with another year of experience. His career will be fine."

"What about *him?*"

"I think he blamed himself more than he should have. It'll take a while, but he'll be okay."

"So," Dad said after a few moments, "what have we decided to do with our younger son?"

"He suggested we might already be searching for a way to get rid of him without getting caught," Mom said.

"Hmm," Dad said, chewing thoughtfully. "That sounds like too much work on our part."

I sighed. "I guess I'm grounded until I graduate."

"That sounds like a lot of work for us too," Mom said. "How about until Christmas?"

"Oh, why not round it up a little?" Dad asked. "He can finish this calendar year doing penance and start next year with a clean slate."

I held my breath. Getting out in January was more than I had been hoping for.

"Okay," Mom agreed. "Grounded till the New Year. What level of grounding? Stuck in his room? Are we taking his Xbox? His computer?"

I tried not to whimper. Losing my computer till New Year's would probably kill me.

"How about putting him under house arrest?" Dad suggested.

Mom was quiet for a moment. "I suppose that's enough," she said. "He's already put himself through a lot of grief." Suddenly I could breathe again. "But more importantly, he's not to say a word about getting his driver's license for a long, long time."

"Absolutely not," Dad said, nodding.

"Stuart?" Mom said after a few moments of quiet. "Do you have anything to say?"

I looked at the two of them sitting next to each other. "I'm sorry again about everything, and I'm going to do my best to earn your trust again. I'm so glad to have you both home that I won't complain about anything. In fact, I'll enjoy having you guys chauffeur me around."

Mom and Dad went to a Halloween party at the Officers' Club, and I stayed home handing out candy. It was only thirty degrees, but it was much warmer than the high of negative fifteen degrees we'd had the week before, and the neighborhood kids were all out in force.

Billy came by dressed as a cowboy, and Vinson had Midge on her leash. There was a bandana around her neck. I gave Billy two handfuls of candy and offered his dad a cup of hot coffee.

Later, I watched a group of kids make their way down the driveway. A little pirate had stopped in the middle of our yard. "You okay?" I called.

"Dropped my mitten."

"That's not good," I said, pulling the door shut behind me.

I hurried over, and when I got closer I realized that it was actually a pirate princess. She looked like she was maybe seven.

"Where's your group?" I asked. There were roaming Security Forces to ensure everyone's safety, but young kids were supposed to be with a group.

The pirate princess gestured toward the next house. "They went that way."

"Then we'd better hurry and find your mitten," I said. The snow reflected enough of the porch light for me to see that her bare hand was already turning pink from the cold. She had a white mitten on her other hand.

I began walking circles around her in the snow, looking for the missing mitten.

"Found it!" she exclaimed.

As I helped her shake the snow out, a voice called, "Katy?"

"Over here!"

Three or four shadows about Katy's size walked toward us, with two taller shadows behind them.

"I lost my mitten," Katy said. "He helped me find it." She pointed to me. "Thank you," she added.

"No problem," I said. "Stay warm tonight, okay?"

"Okay," she said, trudging through the snow to her group. "Next time, Zach," she called, "you should wait for me."

I waved and walked back to the house.

"Happy Halloween, Stu."

I turned back and discovered that one of the taller shadows was Lindsay. She was wearing a black witch's hat and robe.

"You too," I said.

1 November

The Wing Commander oversees punishment for defendents, but since that was Mom and she wasn't around when everything happened, she left it up to Lt. Colonel Porter.

Porter let me off pretty easy, all things considered. In addition to losing my base driving privileges, I had to do ninety hours of community service at the base elementary schools, mentoring kids and assisting the DARE officer with presentations and fundraisers. But I didn't have to do any time at a detention center, and when we left Minot, there wouldn't be any record left.

Except in my heart.

When the moving truck pulled away from the Vinsons' house for the last time, I felt a bigger sense of loss than I had in a long, long time. Billy and Captain Vinson were still around, for a few more days anyway, as Vinson finished his separation paperwork and got the house clean enough to turn back over to housing. They were staying at TLF, and Billy came over every day after school. I watched him and Midge until Captain Vinson came to get him shortly before dinner.

The day the Vinsons finally left, Billy cried on my shoulder.

But I waited until he was gone and I was alone in my room.

I sat staring at an empty computer screen, trying to visualize what my life was going to be like until January. I leaned forward, dropping my head into my hands. How could I get past all this? I'd been over the bad decisions I'd made a thousand times. I'd replayed the "if only" scenes in my head over and over again.

I knew there must be a way to become friends and care for people without losing yourself. I thought about how Mom and Dad had friends scattered around the world, yet they stayed closely connected to them. They kept in touch, and they always took time for a visit if someone came through town, they supported them through tough times and made sure to be at weddings, christenings, and anniversary parties if they possibly could. They cared about their friends without losing themselves in them.

I figured I'd write Billy a letter tonight, telling him about my first day without him on base and asking after Midge. Then I'd e-mail to see if Taylor had any more questions about things here in Minot, and to let him know that the first practices for the high school season were starting next week. I got up to get a snack first, and when I came back I looked out my window. A moving truck had pulled up in front of the Vinsons' house. I watched for a minute. The movers were taking the boxes into the other side of the duplex.

I leaned forward, pressing my forehead against the window. I could see a man making checks on the clipboard, a woman with a toddler in her arms, and a girl who looked to be about six.

Making up my mind, I left my room quickly, trying to get my words right. "Hi," I muttered to myself. "I'm Stuart Ballentyne, and I live across the street. If you need help with anything, just let me know." It wasn't groundbreaking, but I didn't know what else to say.

Fortunately, the Slye family was really nice. I could tell that they were used to moving and meeting new neighbors. I felt a little strange, but also good, when I offered to babysit and then left them our phone number so they could call if they needed anything else.

As I crossed the street to go home, I saw a girl who looked about my age walking up from the corner. I hadn't seen her around before, and I wondered how many other new neighbors were moving on base this week.

A lot, I thought as I went inside, *and they're all probably better at taking care of their friends than I am.*

I had just finished the first problem from my trig homework when the doorbell rang.

The girl who had been walking up the street was now standing on my front porch. Her straight blonde hair hung past her shoulders and she had an anxious expression on her face.

"Hi," I said.

"Are you Stuart?" she asked.

"Yeah," I said.

"Stuart Ballentyne?"

"Right," I said, stepping out on to the porch and pulling the door closed behind me. There was a sign in our front yard that said "Colonel Ballentyne," so I wasn't sure why she sounded so hesitant. "Do I know you?"

She was blushing. "Um...yes and no," she said. "I promised I'd be bringing more drama into your life."

I stared at her. "More drama?"

She sighed and twisted her hands. "Oh, this is even harder than I thought it would be." She looked up through her bangs at the sky, shook her head, and then looked back at me. "When you first e-mailed, I realized you thought I was a guy, and I was afraid you wouldn't want to be e-mail pals if you knew I was a girl. You were the only one who kept writing back. So I just let you think I was a guy."

I felt my eyes getting wider. I couldn't speak.

"But I thought...I thought we'd never see each other. I convinced myself that it didn't matter if you thought I was a guy. And then, when I found out we were moving here, every time I tried to tell you...well, I just...I just didn't know how." She looked down at her hands. "I still don't."

"There are a lot of Taylors in the world. You could have just kept e-mailing and let me think you were still in D.C."

She wrinkled her nose. "That would've been down-right creepy. Stalkerish, even. What if we'd ended up with classes together? I knew we'd be on the same year-round swim team. How could I e-mail and act like I didn't know who you were in real life?"

"But you do know who I am in real life."

"Come on, StuForce. You know what I mean."

My front door swung open, preventing me from saying what I was thinking: *Taylor's probably the only one who really does know me.*

"Oh, I'm sorry," Dad said. "I didn't know you had company." He frowned at me for a moment. "I don't think you're allowed to have company until after New Year's."

"Dad, this is—" I paused, still disbelieving.

"I'm Taylor," she said shyly. "Taylor Tatarka."

"Taylor?" Dad repeated, looking at me. "Not—"

"My e-mail pal," I confirmed.

"Oh. Well. Oh." Dad seemed almost as shocked as I was.

"I just wanted to come say hi," Taylor said. "We got in last night. Mom and Dad are at the BX, picking up supplies for the new house."

"So you finally got here," Dad said, smiling.

"Yes," she said. "Finally."

"Where are you living?"

"We're on Sirocco, down past the school."

"You got into the new housing. That's good."

"Yeah."

"So...will you e-mail me as soon as you get your computer set up?" I looked at Dad. "I told her that I have to wait until after New Year's to talk on the phone and hang out in person, but we can still e-mail, right?" I turned back to Taylor. "And I'll see you at school."

"And at practice," she added. "I knew I couldn't stay today. I just wanted to say hi. But e-mail's worked well so far."

"Yeah. I'm looking forward to actually talking to you," I said.

"Me too." The relief was clear on her face. "I'll see ya—e-ya—later." She turned to leave.

"Oh, don't go," Dad said. "Why don't you hang out here with Stuart?" He looked at me. "Just for the afternoon."

I grinned.

"I'm sorry," Taylor said when Dad had gone back inside. "I swear, it's the only thing I lied to you about, although it really wasn't a lie so much as just a not telling. I didn't mean to put off telling you for so long, I just couldn't figure out how to—"

"Taylor," I cut in, "you're babbling, just like you do in e-mail."

"You're not too mad?"

"I don't know," I said honestly. "I mean, you're a friend, right? Does it matter if you're spotted or purple or female?"

"Maybe you should draw the line at the purple spotted females," she advised.

I laughed.

"Seriously," she said, her blue eyes looking anxious, "I'm waiting for you to say how much this sucks."

"Seriously," I replied, "it doesn't. It's a little weird, yeah, but I promise you it definitely does not suck. It's...it's good to have friends."

I smiled. "I'm really glad you're here."